AD

OUR

LAST

ECHOES

KATE ALICE MARSHALL

OUR LAST ECHOES

VIKING

VIKING
An imprint of Penguin Random House LLC, New York

First published in the United States of America by Viking,
an imprint of Penguin Random House LLC, 2021

Visit us online at penguinrandomhouse.com.

LIBRARY OF CONGRESS CATALOGING-IN-PUBLICATION DATA IS AVAILABLE.

Printed in the United States of America

ISBN 9780593113622

10   9   8   7   6   5   4   3   2   1

Design by Jim Hoover
Text set in Apollo Mt Std and Futura Bold

This book is a work of fiction. Any references to historical events, real people,
or real places are used fictitiously. Other names, characters, places, and events are
products of the author's imagination, and any resemblance to actual events
or places or persons, living or dead, is entirely coincidental.

The publisher does not have any control over and does not assume any
responsibility for author or third-party websites or their content.

To my mom,
who is brilliant and funny and wise,
for all of the love, support, babysitting,
cheerleading, and snacks.

OUR
LAST
ECHOES

We have retrieved the following file from Dr. Andrew Ashford. As before, audio and visual content has been transcribed, as original materials could not be removed without raising further suspicion.

Be aware that Dr. Ashford is aware of the interest in his work, though we do not believe that he has identified either you or our agent. Proceed with caution.

THE
ASHFORD
FILES

File #77

"The Disappearances
at Bitter Rock"

Bitter Rock, Alaska
June 2018

PART ONE

THE FOLLY
OF THIS
ISLAND

EXHIBIT A

Final radio broadcasts of the
Landontown residents

From the island of Bitter Rock, Alaska

12:48 PM, SEPTEMBER 9, 1973

> UNKNOWN: . . . if anyone's hearing this. This is [indistinct] of the Landontown Fellowship on Bitter Rock. Our phone is out. The winds and rain are violent. Mist everywhere. Can't [indistinct] evacuate. Everyone on Belaya Skala has taken shelter in the church. I—

3:45 PM, September 9, 1973

> UNKNOWN: Storm is continuing. Flooding is becoming a concern. We don't know if—

<Transmission cuts out. It resumes a few seconds later.>

> UNKNOWN: We thought we were alone, but—

5:34 PM, September 9, 1973

> UNKNOWN: There are figures in the mist. They're everywhere. Can anyone hear me? Is anyone there? You need to come for us.

\<A long pause is interrupted by a distant rumbling.\>

UNKNOWN: They have our voices.

12:03 AM, September 10, 1973

UNKNOWN: If anyone can hear me, do not come to Bitter Rock. Do not come to Belaya Skala. Do you hear? Don't come! Don't—

\<Frantic voices shout in the background. There is a loud crack, like splitting wood.\>

UNKNOWN: He's here. God help us. God help us, he's here!

1:13 AM, September 10, 1973

\<At first there is only the sound of static crackling. And then labored breathing. A voice—perhaps the same one, but strained almost beyond recognition, speaks slowly.\>

UNKNOWN: There is no salvation.

Note: Landontown was located on the island of Bitter Rock, Alaska. Thirty-one residents were present on September 7, 1973. Only Theresa Landon, wife of founder Cole Landon, was absent. Multiple attempts were made to respond to the final radio calls of the residents, but none of these attempts appear to have succeeded.

All thirty-one residents vanished without a trace. No further communication was received. No bodies were ever recovered.

They were not the first.

They would not be the last.

INTERVIEW

Sophia Novak

SEPTEMBER 2, 2018

The camera is positioned to one side of a study. Bookshelves line the walls; a heavy wooden desk in the center of the room is covered in orderly but prolific stacks of folders, books, and papers. A photograph on the desk shows Dr. Andrew Ashford standing with Miranda and Abigail Ryder, his wards, in front of a sycamore tree.

In the chair in front of the desk sits a young white woman: Sophia Novak. She is blonde, in her late teens. Her features are solemn, her skin sun-weathered. Dr. Ashford appears from behind the camera and sits opposite her, in the chair behind the desk.

ASHFORD: There we go. Ms. Novak, was it? Is it Sophie or Sophia?

SOPHIA: Either one is fine.

ASHFORD: I see. Thank you for coming all this way.

SOPHIA: I thought I should. Abby said—she talked about you a lot.

ASHFORD: The file Ms. Ryder compiled is incomplete. Her notes are fragmentary and I'm having trouble piecing together exactly what occurred. I hoped you could fill in the blanks.

Sophia seems to have expected this. She reaches down to a backpack beside her chair and pulls out a spiral-bound notebook.

SOPHIA: I wrote it all down. Abby asked me to, but I didn't get the chance to give it to her.

She slides it across the table to him. Ashford rests his hand over it but doesn't open it yet.

ASHFORD: What happened on Bitter Rock, Ms. Novak? What did you two find there?

Sophia smiles a little, almost sadly.

SOPHIA: Nothing but echoes.

SOPHIA NOVAK

WRITTEN TESTIMONY

1

MY EARLIEST MEMORY is of drowning.

I only remember bits and pieces. The darkness of the water; the thick, briny taste of it; the way it burned down my throat when I gasped. I remember the cold, and I remember hands, impossibly strong, pushing me under. And I remember my mother lifting me free. Her voice and her arms wrapping around me before the warmth of her slipped away.

But I've never been to the ocean. Never choked on salt water. So I have been told all my life. My mother died in Montana, hundreds of miles from any ocean. The water, the darkness, the cold—they're nightmares, nothing more.

Or so I thought, until Abby Ryder asked me what I knew about Bitter Rock.

The first tendrils of mist seethed past on the wind as the boat bucked. Droplets trembled on the few strands of hair that had escaped my tight braid.

"It's just ahead," Mr. Nguyen shouted unnecessarily: there was no way to miss the island, as grim and foreboding as the name Bitter Rock suggested. But I would have known we were approaching the shore even with my eyes closed. The sea had been a constant since we left the shore; the water had sloshed, sucked, and slapped at the sides of the boat. But now a new sound reached us: a sibilant crashing of water meeting rock.

The engine thrummed through me, singing in my bones. I knew this place. I knew those sounds, even though I shouldn't. The thought sent a shiver through my core, but I couldn't tell if it was fear—or relief. I knew this place. There had to be a reason— an explanation. An *answer*. In my pocket, my hand closed tightly around the small wooden bird that was all I had left of my mother. *We're here,* I thought.

Mr. Nguyen piloted us past sharp black rocks to a tongue of weathered wood—a dock, but not much of one. The engine puttered, then cut out, and Mr. Nguyen leapt to the dock with a nimbleness that didn't match the ash-gray patches in his hair. He didn't bother to tie the boat off. He wouldn't be staying. He hadn't even wanted to bring me in, not with the storm threatening to sweep down and cut off the island from the mainland, but I'd talked him into it.

"You're sure this is where you want to be?" he asked.

Was I sure? Was I sure that I should be here, three thousand miles from home, chasing the memory of dark water? Tracing the footsteps of a dead woman?

Yes.

"I'll be fine," I told Mr. Nguyen. "Will you be okay getting back? That storm looks bad."

"I'd rather face the storm than stay here." He helped me off the boat, catching my elbow when my foot skidded on the wet boards.

"Thanks," I told him, pulling away. "I've got it from here."

He gave me a long, unblinking look. Like he was trying to decide whether to talk me out of it. But he'd tried on the mainland and he'd tried on the way over. I guess he decided he'd done all he could. "Be careful," he said at last. "Nothing good happens here."

I could have told him, *I know*. I could have told him, *That's why I've come.*

Instead I only nodded and turned away.

I didn't have directions to the house where I would be staying, but it wasn't like there were many options. The beach led to a road, and the road led in two directions: west, to the Landon Avian Research Center; or east, where the few houses on the island were located. It was after hours, so no one would be at the Center. I turned east.

The island was equal parts rock and clinging grass. The wind made the grass hiss, like the island already disapproved of my presence. I kept my head down. The strap of my bag dug into my shoulder and across my chest.

If I hurried back, I could still catch Mr. Nguyen. I could tell him that I'd made a mistake. I could go home—except there was no home to go back to. Now that I'd graduated high school, I was officially aged out of the foster system. The only thing I had left was a ghost, and this was the only place I knew to look for her.

I remembered almost nothing about my mother. A blue jacket. Her hand cupping the back of my head as I pressed my face against her thigh. Her voice barely hiding a laugh. *Come on, little bird. Bye-bye, little bird. Good night, little bird.*

Joy Novak died in an accident, fifteen years ago. I was three years old, and I didn't remember any of it. I only knew what they told me in foster care, and it wasn't like my foster parents knew any details. I wasn't able to find any either, when I went looking. One dead woman didn't make a ripple in a world where worse things happened every day, and I'd started to accept a future in which I never knew what her last moments had been like, or what kind of accident had claimed her.

And then I'd gotten a phone call. The girl on the other end had asked what I knew about my mother's disappearance. The word had been so unexpected that at first I hadn't heard it at all. I assumed she was asking about her *death*. So when Abby asked me about what my mother been doing in Bitter Rock, Alaska, I'd told her she'd made a mistake. *My mother died in Montana*, I'd told her. *I don't think she'd ever been to Alaska.*

So you believe she's dead, then?

That's when I realized what she'd said. *Disappearance.*

I still didn't believe her. Not until she sent me the photo: my mother and three-year-old me on a beach.

Turns out there were answers. I was just looking in the wrong place.

Gravel crunched under my feet. A pale bird winged toward me. The splash of red at its throat was vivid as fresh blood. A red-throated tern—the bird Bitter Rock was famous for, in certain scientific circles. It was a perfect match to the wooden bird in my pocket, its wings barred with black and white. The colors flashed at me as it flew overhead, and I tracked its progress.

The western point of the island rose in a hill, and at its top crouched a blocky gray building—the Landon Avian Research Center, or LARC for short. It was the only reason anyone came to Bitter Rock. It was the reason my mother had been here, at least according to Abby, and so I'd lied and wheedled my way into a summer job interning for one of the lead researchers.

The tern flew over the hill and disappeared northward. Heading, I assumed, toward Belaya Skala—Bitter Rock's headland, connected to the main island by an unnavigable isthmus of sheer rock and home only to birds. Though that hadn't always been the case. At least three times before, people had tried to gain footholds of one kind or another on that side of the island.

Every time, it ended in disaster. Disaster that left not corpses, but questions—which had never been answered. This island had swallowed up dozens of people. Now I was here, alone and unsure of what I was facing.

Suddenly it crashed over me, the immensity of what I was doing stopping me in my tracks. My mother was just one name among many, and these islands had eaten them all, and left behind nothing—not even bones. Who was I against that?

I turned on the road, a plea on my tongue— *Wait, I've changed my mind.* But Mr. Nguyen was a blot on the sea, too far for my voice to reach. I dug my fingers into the strap of my bag, sick with the sudden conviction that this had all been a mistake. There was a strange vibration in the air that seemed to settle in my chest and radiate out through my limbs. It made me queasy, like I stood on the lurching deck of a boat with the rumble of the motor beneath me.

I blinked. Mr. Nguyen's boat was gone. I searched the horizon for him—he couldn't have gotten far enough to vanish, not yet. Fear skittered over my skin. I gritted my teeth. It was fine. I wasn't leaving anyway. I was letting my nerves get the better of me, that was all.

My eye caught against a shape jutting up from the waves.

It was a man standing in the water. He was up to his thighs in cold surf, facing away from me. He wore an old-fashioned army jacket that flapped in the wind. He stood canted to one side, like he had a bad leg, with his arms dangling into the water. His head hung forward.

That water had to be freezing. What was he doing? I stood rooted for a moment, torn between concern and caution. I drew forward haltingly. That buzzing in my bones was almost an ache. I licked my lips, wanting to call out, but afraid to. "Hello?" I managed at last, still far away, lifting my voice above the crash of the surf.

His shoulders jerked back. His head snapped up. He started to turn.

I knew immediately I'd made a mistake. I scrambled backward, a yell lodged in my chest, desperately wanting to steal back that word, to stop him from turning, because I was sure, in a way that I could not explain or defend, that I did not want him to turn.

Rough hands seized my arm and yanked me around, and now I did yell. A huge man loomed over me, his hand gripping the meat of my upper arm. His face was half-hidden behind a huge gray beard, an orange knit cap jammed down over his blunt forehead.

"You," he growled, brow knit. "What are you doing out here?" His voice was thick with a Russian accent. He smelled of damp, salty sea spray and stale cigarette smoke. Drops of moisture jeweled the bristles of his beard. A half-healed blister balanced at the edge of his bottom lip. One of his eyes was almost entirely white, the skin around it ropy with a starburst of scarring.

"I—I—" I stammered. Fear surged through me, and my breath caught in my throat.

But fear wasn't useful. Not now. I shoved it away—not just repressing it, but flinging it away from me, into the void—the other place that was always waiting. It bled away in a rush, and I gave a small shudder of relief.

"Get your hand off my arm," I said, cold and flat.

He peered at me through his good eye. "Do you know me?" he asked.

"No," I said, bewildered.

He let go abruptly and took a half step back. I just stared at him. I wasn't afraid, and there would be a price for that later, but for now I needed the calm. The empty. I did know him, though—didn't I? It was like I remembered him from a dream. Or maybe a nightmare. "What were you looking at?" he asked, brusque and demanding.

"I saw—" I twisted back toward the water. The man was gone. In his place was a tree that must have been uprooted on some other shore and dragged here by the tides, blackened by the water and pitching as the waves rolled it. Out in the distance, Mr. Nguyen's boat continued its steady retreat. Not vanished at all. The tree— I'd seen the tree, and somehow I'd thought it was a man.

The explanation leapt into my mind, comfortable and reassuring and false. I swallowed. No. I knew what I'd seen.

"Hey," someone called.

The speaker was a young man—I blinked in surprise. I hadn't expected to find anyone my age here, but he was eighteen or nineteen at the most, with black, tousled hair and a lip ring. His skin was light brown, his frame borderline scrawny; he wore a T-shirt printed with a caffeine molecule over a long-sleeved shirt. He loped up the road and slowed as he approached, the slight laboring of his breath suggesting he'd run a fair distance. When he spoke, it was with a British accent. I didn't know enough to tell what kind, but it made him sound a lot more refined than he looked in this state.

"Everything okay here?" he asked.

"Yeah," I said, tearing my eyes away from the ocean. If I said anything about a man in the water, they'd think I was delusional.

"You're all right?" the boy pressed, looking between me and the big man, who still stood closer to me than I liked. "I heard a shout."

"I'm fine." True enough, with my fear neatly excised. But that glassy calm made people nervous, and the young man's eyes were uncertain as he looked me up and down. I forced myself not to glance over my shoulder. Not to wonder if someone was behind me. "It was just a misunderstanding."

The big man's eyes tracked out past me, at the driftwood tree, and he gave me a narrow look. "You two, you should get inside. The mist is coming. It's very dangerous."

"Yeah, we'll do that," the boy said. The big man muttered something under his breath and walked past us, heading down the road. The boy waited for him to get a good distance away before he turned to me. "You're the intern, then. Sophia Hayes."

Sophia Hayes. I'm Sophia Hayes. I'd practiced it in front of a mirror until it felt natural. One of many lies I'd have to tell. "Yeah," I said. Empty of fear, I could tilt my lips in a faint smile. "How'd you guess?"

"It's not exactly a huge deductive leap," he said, smiling back. It made his lip ring click against his teeth. "I'm Liam. Liam Kapoor. My mother's your evil overlord." Liam stepped forward with his hand outstretched and I took it. His skin was cool, his palm lightly callused. The motion pulled his sleeve up at his wrist, baring the edge of a bandage taped down over the back of his arm.

"You mean Dr. Kapoor?" I asked. She was one of the two senior staff members who ran the LARC, and the one who'd hired me.

"That's the one. I'm spending the summer out here with her as punishment for a few minor transgressions."

"Poor you," I said. I wondered if those transgressions had anything to do with the bandage. "That guy . . ."

"Mikhail? He's the caretaker. Or groundskeeper. Or something," Liam said. "Wanders around the island with a shovel, glaring at people. He's not what I'd call friendly, but I've never seen him accost anyone like that."

"I think he just—wasn't sure who I was," I suggested.

"There's a way of saying hello without coming off like a total creeper, and that wasn't it," Liam said, eyeing me with an uncertain look. Like he was wondering if he needed to be more forceful, more comforting, or something else entirely. "You're sure you're okay?"

"I'm totally sure. Completely sure. Absolutely—"

"Got it," he said with a laugh. I crafted a smile, false and crooked.

"Although I am exhausted," I confessed. It wasn't a lie—I'd been traveling for more than thirty-six hours, crammed on planes, jostled on buses, and pitched around in Mr. Nguyen's little boat. "Dr. Kapoor's instructions said to head down the road until I reached Mrs. Popova's house."

"You're on the right track. Dr. Kapoor's place is right up there." He pointed in the direction he had come from. "I was out for a walk when I heard you. Mikhail's place is by the water nearer the LARC, and Mrs. Popova's is straight that way, at the eastern end of the island. Come on, I'll walk you there."

I nodded. I didn't look at the water, at the tree, at Mr. Nguyen retreating. I kept my eyes fixed on the gravel road, and on the sky ahead, where a dozen birds wheeled and cried.

I'd done my research before I came here. I knew my mother wasn't the first to disappear from Bitter Rock. There was the *Krachka*. Landontown. And, in 1943, there was a tiny army outpost. Thirteen men, an airstrip, and a few planes.

Like my mother, they had come to Bitter Rock.

Like my mother, they had vanished.

I kept my eyes on the road, and I wondered what if they weren't gone at all?

EXHIBIT B

Post on Akrou & Bone video game fan forum

*"Off Topic: Urban Legends & Paranormal Activity"
sub-forum*

JUNE 3, 2016

My grandpa was in the air force during World War II. He always said that the scariest story he had wasn't from his days dodging German Messerschmitts over Europe, but on our own home turf. Early in the war, he was stationed at an airstrip on a tiny Alaskan island. They dubbed it "Fort Bird Shit." It was a boring assignment. The Japanese threat was farther west, so the biggest problem they had to deal with was the salt water in the air corroding the metal on the planes.

Some weird things happened, but nothing that couldn't be chalked up to men being drunk, bored, and isolated. Seeing people who weren't there, hearing weird noises, that sort of thing. One man insisted that someone was speaking Russian to him whenever he started drifting off to sleep. Then one day my grandpa gets the job of taking the ranking officer back to the mainland. There was a thick mist that night. They headed back the next day—and everyone was gone. *Everyone.*

Whatever happened, it was just after dinner, because the dishes were being washed. They were abandoned in the tubs. Some boots and rifles were missing, but not all of them, which meant that some of the men were barefoot and unarmed. One of the planes was crashed in a ditch, like someone had tried to take off. A wall nearby was riddled with bullet holes.

They never found out what happened. The official report said a storm killed everyone, but Grandpa insisted the night was calm. Not even a breeze. Just fog.

I would say he was pulling my leg, but I have to be honest— my grandpa didn't have a sense of humor. At all. And when he told me the story, he seemed terrified. Whatever happened, he was still scared seventy years later.

2

LIAM GAVE ME an amused look as we started off toward Mrs. Popova's. "So you must really love birds," he said.

"I guess," I replied, then cursed myself silently. If I wasn't careful, I was going to give myself away before I ever stepped foot in the LARC. And then I'd get sent home without finding out anything about my mother.

"Is there another reason you'd want to fly out to the edge of the world for an entire summer? Because if you came for the nightlife, you are going to be deeply disappointed," he said, his tone teasing. "And according to Dr. Kapoor, you were *extremely* persistent. I don't think I've ever met someone who could wear her down before."

"'Persistent' is one word for it," I said. My teachers tended to go with "stubborn." My last foster mother had preferred "goddamn pigheaded." I'd been emailing Dr. Kapoor for months, trying to convince her to let me work for the LARC over the summer. Nobody just visited Bitter Rock. I needed a reason to be here. But I couldn't tell Liam any of that, and he was still looking at me like he was waiting for an explanation. "So you call your mom Dr. Kapoor?"

"Since I was five," he said. "She's never seen fit to correct me."

"Should I check in with her? Before I turn in?" I asked.

"She and Dr. Hardcastle are over on Belaya Skala doing their science . . . stuff," he said, waving a hand vaguely. "Dr. Kapoor meant to be back to greet 'our wayward intern,' but then we heard the storm warning, and we *assumed* you'd be delayed." He raised an eyebrow, like it was a downright supernatural phenomenon that had ushered me here in defiance of bad weather.

"I talked Mr. Nguyen into it," I said with a half shrug.

"That would be why I'm staring at you. Mr. Nguyen's from the mainland. And nobody from the mainland comes out here if they can avoid it when there *isn't* a storm." He looked like he was going to say something more, but then the radio at his belt crackled to life.

"Liam?" it was a woman's voice, distorted by static.

Liam held up a finger to ask me to wait as he replied. "Here."

"That storm's staying offshore, but the mist's coming in quick. Where are you?"

"Walking toward Mrs. Popova's. The intern got here. Sophia."

I wasn't sure if I should say hello, but the voice continued without giving me the chance. "Get yourselves back to Mrs. Popova's and stay there. I don't want you to get caught out in the mist trying to get back to the house on your own."

"What about you?"

"We'll be fine. I'll see you in the morning." There was a finality to the clipped words.

"You heard the boss lady. Mist's coming," he said. "Best hurry."

"What's the big deal?" I asked. "Can't you just walk home?"

"Nobody goes out in the mist. There are so many sharp drops and rocky hills around here, even just walking around when the mist is up is dangerous. Driving is worse, given the quality of the roads. Driving in the mist in the dark is suicidal."

"It doesn't get dark this time of year," I pointed out.

"Then we may yet survive our journey," he told me, mock-dramatic. I chuckled, amusement cracking through my tension for a moment, at least.

I was actually relieved that I'd beaten Dr. Kapoor back to Bitter Rock. My exchanges with her had all been over email, but even in text you could feel her glaring at you. I had to keep fooling her into thinking I was just a bird-obsessed teenager trying to "get some real-world experience." I'd already slipped up with Liam. I had to be more careful.

We trudged down the gravelly, pockmarked road, the only one that wound along the length of Bitter Rock's main landmass. There were no trees on the island, but the rocks and hills hid our destination from view until we were almost on top of it. "This is it," Liam said as we approached. In another setting, the cottage-style house might have looked cute, but the salt had stripped its paint until what was left hung in tattered strips from gaunt gray boards, and the roof shingles were patchy. Not even the floral curtains in the windows could rescue it from looking on the

the brink of ruin. "The Bitter Rock Chalet, aka Mrs. Popova's house. Everyone from the LARC stays here. Except Dr. Kapoor, who has her own house, and Dr. Hardcastle, who claims to have a cot in his office but I'm pretty sure sleeps upside down in the closet like a vampire."

"I think vampires sleep in coffins," I said.

"He might have one of those in one of the storage rooms, actually," Liam said. "The only people who ever come here are LARC researchers or really, really dedicated bird-watchers. The only place to stay is Mrs. Popova's. So it doesn't need a sign or anything."

The front door opened, and a sprig of a woman, gray-haired and with glasses that took up half her face, stepped out and crossed her arms. Her tan cardigan hung to her knees, emphasizing her thin build. Her face was creased and wrinkled, her skin light brown and decorated with liver spots. "Liam Kapoor," she declared as we approached. "What are you doing out with the mist coming in?"

"Fetching lost interns," Liam said. "I'm thinking of starting a collection. Mrs. Popova, Sophia. Sophia, this is Mrs. Popova."

"I knew a Sophie once," she said. There was something odd in her voice—almost grief and almost anger. Sophie—I hadn't gone by that since I was little, and there was something unsettling about hearing it now.

"It's a pretty common name," I replied. In the top fifty the year I was born, a fact I had confirmed before deciding to keep my first name for this deception. It was too hard to train myself to react properly to a false one.

"Wait, you mean the girl in the boat?" Liam said, sounding startled.

"Who's the girl in the boat?" I asked.

"It's nothing," Mrs. Popova said with a sigh.

"It's sort of like a ghost story," Liam said.

"And not a pleasant one," Mrs. Popova added, in a tone that precluded any further discussion. She waved both of us toward the house, eyeing the mist with more wariness than I thought was warranted. "Best get inside quickly, before this gets any worse. I'll make cocoa."

I followed Mrs. Popova inside. *A ghost story. The girl in the boat.* So the memories haunting me had a name.

A clatter of voices greeted us in the entryway. By the time I'd stripped off my shoes, I'd sorted them into two speakers, one male and one female.

Mrs. Popova ushered me farther in. The kitchen was a mix of weathered practicality and grandma flourishes, much like the exterior. A rifle sat propped against the back door; every cup and kettle had a lace doily to rest on.

Two people sat at the kitchen table. The first was a tiny white woman, a brunette with hair that stuck up in a way that made her look perpetually surprised. Even indoors she wore a puffy blue coat that seemed on the verge of swallowing her up and digesting her. The man, who had East Asian features, was short and solidly built, the sides of his head shaved and the rest of his hair swept back in a startled swoop.

"Hey, you found the fledgling," the man said. He had a Midwestern accent that charmed me instantly.

"Is the queen back in her castle?" the woman asked. Her chirpy voice held hidden barbs.

"She's up at the LARC by now," Liam said. "She said they'd stay there for the night, and I'm stuck with you lot."

"Poor thing." The woman tutted, and laughed.

"I'm making cocoa for anyone who wants it," Mrs. Popova declared. "And tell the poor girl your names."

"Kenny Lee," the guy said. "We had a bet going on whether you'd show up, you know. Figured it was even odds you were a prank."

"I'm Lily," the woman said.

"Lily Clark, right?" I asked.

"That's right." She stuck out her hand and I had to step up to take it. Her skin was startlingly cold, her handshake firm enough you knew she'd practiced it. "How'd you know?"

"Your pictures are all up on the website." Except for Liam's; he'd surprised me. And I didn't like surprises, not right now.

"We have a website?" Kenny asked. "Why didn't I know about that?"

"Because Will had me put it together without telling Dr. Kapoor. Something about dragging her kicking and screaming into the modern era," Lily said.

"What picture did you use?" Kenny asked suspiciously.

"Just one I grabbed from Facebook," Lily said.

"They're nice photos," I supplied.

"Probably not very accurate, then," Kenny said with a laugh. "We're usually bedraggled, muddy, exhausted, or all three at once. You can identify a LARC employee by the dark circles under our eyes and the stray feathers tucked in odd places." He leaned back in his chair and waved at us to take our seats. The chair creaked alarmingly under me, but held up. "This is great, you know. I don't have to be the new guy anymore. You get all the abuse."

"Nah, she's just a kid," Lily said. "I'll be nice to her." Kenny groaned good-naturedly.

"How long have you been at the LARC?" I asked him.

"Two summers, but I got here a week after Lily. I've been 'new guy' ever since," he said. "It'll be great having some extra company, at least. Especially since Liam's leaving."

"What?" I asked, startled and, I had to admit, a bit disappointed.

Liam gave a too-casual shrug, slouching in that boneless, expansive way that only tall, skinny guys can manage. "My mum— my other mum—didn't precisely check with Dr. Kapoor before she put me on a flight to Anchorage. The only reason I've been here this long is that Mum took off for a research trip to Morocco for a book, and my grandparents are visiting my cousins in Delhi and can't get a flight back until next week. I think Mum was trying to force us into some quality time together, but Dr. Kapoor's busy with her feathered children. And I know better than to compete with them for her affection."

Mrs. Popova whisked the cocoa and pursed her lips, shaking her head as if in regret.

"I'm sure your mom loves you more than birds," Kenny said awkwardly.

"More than any one of them, to be sure," Liam said. "But in the aggregate, sometimes I wonder." He smiled that easy smile to take the edge off his comment.

The silence threatened to get truly excruciating, and I cleared my throat. "You mentioned a ghost story?"

"A ghost story?" Kenny asked, perking up.

"I said it was *like* a ghost story," Liam hedged.

Mrs. Popova clicked her tongue. "All stories turn into ghost stories if you wait long enough," she said. She paused in the midst of stirring the cocoa, looking out the kitchen window at the gray of the mist. "No, she wasn't a ghost. She was just a child."

"The girl in the boat?" Kenny guessed.

Mrs. Popova sighed. "It's not a story I care to tell or hear without a bit of whiskey in me, and I haven't got any. So if you'll excuse me, I'll get myself to bed. Enjoy your cocoa. Lock the doors. And—"

"Don't go outside," Kenny and Lily chorused. They laughed, but my skin prickled.

Once Mrs. Popova was in her room, I turned my gaze on Liam. "So. The girl in the boat," I said, ready to shake him by the shoulders until he explained what the hell he was talking about.

"You're not saying it right," he informed me.

"How am I supposed to say it?" I asked.

"Like this: the Girl in the Boat," he intoned. Like a title. Like a figure from myth. Like, I thought, a ghost story.

"It's kind of LARC legend," Kenny said. "Passed down to the new grad students and post-docs."

Liam nodded. "I heard it from one of my mom's students at the University of Alaska when I was a kid. It's been around awhile. There are a few different versions."

"And what version would you tell me?" I asked.

"The spooky version, of course," Liam said, and grinned. He sat up, leaning forward a bit and holding up his hands as if framing the scene. "A fisherman is out on the ocean. No one for miles around, as far as he knows, and fog all around him, so thick he can't see. And he starts to hear this bird. Like a loon, maybe. Mournful, sad. This broken cry calling out again and again. He tries to ignore it. It's just a bird, and he has a catch to haul in. The cry starts to fade. Like it's getting weak. And he doesn't quite know why, but he starts heading toward it."

I shivered. The cadence of Liam's voice had changed. It was low and haunting, his eyes fixed on mine as he spoke. Kenny and Lily seemed just as spellbound, leaning forward in their seats, even though they knew the story.

"Then he can't hear it anymore. And he can't see anything through the fog. So he cuts the engine. All he can hear is the water against the hull of his boat, and his own heavy breath." He let the silence hang, leaving us to imagine that eerie stillness. When he spoke again, it was softly. "And then . . . he sees it. Emerging from the fog. A low shape on the water. A boat. Just a rowboat, but it hasn't got any oars. He draws up alongside it and looks inside. And he sees a little girl, curled in the bottom of the boat. So cold and so tired and so hungry that she's lost even the strength to cry. He takes her back to shore, and bundles her up, and gets her help. If he hadn't come upon her then, she would have died."

"But she didn't," I said. My mouth was dry. I struggled to keep my voice even, the normal level of curious. "So it isn't a ghost story after all."

"I don't know," Liam said. His head tilted. "Maybe you don't have to die to be a ghost."

I couldn't tell if he was joking. And I didn't know what my

answer might be if he wasn't. Was that what I was? A ghost? "Did it really happen?" I asked.

"Maybe?" Kenny said, but Liam looked thoughtful.

"There was this thing," he said. "When I was little, Dr. Kapoor was a postdoc, and she was spending the summer here. When she got back, she was really . . . withdrawn, I guess? I was too little to know why, but I heard her talking with Mum once. I remember something about a girl, and I remember having the impression something bad had happened to her. That would have been . . . 2003?"

"That's the year that storm happened," Lily said.

"What storm?" I asked. As if I didn't know.

"It was this awful accident," Lily said. "Some idiots went out on the water during the mist, and the weather turned. The boat sank, or something? Three people died. They never even found the bodies. But I don't remember there being a kid involved."

"No one really talks about it," Kenny pointed out. "Could be we don't have all the details. The only people around from back then are Hardcastle and Kapoor, and good luck getting anything out of *them* about it."

"Ah," I said, as if that satisfied my curiosity, as if it didn't really matter to me at all. A storm. Three people dead. Just a number, some faceless figures. But I knew their names. Joy Novak. Martin Carreau. Carolyn Baker. The coverage was obscure, the records thin, but I knew they'd been here. And then . . . they weren't.

"Are you all right?" Liam asked.

"I thought we agreed you wouldn't ask me that," I replied. I wasn't all right. My nerves jangled, and a familiar vertigo swept over me, the prelude to the crash that always came after I pulled my little trick with unwanted emotions. I was out of time. "I'm just tired. I think I should get some rest," I said. Was my voice too loud, too frantic? Liam frowned slightly, but the others looked unconcerned.

"You're the third door on the left," Lily informed me. "Bathroom's at the end of the hall."

"Thanks." I stumbled as I stood, but I hoped they'd just pass it off as weariness from a long trip. I offered an anemic wave and hurried down the carpeted hallway, hearing my breath too loudly in my ears.

I barely got the door closed behind me before my knees went out. I sagged and slid, letting my bag fall to the ground beside me, as the fear I'd pushed away less than an hour ago slammed back into me.

I screwed my eyes shut. I shoved one hand into my pocket and wrapped it tight around my mother's wooden bird, letting the sharp points of the wings bite into my palm. I sucked in breath after breath through my nose, and told myself I was safe, that there was no reason for this surge of adrenaline, this racing pulse, this wild, untamed fear.

I counted breaths. Fifteen. Thirty.

By forty-five, I was something approaching calm. I relaxed my hands, opened my eyes, and let my head loll against the door. That hadn't been so bad. I hadn't felt like I was dying. I hadn't thrown up. And no one had seen.

I stood up shakily. The window threw my reflection back at me—hollow eyes, hair like a mass of briars around my face. I looked away quickly. I hated seeing my reflection. Especially after one of my crashes—that emotional collapse that inevitably followed after I'd shoved away fear or sorrow into that empty void-space. Though sometimes the blinding fear or anger or rending sadness rushed over me like a wave with no reason at all. I was lucky this time. I'd had warning and somewhere private to ride it out.

I dropped my bag on the bed and sat next to it. I pulled out my clothes, stacking them side by side on the bed to store later, and reached to the bottom of the bag, to the most important object I carried with me: a printout of a scanned photograph.

The phone call had come late at night, when I was leaving my shift at the burger place near my school, walking back to my foster home. It was short-term placement—three months left and I'd be out on my own, eighteen and done with high school. I never answered unknown numbers, but for some reason I picked up.

What do you know about Bitter Rock?

I was sure Abby had the wrong person. Or that it was some kind of prank. And then she texted the scan to me: a photo, front and back.

The photo showed my mother and me. I was maybe three. Small, but I always have been. I was pressed against her side, grinning up at her. I'd had brown hair as a kid; it had only lightened to blonde as a teenager. The same as hers, which was pulled back in a braid, the same way I wore mine now. A close-mouthed smile made her look like she had a secret and wanted you to know it. Her hands were in the pockets of a puffy vest; her gaze was fixed squarely on the camera. Behind her was the sky, and scrub grass, and a rocky cliffside. And in the corner of the photo was the edge of a sign. LANDON AVIAN RES—

That's all you could read. There was a date scrawled on the back of the photo, next to our names. August 10, 2003. Days before she died. She looked happy. She looked well. She looked a world away from dying in a Montana hospital.

I lay down on the bed, holding the small wooden bird between my thumb and forefinger. Now that I'd seen one in person, there was no mistaking that it was a red-throated tern. A bird that only came from one island.

I knew a Sophie once, Mrs. Popova had said. Who else could she mean? I didn't remember her. Did I? I shut my eyes and summoned up an image of Mrs. Popova's face, and something kicked hard at my gut, the same not-quite-memory that I'd gotten looking at Mikhail.

Abby, the girl who called me, had told me about 2003, the summer when my mother, Martin Carreau, and Carolyn Baker went missing. Their deaths—or disappearances—were strange enough on their own, she said, but it wasn't the first time it had happened.

She didn't tell me more than that, so I found it on my own. The disappearances weren't tied to Bitter Rock directly, not overtly, but you could make the connection if you knew what you were looking for. A small island. People missing. Investigations that petered out far too soon.

The *Krachka* first—a fishing boat. The crew missing and an entire village with it. An airbase in World War II abandoned without explanation. A back-to-the-land commune wiped off the map.

And three vanished ornithologists in 2003.

Abby wasn't the first to put the pieces together and see the pattern. I'd found other theories—internet forums teemed with posts suggesting the missing were the victims of aliens, government experiments, the Rapture in miniature. And then the voices of reason always chimed in: *coincidence.* It was a dangerous part of the ocean. Lots of storms and lots of rocks. It was too remote for emergency services or search crews to get out there, increasing the chances of bodies going unrecovered. And, of course, some of it could be made up or exaggerated. It was the obvious explanation. The one that didn't require you to believe in the impossible.

But I already believed in impossible things.

Because I was one of them.

EXHIBIT C

*Video recording posted to Facebook
by Angela Esau*

POSTED OCTOBER 18, 2013, 9:43 AM

Caption reads: what a FREAK

The video is from a high angle, a phone lifted above the heads of a crowd of middle school students. They're shouting, some of them laughing, most of it unintelligible or profane. They've formed a tight ring in a hallway lined with blue-gray lockers, and in the center of the ring, a girl is on her knees. She hunches, screaming and tearing at her wheat-colored hair, pulling it free of the braid that hangs to the middle of her back.

STUDENT 1: What's wrong with her?

STUDENT 2: Someone get help!

STUDENT 3: Holy shit! She's going crazy!

The girl turns her face toward the camera. It is Sophia Novak, age thirteen. Her face is raked with red lines where her nails

have dug into her cheeks. Her lips are skinned back in a ric-
tus of fear and rage, and the whites of her eyes show as her
gaze roves blindly over the students. And then she lunges.
Not at the students, though they lurch back in a wave to get
away, but straight into the bank of lockers.

She rams her head against them, and then her fists, pounding
the metal.

TEACHER: Move! Get out of the way!

The male teacher pulls her away from the lockers. The locker
doors are dented, smeared with blood. She wrenches away
from him and then stops.

She freezes, the rage falling from her face like a mask cast to
the floor. She blinks, looking dazed. She spreads her hands
and looks down at them.

TEACHER: Sophia?

She turns and walks calmly away from him. The crowd of stu-
dents parts hastily to give her room.

The video ends.

3

I MUST HAVE dozed off, because then I was dreaming. The dreams were always the same, a tangled knot of memory and nightmare—the sea, the cold, the shore. A sky empty of stars. And lastly, always, the dark angel.

The dark angel was a hole in the world in the shape of a man. Six wings grew from its shoulders, and it hung above me, its outline surrounded by streaks of light like fractured glass. It pointed at me—

And I woke. I sat panting in bed, sweat sticking my shirt to my skin. The light in the hall was off, and I glanced at the alarm clock beside the bed. Just after two a.m. It was dim outside, though not quite night. There was no true night in the summer here.

Something clicked softly against the window.

My head whipped up. For a moment all I could see was my startled reflection. Outside there was only the sound of waves and wind, of rock tumbled against rock, scrape and hush, and of the terns calling.

Or was it more? The scrape of rocks became a footstep; the tern's scream became the wail of someone crying. Then back again. I crept from the bed and turned off the light. When I turned to the window, my twinned self in the reflection had vanished. In its place was the mist.

And in the mist, a shadow. Someone was outside.

I bolted to the window, but the shadow had receded into the gloom.

I bit my lip, my mouth dry and sour with adrenaline. Everyone I'd met so far had told me this place was dangerous. Mr. Nguyen, refusing to set foot on the shore. Mikhail, with his parting warning. Mrs. Popova, locking the doors against an empty island. I should stay put. Any sensible person would stay put.

But I wouldn't find out anything by staying safely indoors. And it wasn't like I had anything to lose, except my life. And it wasn't a life worth fretting over.

I grabbed my phone for its flashlight and hurried for the back door, doing my best to move quietly. The house was old and creaked with every step, but no one stirred. I twisted the deadbolt on the back door and yanked it open. Frigid air blasted me immediately, but at least there was only fog. The storm had stayed out east after all.

Mrs. Popova's house backed up to the water. I walked slowly toward it—between the darkness of the cloud cover and the mist, I could barely see my own feet. It would be easy to fall, crack my skull on the rocks, and be carried away by the hungry tide. Just another one of the vanished.

I'd reached the edge of the water. The surf slapped at the pebbles just ahead of me, foamy, flecked with grit and bits of seaweed. It sloshed, shushed—dripped. But no, that last sound was behind me, and with it the scrape of rocks. A footstep.

Fear jolted through me, rooting me in place. I should have turned, but the terror held me still. Another footstep came, and with it a soft exhalation of breath.

Angrily, I shoved my fear into the emptiness of the void. For an instant, it vanished—and then it rushed back, like a wave retreating only to crash against the shore once more. I sucked in a startled breath, and bit down against a low moan of animal panic.

"Who's there?" I whispered. My voice was too weak to overcome the ocean.

Fingertips brushed the back of my neck. I held myself perfectly still as they trailed lightly down my back to a point between my shoulder blades, then fell away. The person behind me sighed, and their footsteps fell back. I forced myself to turn slowly, my heart hammering.

The mist was thick. Thicker than any fog I'd ever seen. The figure in front of me stood no more than four feet away, but all I could see was a gray shadow through the mist. A person, but featureless, nearly formless. Silent, except for the persistent drip of water. A damp, earthy smell seemed to emanate from them.

"Who are you?" I asked.

"Who are you?" the figure repeated. Voice a croak like a raven's.

"What do you want?" I asked.

"What do you want?" Less of a croak now. Almost human.

The figure faded. It took me a moment to realize they had stepped back—and back again, the mist swallowing them until all that was before me was a featureless expanse of gray.

I was alone.

VIDEO EVIDENCE

Recorded by Liam Kapoor

JUNE 28, 2018, 2:34 AM

Liam sits on his bed in one of Mrs. Popova's room. He rakes a hand through his hair.

LIAM: Hey, Mum. Here's your daily message, as commanded. I can't sleep. Still. So that's fun. Dr. Kapoor doesn't want me here. Still. So that's also fun.

He sighs and looks away from the camera, toward the window. He frowns.

LIAM: Hold on. Someone's out there.

He walks to the window. The camera captures his face from below as he peers into the mist. Then he mutters something and switches to record with the rear-facing camera.

A figure walks past the window—a young woman, indistinct in the mist. She pauses directly in front of Liam and looks toward him, her features obscured.

LIAM: Sophia? What is she—

The girl walks away swiftly.

LIAM: She shouldn't be out there.

He moves quickly, dashing out of his room and down the hall. The backdoor gapes open. Liam swears and pauses to shove his feet into his boots.

LIAM: Just my luck if the new girl falls and breaks her neck on the first night. And it'll be my fault somehow, I guarantee you . . .

He jogs out into the mist.

LIAM: Sophia? Sophia, are you out here?

The mist is growing thinner, a stiff breeze carrying it away, and a gap reveals the slim figure out on a spit of rock, arms wrapped around herself and hair whipping in the wind.

LIAM: Sophia!

The girl looks back. For an instant, Sophia's strange, solemn features are clear—and then she turns away and steps into the water.

LIAM: What the hell . . . ?

She takes a step deeper into the surf.

LIAM: Stop!

Liam runs forward, but his untied boots skid out from under him, and he falls with a yelp and a clatter of rock. By the time he scrambles upward, there is no sign of Sophia. And then the camera focuses, and Liam swears again. Sophia stands up to her rib cage in churning water. A swell engulfs her to the neck as it passes, and then she takes another step, farther from shore.

LIAM: Sophia! Come back! What are you doing? Jesus, that water's freezing, you're going to—

But she only walks onward, and the water folds over her. She vanishes—and does not emerge again.

LIAM: No. No, come on . . .

He breathes heavily, stepping toward the water before shying away again. At this point in the summer, water temperatures remain dangerously cold. Yet Liam steps closer to the water's edge.

SOPHIA: Liam! I'm here.

He whirls around. Sophia staggers out of the mist from the direction of Mrs. Popova's, looking dazed.

LIAM: What the—?

He looks again toward the ocean, but there is only black water and white foam, and the mist, growing thicker with every breath.

Of the girl who walked into the ocean, there is no sign at all.

4

I HEARD LIAM calling my name, but I was still rooted in place. It took me what felt like an eternity to start moving. Longer to get my voice back and call to him. He looked at me wildly, like it was impossible that I was standing there.

Then he grabbed me in a tight hug, releasing me before I could decide how to respond. He cleared his throat, looking awkward. "Sorry. It's just I saw—I thought I saw—"

I didn't get to hear what he was going to say. From farther along the beach came a crash and a scream. We exchanged a look that meant something like *Now what?*

Liam sprinted toward the sound, awkward in his unlaced boots. I followed a beat behind. The sound had come from the end of a spit of rock, and as we drew closer a light stuttered near the water, accompanied by a string of frantic cursing.

A small motorboat had slammed up against an outcropping of sharp black rocks about ten feet out from where we stood. Razor-sharp barnacles studded the slick rocks. The boat was taking on water rapidly, sinking, and a girl who looked about my age had flung herself up on the rock, scrambling for purchase, a heavy bag slung over her shoulder. Her foot slipped, and she plunged up to her waist in the water with a yelp.

"Hang on," Liam called to her.

"What d'you think I'm trying to do?" she hollered back. Her voice sounded familiar. She braced and hauled herself upward again, but she was still submerged to her knees, and her hands were bloodied.

Lily and Kenny came racing into view. "What's going on?" Lily asked, and then she saw the girl. "Oh, shit."

The boat listed and slipped out of sight beneath the water. Beyond the girl, the water was deep, but between her and us I could see the shapes of rocks maybe a foot or two below the surface. Slippery, but better than plunging into ice-cold water. Hopefully.

Automatically, I started to push aside my fear, but then I remembered how it had rushed back into me immediately, worse than before, how it had left me frozen. So I let it stay.

"Liam, grab my hand," I said, voice shaking but determined. I didn't wait for anyone to object. I stepped out into the water. Liam lunged to grab me, getting his hand around my wrist to steady me as I balanced, my bare feet going instantly numb. I met the girl's eyes. "You're going to have to get closer," I said.

She began to inch around the rock. I stepped out as far as I could, Liam leaning to support me while Kenny grabbed his elbow to steady *him*. The girl reached toward me. Our hands met, her frigid, wet fingers closing over mine. "Got it?" I asked, teeth chattering.

"I'm good," she said tightly, hiking her bag up higher, and levered herself carefully off her perch, stepping onto one of the submerged rocks. She wobbled. I wobbled. But Liam steadied me, and none of us fell. We picked our way carefully to dry land. Liam let go of my hand as soon as we were safe, but I kept my grip on the girl until she straightened up, pale and shivering.

"Thanks," she said, giving me an odd look. I knew where I'd heard that voice before. Abigail Ryder. The girl who'd told me about my mother. I stared at her. And she—winked.

"Who the hell are you?" Lily demanded. "What are you doing out here?"

I didn't want her answering that question. Or giving me away. "Maybe we can hold off on interrogating her until she's inside and not hypothermic," I suggested, putting the kind of steel behind the words that tended to make people hop into action without questioning. Kenny gave a little jerk and nodded, but Lily's look was skeptical. Abby shivered theatrically.

"G-good idea." She might have been playing it up, but her lips were turning blue.

Of the four of us, only Kenny had managed to grab a coat on his way out the door, and he hung it around Abby's shoulders as we helped her toward the house. Mrs. Popova stood on the back porch, holding her rifle loosely.

"She crashed on the rocks," Kenny said. "We've gotta get her warmed up."

Mrs. Popova's lips thinned. She looked out past us—at what, I couldn't imagine.

"S-sorry to impose," Abby said, teeth chattering.

For a wild moment, I thought Mrs. Popova was going to refuse. But then she stood aside. We trooped in and Kenny settled Abby on the couch before going to get the fire started. Mrs. Popova looked outside one last time, then closed the door and threw the deadbolt.

I stood a few feet away from Abby as she stripped down to her underwear, the guys turning tactfully away, and wrapped herself in a heavy quilt. What was she doing here? No, that was the wrong question—I knew what she was doing here. She was chasing the same answers I was. But I didn't know why, and that worried me.

"Liam," Mrs. Popova said, her voice clipped, "call your mother and tell her about our guest. And you." She looked at Abby. "Who are you and what on earth are you doing out here?"

"Abby. Abby Ryder. Nobody would take me, so I had to find my own way here," Abby said. "I was trying to beat the storm, but I got a bit lost. With all the mist I didn't even know I'd found the place until it busted a hole in my boat."

"You were *trying* to get here?" Kenny asked, mystified.

Abby gave a sharp little laugh. "Assuming this is Bitter Rock, yeah."

"But *why*?" Kenny pressed.

Abby's eyes flicked to me for a split second. "I'm doing this school project. About mass disappearances. I was in Juneau visiting my aunt and I heard about the whole Landontown thing. I wanted to visit and check it out, and, well . . . I guess I got carried away?"

She was lying. She'd called me about Bitter Rock months ago, and she hadn't said anything about a school project then. She'd said she worked for a professor or something—Dr. Ashford. She said he investigated "this kind of phenomenon."

"So you're one of those," Mrs. Popova said, shaking her head with obvious disapproval. Abby had opened her bag and pulled out a wad of wet clothes, grimacing.

"I'll grab you something to borrow," Lily said. "Put those by the fire to dry."

Liam was speaking quietly on the phone in the kitchen. He hung up and joined us. "Dr. Kapoor says to stay put. Bring her to the LARC in the morning," he said.

"For now, everyone should get some sleep," Mrs. Popova said. "And get out of those wet clothes. Especially you, Ms. Hayes."

Abby's eyebrow quirked at the surname. I looked down at my soaked jeans and bare feet, the latter of which were an unsettling shade of gray. "Right," I said.

"Where's she going to sleep?" Lily asked, returning with the offered clothing.

"She can bunk with me," I said immediately. "I don't mind."

"Sounds good to me. Sorry again. And thank you guys for saving my ass," Abby said.

"There will be a reckoning in the morning," Mrs. Popova said, more a warning than a threat. Dr. Kapoor, I imagined, was *not* going to be pleased.

And I could be sunk before I'd even gotten started.

I pointed Abby toward the room and started to follow, Abby

awkwardly carrying Lily's borrowed clothes and her own bag while keeping the quilt wrapped around her. Liam grabbed my arm. "I know I'm not supposed to ask if you're okay, so this is me not asking if you're okay," he said quietly.

"Why wouldn't I be?" I asked. I didn't ask it dismissively—I needed to hear the answer.

He swallowed. "Something happened out there."

"You saw something?" I wanted the answer to be yes. Because that would mean it wasn't just me, letting my imagination run wild.

"There was someone out there," he said. "And she looked . . ."

"What?" I asked.

His hand dropped from my arm. "I don't know. The mist was really thick."

Disappointment and something deeper sang through me. For as long as I could remember, I'd been waiting for someone to tell me that they saw what I did. That I wasn't alone. Or delusional. But anytime anyone came close, it ended like this. They saw something they couldn't explain, and they ran as fast as they could in the other direction.

At least, that was what it had been like when I was younger. Before everyone figured out what a freak I was and stayed away in the first place. Liam would figure it out too.

"Good night," I said, and told myself I was used to it. That I didn't care what Liam Kapoor thought about me.

"Pardon my nudity," Abby said once the door was closed, and dropped the quilt. I turned away while she shimmied into the sweats and long-sleeved tee that Lily had offered. Lily was shorter and stockier than Abby, and the sweats hit awkwardly above the ankle.

As I stripped off my own sodden jeans, she unpacked the rest of her bag. There was a camera case and a notebook, along with a three-ring binder. The camera case was damp but the interior looked dry, and the notebook and binder were in plastic bags. She let out a sigh of relief.

"Nothing vital lost," she said. "So, Ms. *Hayes*. What brings you to Bitter Rock?" I glared at her, but she just smiled a little. "Sorry. I'm assuming you being here is my fault."

"Keep your voice down," I hissed at her, but she was almost whispering already. I was just nervous. I perched on the bed opposite her. "What are you really doing here?"

"The same thing you are, I'm guessing. Trying to find out why people keep disappearing from this place, and why no one else seems to care," Abby said.

"Why do *you* care?" I demanded, then shut up as I heard Kenny and Lily head down the hallway, chatting.

Abby shrugged. "Curiosity, same as you."

I stared at her a beat, rage rising behind my breastbone. "Curiosity? I've spent my entire life wondering how my mother died. And it doesn't make any sense. There's no reason to hide the truth if all that happened was that she died in a storm. Why hide the fact that she was here? Who's hiding it? What happened to her? What happened to *me*? I have to know, because until I do, I don't even know who I *am*. I've got nothing. No family. No friends. I don't even have a home to go back to. All I've got is myself, and

I don't know what 'myself' *means* if I don't know why I lost everything else. So that's why I care, *Ms. Ryder.* It's not *curiosity.* It's . . . everything."

I let out my breath in a rush and looked away, my eyes pricking. I resisted the urge to shove that emotion away, force it into the void. It always felt like the easier way out, in the moment. But some hurt was worth feeling.

"Okay," Abby said softly. "You're right, that was flippant. I'm sorry. I came because of this." She unzipped an inner pouch in her bag and pulled out a small cardboard box. She opened it carefully and emptied the contents onto her palm, holding it out to me.

It was a wooden bird. A red-throated tern. Almost every detail was the same as the one in my jacket pocket: the red patch on its throat, the angle of its wings. But one wingtip had been broken off, and a brown stain marred its side.

"It's a red-throated tern. They only live here," Abby said.

"I know," I said. "I . . . I've seen one like that. Where did you get it?"

"My sister gave it to the man I work for, Dr. Ashford."

"And that made you want to come here?"

"Yeah. See, the thing is, my sister gave it to him in September. When she'd been dead for almost a year." I stared at her. She gave me a crooked smile. I didn't believe in ghosts, exactly, but I was ready to accept them as part of a world that included me. "I've got no idea why Miranda sent me here. But you're not the only one with personal business on this island, Sophia. Which means you're not on your own."

I drew in a stuttering breath, relief that felt like sorrow

sweeping through me. It seemed too dangerous to believe. I had always been alone. Always. "I need to find out what happened to her. To us," I said.

"I know. And I'll help you," Abby said. "I'll tell you everything I know. But first, I need you to tell me something."

"What?" I asked, wariness stealing back into my tone.

She tilted her head a little. "Why don't you have a reflection?"

EXHIBIT D

*Photograph from the Instagram account
of user @missoulamont_anna*

POSTED MARCH 7, 2018

*Image shows a young woman with curly brown hair and a ma-
roon coat standing in front of a pizza parlor, offering the
camera a practiced smirk. To the right of the frame, captured unintentionally in the background, is a second girl,
this one with a long plait of blonde hair hanging to the middle of her back. She is looking at her reflection in the mirrored windows of the restaurant.*

*Except that it is not a reflection at all, or not a proper one. The
girl in the mirror is also blonde, also with her hair braided,
also with a gray coat and jeans.*

*And like the girl who stands at the edge of the frame, the reflec-
tion is facing away from the camera.*

5

ABBY LOOKED STRAIGHT at me. People didn't often do that. Something about me didn't invite direct scrutiny. But she'd seen. She'd seen what no one else had, my whole life.

I don't know when I first realized that I didn't have a normal reflection—or rather, that other people *did*. That their reflections didn't move out of synch, face the wrong way, get details wrong.

"I have a reflection," I said to Abby. Not because I thought I could fool her, but because I needed her to say it, the way I'd needed Liam to tell me what he'd seen. I needed to be sure. And so I waved at the window opposite us, and my reflection waved back.

"Yeah, no," Abby said. "That's not a reflection. A reflection is a *mirror image*. You have a mole on your right cheek. Which means it should be on your reflection's left cheek, but it isn't. It's on the right. Your jacket has a pocket on the left. So does the one in the reflection."

I gave a strangled laugh. "This is tame, for me. Sometimes she does what I do, only a second too late. Sometimes she's wearing different clothes. Or her hair is all wild, even though I always keep mine braided. Or she's looking the wrong way."

"Why?" Abby asked.

"I don't know," I said. "I'd almost convinced myself it was all in my head."

"It isn't," Abby said. Her eyes were still locked on mine, and when she spoke, each word was deliberate and clear. "Sophia, I believe you. You never have to worry that I'm going to call you crazy or think you're seeing things that aren't there. You are not the strangest thing I've come across, I promise. Okay? I believe you."

I looked away, and bit my lip to try to hold back the tears that threatened to fall. I hadn't realized how much I wanted to hear those words. How much I *needed* to, after all these years knowing there was something wrong with me. Instead, I'd only ever gotten frightened looks—or disgusted ones. Medication I found ways to throw away. And eventually, I'd gotten the same speech, over and over— *We think you'd do better with a different placement.*

"Thank you," I said. I sank down onto the bed, my legs suddenly unable to hold me up.

She shifted, a little uncomfortable. "You should hear it when Ashford does that speech. Makes *everybody* cry."

"Ashford—that's your boss?" I asked. "He investigates, what, paranormal stuff?"

"Dr. Ashford would say 'inexplicable phenomena of potentially extra-natural origin,'" Abby said. "In layman's terms, spooky shit. Most of the time it's bunk, or else a sad lesson in the evils of totally normal human beings."

"So how are you so sure it isn't this time?" I pulled my feet up under me on the bed.

"My gut," Abby said. "And that my dead sister gave me that bird. Or gave it to my boss, anyway, and I kinda stole it."

"Stole it?" I repeated. "Wait, your boss doesn't know you're here?"

Abby started to pack away the things that were dry, not quite looking at me. "He tried to hide it. And then when he realized that I'd found it, he tried to forbid me to go. Wouldn't tell me why. He just said to trust him. And I do, but . . . She gave it to me for a reason. She's my sister. Was. If she wanted me to come here, I had to. So I waited until Ashford was out of town—out of the country, actually—and came by myself." She said it lightly, but I could hear the thread of hurt beneath her words.

I shivered. "Does your sister do that a lot?" I asked. "Boss you around?"

"She's only shown up twice since she died," Abby said.

"What happened the first time?"

"Four people died," Abby replied matter-of-factly. She finished with her things and hopped up into the bed, sitting at the foot while I scrunched up near the pillows. She combed her fingers through her chin-length brown hair, which only succeeded in leaving it in slightly less random clumps. "But they didn't have me around to watch their backs. I only got there after the fact."

It wasn't entirely reassuring. "So how are we supposed to do this?"

"Ask questions. Investigate. Research," she said. "This place is so full of secrets, any amount of digging should turn something up. And then we just chase whatever lead we can find." She looked at me thoughtfully. "The reflection thing. Did that happen before you came here? When you were a kid, I mean."

"I don't know. I don't remember it happening, but I was only three. I don't really remember anything from that far back."

"Still. There's a good chance that whatever *that* is," she said, pointing at the window, "started here." She tapped a finger against her lips. "We need to talk to the other people who were on Bitter Rock the summer your mother disappeared."

"Dr. Kapoor and Dr. Hardcastle," I said. "But I don't know if they'll talk."

"Don't worry. I'll do what I do best—bother people until they let something slip." She gave me a wry smile. I decided I liked her then. I didn't trust her, exactly. But I liked her.

What did it say about me that the first time in my life I had an easy time making friends, it was on a haunted island in the middle of nowhere?

"Be careful when you meet Hardcastle and Kapoor," Abby added. "You don't know how far people might go to protect their secrets."

"But if whatever happened was supernatural, then they didn't do anything," I said. "Why would they need to hide it, other than people not believing them?"

"We don't know what happened," Abby said gravely. "And we don't know who's to blame."

INTERVIEW

Sophia Novak

SEPTEMBER 2, 2018

ASHFORD: Abby told you she'd stolen the bird.

SOPHIA: She told me that you'd hidden it from her.

ASHFORD: It was for her own protection.

Sophia looks unconvinced.

SOPHIA: You took her and Miranda in after their parents were killed. You raised them. I imagine you got to know them pretty well in that time.

ASHFORD: What is your point?

SOPHIA: How exactly did you think that forbidding Abby from going to that island, and refusing to tell her why, would play out? Of course she went.

ASHFORD: I hoped that she would trust me.

Sophia sits back. Her gaze is cool, unimpressed with this declaration.

SOPHIA: And should she have trusted you, Dr. Ashford? Or was she right to question?

Ashford doesn't answer. He folds his hands.

ASHFORD: Do you know how Abby and her sister came to be in my care, Ms. Novak?

SOPHIA: Their parents died.

ASHFORD: Their parents were torn apart. I was already pursuing the creature responsible, but I was too late. I found the girls on the road, screaming for help. By the time I got to the house, there was little left. Their father had to be identified through DNA. I did everything I could to keep them safe, but the Beast found them again. Killed Miranda. So perhaps you can understand why I might have been a bit overprotective of my other—

SOPHIA: Daughter?

Her voice is soft, not cowed but kind.

ASHFORD: Charge.

SOPHIA: Except you weren't just protecting her. Maybe it started that way. But by the time Miranda gave you that bird, you'd been lying to protect her so long that you had to keep lying. You had to lie to protect yourself. Because if she found out the truth, she would never trust you again.

6

I STOOD OUTSIDE Dr. Kapoor's office, the muffled voices inside offering only scattered intelligible words. Liam leaned against the wall opposite me, his arms crossed and his tongue worrying at his lip ring in a nervous habit. Every once in a while it clicked against his teeth. I should have found it annoying, but on Liam it was endearing.

"What do you suppose her odds of survival are?" I asked him, trying to break the tension.

"Oh, fifty-fifty," Liam said. "In her position, I'd rather try swimming back to the mainland than be in there with Kapoor."

The door opened, and Abby stepped out, followed by Dr. Kapoor. Dr. Kapoor looked distinctly irritated, which Abby seemed accustomed to.

"Ms. Ryder will be staying at Mrs. Popova's until Mr. Nguyen can pick you both up." I twitched, dismay running through me, and then I realized she was talking to Liam. Of course. He was heading back. "The weather still isn't clear for a crossing, but it should be tomorrow," she concluded. Dr. Kapoor's accent was solidly American, without any of the clipped precision of Liam's British accent. She was short, barely coming up to Liam's shoulder, and her brown-black hair was cropped within an inch of her scalp. She had a glare that would intimidate a wolverine, and currently it was fixed on me.

Abby didn't look concerned. She had twenty-four hours to figure something out, and she struck me as the sort of person who could do a lot with far less time.

"Ms. Hayes," Dr. Kapoor said sharply, startling me back into the present. "Do you need a printed invitation?"

I realized she was holding the office door open for me. I slinked in past Abby, who gave me a little wave. Lily was coming down the hall to collect her. Even after a single night of acquaintance, she felt like the best ally I had, and I didn't want to be separated so soon. But I didn't see how to object without raising suspicion. Liam trailed in after me, and I remembered that he, too, would be leaving soon. I'd be alone.

No more alone than I'd always been, I told myself.

"I do not expect you to know anything," Dr. Kapoor said without preamble. "I do expect you to learn. I expect you to ask questions, and not to assume answers. The worst thing that you can do is *guess* at what you are meant to be doing out of embarrassment or fear of looking foolish."

I blinked. Apparently we weren't going to discuss last night.

"Did you hear me?" Dr. Kapoor asked.

"Uh. Yes. Sorry, I thought we were going to talk about—"

"You are here to learn, and to work. That is all you should be worried about, Ms. Hayes," Dr. Kapoor said. She crossed her arms. My gaze wandered hopefully to the chairs by the desk, my legs still achy from last night's strain, but I could tell Dr. Kapoor was the kind of person that thought sitting just invited wasting time. Liam, however, plopped into one and threw his arm over the back. Dr. Kapoor ignored him. "You should know that most of our work is repetitive, tedious, meticulous, and dull. It's also often cold, wet, and physically demanding."

"You mentioned," I replied. "In your emails."

"Seventeen emails," Dr. Kapoor said crisply. "To your thirty-nine. There are birds everywhere, Ms. Hayes, and I have difficulty believing that you are so fixated on a minor tern that you simply had to study these ones. But persistence in the face of repeated failure is an admirable trait in a scientist, even if it is absurdly irritating on a personal level, so. Here we are. Any questions?"

"Hello!" a voice shouted behind me

I jumped and squawked in surprise. I whirled around and came face-to-face with a huge black raven crouched in a cage. Its throat feathers were ruffled, its beak cracked open as it examined me with bright black eyes. Its cage was secured with a fat padlock and covered with toys made of nuts and bolts and carabiners, things to twist and open.

It cocked its head to the side, examining me with my face flushed, the startled exclamation still on my lips—and it broke out into cackling, almost human laughter.

"Asshole," I muttered.

"He gets that a lot," Liam said, deeply amused.

Dr. Kapoor gave the bird a fond smile, and I remembered what Liam had said about her "feathered children." "This is Moriarty," she said.

"Hello, hello," Moriarty croaked, and shifted from foot to foot. Then he chortled, his beak jerking spasmodically, his feathers puffing out around him. He flapped his wings twice, then settled back into a piercing, silent regard.

"Does he have scientific value, or do you keep him around to scare visitors?" I asked, giving him a dire look. He cracked his beak in what I could swear was a mocking smile.

"Mostly the latter," Dr. Kapoor replied. "He's an excellent mimic. He's managed to convince more than one undergrad the LARC is haunted. I trust you're made of sterner stuff."

"I am, definitely," I said, trying to sound both confident and obedient and like I hadn't just gotten panicked by a glorified Halloween prop. Behind his mom's back, Liam threw me an exaggerated thumbs-up and a *great job* nod, and I resisted the urge to roll my eyes at him.

Dr. Kapoor snorted. "Let's see how long that earnestness lasts when you're trying to count chicks from a hundred yards away in a driving rain. All right. The red-throated tern nests in spring. Eggs hatch in May and June. You've come at the tail end of hatching, which means we've got hundreds of gray fluffballs to locate, identify, and document. It is simple and boring work, and I do not yet trust you not to fuck it up. So you're going to observe today, and get familiar with the other side of the island."

"Belaya Skala?" I asked.

"You know why it's called that?" she asked, but didn't wait for an answer. "Whatever idiot 'discovered' this place thought the rocks on the headland were covered in snow in the middle of summer. Thus, 'White Rock.' Turns out it wasn't snow. It was bird shit. But for some reason they decided 'Bird Shit Rock' lacked poetry. So they stuck with Belaya Skala and Gorkaya Skala for the two halves of the island."

"Gorkaya Skala is Bitter Rock?" I asked.

"Indeed. And the translated version stuck as the name for the whole island when Alaska became part of the United States," she confirmed.

"The Russians did have another name for the island," Liam said. His mother shot him A Look, but he just grinned. "Ostrov Dyavola. The Devil's Island."

"Why would they call it that?" I asked, mouth dry.

"Superstition and sensationalism," Dr. Kapoor snapped. "There's no way over to Belaya Skala by foot, so we go by boat. I'll meet you at the dock in ten minutes. Liam? You'll come along." It had a very *so I can keep my eye on you* undertone to it. This was apparently a dismissal, because she headed out the door without another word. My nerves were jangling, but I'd survived my first face-to-face meeting with Dr. Kapoor.

"She has that effect on everyone," Liam said, misreading my expression as general intimidation. "She's not the warm-and-nurturing type, but she's fair and she doesn't get pissed for no reason, and she's always willing to help if you need it. She's just not friendly about it."

I wondered how much of that was different for her son. Something in the tight way he looked at her told me her standards were even stricter for family.

"So. You ready for Belaya Skala?" Liam asked. I must have looked uncertain, because he laughed. "Don't worry. The only thing over there is a bunch of birds and graves."

"Graves?" I asked.

"Well. Not literally, I guess. They never did find the bodies," he said.

"Which ones?" I asked.

"It's a bit unsettling that you have to ask," he replied.

"More than a bit." We stepped out into the hall. "Nice to meet you, Moriarty," I called.

And then in a crooning, feminine voice, plucked from my memory and garbled by time, the raven replied. "Bye-bye, little bird."

7

LIAM WALKED ME out of the building and down a trail that snaked along the cliffside at the northern end of the island. Despite the clouds in the east, the sky above the island was clear, and the sun made the water gleam. Still, the wind threatened to push the storm our way, so we were both wearing rain shells just in case.

"What do you think Abby's deal is?" Liam asked as we walked, picking our steps carefully along the steep path.

I gripped the strap of my bag in a stranglehold and tried to sound casual. "You heard her. Some school project."

"Seems like a lot of effort. And over the summer too."

"Maybe it's one of those funky private schools for rich kids," I said.

"I doubt it. I've gotten kicked out of several of them. I like to think I can spot their denizens, and Abigail Ryder doesn't fit the bill."

I raised an eyebrow. "Does that mean you're rich?" I asked, hoping to get him off the subject of Abby and talking about himself. With most people, it was the quickest way to derail a conversation you didn't want to have.

"Old family money," Liam said. "Tainted money, according to my mother, since the only reason we have it is that my grandfather died before he could disown her. She gave most of it away, but Dr. Kapoor convinced her to use some for my education. Whenever I get kicked out, Mum's torn between disappointment and glee that I'm squandering her father's money."

"Did he disown her because of Dr. Kapoor?" I asked, genuinely curious now.

"No, it was because she argued against the Oxfordian theory of Shakespearean authorship in her thesis." I stared at him, and he laughed.

I rolled my eyes. "You know, it's not fair. With that accent you sound very authoritative."

"Only to an American. Though this country is growing on me for that very reason."

Down at the dock, Kenny was packing gear into a skiff with the name KATYDID stenciled on the side. Kenny looked up as if surprised to see us. For a minute I wondered if he hadn't known I was coming, but then I realized it was his default expression.

"Oh, hey. Good morning, you two. Sophia, I forgot to ask if you like coffee."

"Yep. But I left mine in the car, sadly," I said.

Kenny bent over and extracted a long thermos from an army-green bag. "Vital scientific equipment. Never leave base without it."

"You're a treasure," I told him, meaning it.

Kenny smiled. "We look after our own out here. And you're one of the flock now."

I wished in that moment that I was really the person I was pretending to be—a girl with a passion for birds and a bright future ahead of her. But without a past, I couldn't have a present, much less a future. I didn't know who I was—or who I wanted to be.

I helped hand Kenny the last of the bags, waiting as he maneuvered each into place in an arrangement that seemed to be exacting but looked like a messy heap to me.

"Everything stowed?" a voice said behind us. I turned to see a man in a long-sleeved tee. He was a big man, solidly built, with salt-and-pepper hair that was tousled—not like Kenny's and Liam's genuine *what is this ungodly hour* look, but carefully sculpted with gel, matched by a meticulously trimmed goatee. Abby stood next to him, her hands jammed in her pockets and a knit cap covering all but a fringe of her dark hair.

"You must be Sophia," the man said, holding out his hand. "I'm William Hardcastle. Call me Will."

I should have reached for it. I should have shaken his hand, said it was nice to meet him, smiled. But I was frozen. Because I'd met William Hardcastle, though I hadn't realized it before. I hadn't recognized the photo or the name. But I knew that voice. How did I know that voice? Why did it send a shiver of fear down my spine? The fear was corrosive, acid trailing down my vertebrae. And with it came a whisper, almost real enough to hear—*hide*.

But he couldn't know who I was, could he? Hardcastle had

been here with my mother, but I was only three years old in 2003. My hair had been dark brown, not blonde. You could see the resemblance if you were looking for it, but I didn't think that a shared first name would give me away.

The fear didn't know logic, so I gritted my teeth. My "moods," as my last foster mother had called them, were uncontrollable. Some were backlash, but other times they came out of nowhere. Whatever this was, though, it didn't feel like that—didn't feel like the panic was slamming into me out of nowhere. I didn't know why I was afraid, but the fear was all mine.

Dr. Hardcastle's hand remained extended. One second, two, and I forced myself to come unstuck, to reach out, because if I didn't move, he would know something was wrong.

But then Dr. Kapoor was striding across the beach, Lily in tow, and Dr. Hardcastle half turned, his hand dropping. I curled my fingers under, ignoring the voice in my head telling me to run. Liam gave me an odd look, but I didn't meet his eyes.

"What are you doing, Will?" Dr. Kapoor demanded.

"The same thing you are?" he said, with a chuckle that suggested he knew exactly what she was asking.

"I told Lily to deliver Ms. Ryder back to Mrs. Popova's until we can arrange a ride to the mainland," Dr. Kapoor snapped. "Lily says that you stopped her." Lily looked like she'd rather be a mile out in the open ocean without a boat than here. Abby showed no such distress.

Hardcastle ducked his head with a performative wince. "I know I shouldn't have overruled you like that, but what's she going to do all day? Make doilies with Mrs. Popova? If she's with us, at least we can keep an eye on her. Maybe she can even help count some of your hatchlings."

"I'll be quiet as a mouse. I won't get in your way at all," Abby said.

"She's not LARC staff," Dr. Kapoor said.

"Neither is Liam," Hardcastle pointed out.

Dr. Kapoor's jaw tensed, but she turned to Abby. "Do exactly as you're told, and no straying off on your own," she said.

Abby threw her a salute. "Aye-aye."

"Let's get moving. We've lost too much time with this weather," Dr. Kapoor said, as if the clouds and rain had been arranged to personally inconvenience her. The LARC researchers climbed into the skiff with practiced ease, and Abby followed nimbly.

Liam and I stepped out onto the slick, water-swollen boards of the dock. Liam got in first and offered me his hand. With a glance at the slippery dock, I accepted the help.

The boat rocked as I stepped in, pitching me toward him. He caught me by the arm. "Careful, there. That was very nearly the start of a romantic comedy," he said.

"If it was really a romantic comedy, I would have knocked us both into the water," I pointed out.

"And with that, my hopes are cruelly dashed," he replied.

I stared at him, and suddenly realized there might be a reason besides concern that I kept catching him looking at me. Could he actually be flirting with me? Boys didn't flirt with me.

Of course, all the boys I knew had figured out I was a freak a long time ago, and I'd done little to alter that opinion. Liam might be interested, but it was only because he didn't know me. Still.

It wasn't the worst thing to happen since I came to Bitter Rock. I smiled at him. I was surprised at how easy it was.

"It's a full house, so get friendly," Hardcastle said amiably.

The engine started up, and my smile dropped away. We were going to Belaya Skala.

And somehow I knew, deep in my bones, that whatever had happened, whatever I was trying to discover—it had happened over there.

I watched William Hardcastle, sitting at the prow of the boat and chatting with Lily. I knew something else: William Hardcastle had been involved. That fear started up again, a bitterness at the back of my throat and the sound of my pulse in my ears.

"Sophia?" Liam said uncertainly. It was the second time he'd said my name.

I gave him a wide smile. I couldn't be calm, but maybe I could fake it. "Sorry. I'm still jet-lagged, I guess."

He was looking at me strangely, and I found myself frantically cataloging every aspect of my demeanor, my appearance. What would give me away? What was the detail that would make him start to turn, to dislike me, the way everyone did in time?

"Yeah. The sunlight messes with your circadian rhythms," he said at last.

We rode the rest of the way in silence.

PART TWO

SOMETHING RICH AND STRANGE

EXHIBIT E

Excerpt from the article "Lesser-Known Mass Disappearances"

6. THE VANISHING SHIP: ALASKA

In the fall of 1884, the residents of an island off the coast of Alaska were awakened by shouting. A Russian fishing vessel, the *Krachka*, had run aground on the rocks off the northern point of the island, an area inaccessible except by boat. One injured fisherman was brought by rowboat to the larger town on the southern end of the island. The rest, it was decided, would shelter with the residents of the northern side until the weather calmed.

The island's doctor, along with several others, made their way to the northern end of the island in the morning. But there was no one there.

The ship was mired on the rocks offshore. The two lifeboats had been deployed. One was found on the beach. The other was never located. Several pairs of boots, along with sodden clothing, were discovered drying next to the fireplaces in empty homes.

Supper still lay, uneaten, on the table; cold cups of tea sat on mantels and countertops. A broken lantern was discovered halfway up a hill. In the schoolhouse, a phrase from a Bible verse was written on the chalkboard: И КАЖДОЕ ИЗ ЧЕТЫРЕХ ЖИВОТНЫХ ИМЕЛО ПО ШЕСТИ КРЫЛ ВОКРУГ, А ВНУТРИ ОНИ ИСПОЛНЕНЫ ОЧЕЙ; И НИ ДНЕМ, НИ НОЧЬЮ НЕ ИМЕЮТ ПОКОЯ, ВЗЫВАЯ.[1]

The clearest hint of what had happened was found in the captain's log on the fishing vessel. The second-to-last entry, dated two days before the wreck, read: *We cannot seem to escape the fog. Alexei says he hears music in it, and he stands by the rail to listen and will not sleep. The [damaged, unreadable] throw it overboard, but [further damage] too late.*

The final entry reads only: *I see him now.*

No trace of the townspeople or the ship's crew was ever found.

---

1 Revelation 4:8, partially transcribed: "And the four beasts had each of them six wings about them; and they were full of eyes within: and they rest not day and night, saying."

VIDEO EVIDENCE

Recorded by Joy Novak

AUGUST 14, 2003, 12:14 AM

NOVAK: There we go!

The camera focuses on Joy Novak, who holds it at arm's length. She sits packed into a skiff with several others, who sit behind her: Dr. Vanya Kapoor, Dr. William Hardcastle, Carolyn Baker, and Martin Carreau. The passengers range in age, with Baker, at twenty-one, the youngest, and Hardcastle, thirty-eight, the eldest. It is night, but in summer that means only a slight dimming that barely qualifies as twilight.

NOVAK: This is the entirely illicit voyage of the . . . Does this boat have a name?

CARREAU: The *Oyster*.

NOVAK: The voyage of the *Shadow Oyster*.

CARREAU: The *Shadow Oyster*? Really, Joy?

Carreau's accent is French. He keeps long, dark hair, courtesy of a Moroccan mother, tied back.

NOVAK: We have to add something to make it more badass. We're breaking the law, after all.

KAPOOR: It isn't actually illegal, just against the rules.

She sits stiffly on the rearmost seat, looking as if she is not here entirely by choice.

BAKER: Roughly the same thing where Vanya is concerned.

She giggles, pushing her glasses up. She holds a silver flask in the opposite hand. It's difficult to gauge whether she is intoxicated or simply energized by the illicit nature of the outing.

Novak shushes them.

NOVAK: We, the employees of the Landon Avian Research Center, being of sound mind—mostly—have embarked upon a most scientific expedition of science-ness.

She turns the camera to look out over the front of the boat, revealing Belaya Skala.

NOVAK: As you can see, we have arrived at Belaya Skala. At night—if you can call this night. Technically it's . . .

She glances back at Carreau.

CARREAU: Nautical twilight.

NOVAK: It is expressly forbidden for any man or beast to linger on Belaya Skala at night or in the mist. But thanks to yesterday's storm, all our flights out were canceled, so we're all stuck on the island with nowhere to go. The forecast is clear, we're leaving in the morning, the Perseids are peaking, and tonight is the first time we'll get *true* night all summer. Which means that it's our best chance to see the meteor shower with the least amount of light pollution any of us is likely to experience in our lives.

BAKER: And it's my birthday.

NOVAK: And it's Carolyn's birthday. So we're going to get drunk, watch rocks fall from space, and get eaten by ghosts or aliens or whatever it is out here that everyone's so afraid of.

KAPOOR: I cannot believe I let you all talk me into this.

There's a rustle just off camera. Baker jumps with a squeak of surprise.

NOVAK: What the—

HARDCASTLE: Well, look at that. We've got a stowaway.

The camera swings around to focus on the three-year-old girl uncurling from under a tarp at the far back of the boat: Sophia Novak.

8

LIAM WATCHED ME with a concerned expression as we made the crossing. That, I reminded myself, was a complication I didn't need. Relationships required vulnerability and honesty. And I couldn't offer either.

Our path brought us parallel to the jagged garland of rocks that connected the headland to the main island. Approaching from this angle, Belaya Skala was all tumbled grays and blacks, not the white that had given it its name. I knew from studying maps that the headland was roughly triangular, the tip of the broken crescent that was Bitter Rock. The leeward side—the side sheltered from the wind—was where the terns roosted on white rocks. Like Bitter Rock, there were no trees, and the biggest plants were low-lying bushes.

"Does anyone live here?" I asked as the engine cut and we puttered toward a sliver of shore. I knew the answer, but I was fishing for extra information.

"Not anymore," Kenny replied. "There was the Landontown Fellowship, a sort of commune I guess you could say? But that, uh, didn't last. It's actually better land for building—lots more flat space—but for whatever reason nobody's ever managed to stay there for long."

"Not enough land to keep livestock, and hardly anything grows," Dr. Kapoor added. It was true—but I wondered if that was deliberate, the way she implied that was why Landontown had faded. "Belaya Skala is only suitable for birds, looking at birds, and getting away from people."

"Which is why we love it," Kenny added, and Dr. Kapoor actually chuckled.

We all loaded up with bags and equipment, then hiked toward the eastern side of the headland. We heard the birds long before we saw them. They'd been a constant background chatter since we launched, but the sound became oppressive the closer we got. A thousand conversations in a dialect we didn't understand. Though maybe Hardcastle and Kapoor did, after fifteen years.

The slight curve of the island cupped the remnants of the morning's fog and kept the rocky hillside obscured as Kenny and Dr. Kapoor set up a pair of huge binoculars on a tripod. Hardcastle and Lily busied themselves with some kind of audio equipment—a parabolic microphone, bulky headphones, and a laptop in a waterproof case.

"Ms. Hayes," Dr. Kapoor said, and I snapped to attention. "You'll be assisting with a count today. If you get bored, I don't care. If you have to pee, I don't care. You stand and you watch until I release you. Got it?"

Liam swung a grin toward me, as if he was waiting to see my

reaction. I just nodded. Do the job well. Don't give her reason to question why she's letting you stay.

"What should I do?" Abby asked.

Dr. Kapoor lifted an eyebrow. "Don't wander off," she said simply.

We'd come around to the southeastern tip of the headland. The shore stretching north and west was concave, creating a sheltered inlet of rocky cliffs, a steep snarl of rocks that were, as the explorer in Dr. Kapoor's story discovered, white with bird guano. The angle of the shore and the hill we stood on gave us a clear view of the whole colony.

"Take a look," Dr. Kapoor invited. Or rather, instructed. I stepped up to the binoculars. I could make out the nests tucked among the rocks. They were shallow bowls of twigs and grass. In pairs or singly, adult birds fussed and bobbled around chicks that ranged from grumpy-looking but cute balls of down to scraggly, skin-and-peach-fuzz creatures that looked like aliens.

"And we're just counting the chicks?" I asked.

"No, I am counting the chicks," Dr. Kapoor said. "You are standing right there and not interrupting." She pointed toward an empty patch of grass near Abby. I shuffled over obediently.

Kenny pulled a binder and a laminated map of the nest sites, each numbered, out of his bag and sat cross-legged on the ground. He flipped the binder to a printed chart with empty cells and waited expectantly as Dr. Kapoor scanned the landscape before settling on a target.

"Nest nineteen," she said. "One live chick. One egg, unhatched. Nest twenty . . . the second chick didn't make it through the night;

it's not moving. One chick still living. Nest twenty-one . . ."

It went on like that for a while, with long pauses as Dr. Kapoor adjusted the binoculars and checked with Kenny that he was caught up. I shifted from foot to foot to keep my circulation going. Liam had put in earbuds and found a rock to sit on. Abby paced a short distance away, her camera out and clicking away as she took landscape shots.

Hardcastle had the headphones on, pointing at something on the laptop screen and talking to Lily. I tried not to watch him too carefully, too obviously, but I couldn't help it—looking at him made my skin crawl, but looking away made me feel like I was turning my back on something dangerous. When he took off the headphones and looked up at me, I jerked, certain that my suspicion was written on my face.

"Why don't you three go explore the rest of the island?" Hardcastle asked.

Dr. Kapoor's head whipped up. "I don't think that's a good idea," she said.

"Why not?" he asked. "Sophia should know the lay of the land, at least, and Liam's gotten the tour already, so he can show the ladies around."

Liam popped out one earbud, looking hopeful. Abby kept her back to the adults, studiously examining her camera, but she looked as hungry as I felt to see this place.

Dr. Kapoor considered. Then she relented. "Keep your radio on you," she told Liam.

"Got it." Liam straightened up, stretching. The movement emphasized his long frame. My own build could generously be described as skeletal, but the rain shell I'd donned over my usual uniform of a T-shirt and jeans made me look shapeless.

We left the others and tracked over the back side of a hill. It was good to move after standing still for so long, and it must have shown.

"I thought she'd leave you stood there all day," Liam said. "You know, if you're lucky, maybe she'll let you look at a bird for more than two seconds by the end of the summer. But you have to establish that trust first. Prove yourself."

I snorted. "I guess I was expecting things to be a bit more hands-on."

"In a week or two they'll do the banding on the chicks. That's a lot more interesting, Kenny says. But most of the action happens back at the LARC itself. Kenny's doing something with DNA, and Lily and Hardcastle are doing this whole study on the bird calls— apparently they're unusually varied, or something? I was sort of tuning her and Kenny out at that point, I'll be honest. They get a bit overexcited. Tend to ramble. Then again, I seem to be rambling, myself. So stones, glass houses, et cetera." He slanted his smile at me.

"So can you show us around town?" Abby asked. She'd stopped to take a picture of Bitter Rock, beyond the channel of gray water and the black fangs of the isthmus, and she hustled to catch up.

"You mean Landontown?" Liam said with a frown. "There's not much there."

"But it is why I came," she reminded him.

"I suppose it's either that or an exciting tour of the island's best rocks," Liam said with a shrug. "This way, then. So you know about the Cole Landon debacle?" He was asking me.

I feigned ignorance, shaking my head. "Isn't that the guy who founded the LARC?"

"His widow founded the LARC, actually. He was an eccentric millionaire. He had this group of what you might call followers. They were all into this idea of getting back to the land and living communally. He bought Bitter Rock and brought all his people here. They built the Landontown Fellowship." He pointed down the hill. It dropped away for a bit, then leveled out into a plateau before the hill fell away again to the sea and a barren beach. There were only a dozen structures standing; a few more that had collapsed or burned down.

"And they all vanished," Abby said. Her camera clicked.

"Right," Liam said. "There are lots of theories. Mass suicide—they *were* kind of a cult. Storm. Murder. Cole Landon's widow was the only survivor. She was visiting relatives at the time. She established the LARC and never set foot here again."

Above the town to the north was a short, curved concrete wall with a gap running along the center. Something metal stuck out from the gap. "What's that?" I asked.

"Artillery," Liam said. "Don't worry, it's just decorative at this point. There's a bunker, too, right over there." He pointed out along the hillside. A metal door was set into the hillside, surrounded by more concrete and rubble that indicated there must have once been a wall a few feet in front of the door. "There was an airstrip here during the second world war. The bunker's flooded or something, though—can't get in."

"Have you tried?" Abby asked.

"No," he said. "Not being a *huge* fan of tetanus, I have some-how resisted the allure of a ruined hole in the ground."

Abby raised her eyebrows. "I've got all my shots." But she didn't press the issue. We headed down the hill, taking short, careful steps over the dew-slicked grass. A signpost stood at the entrance to the town, but the sign itself was long gone. Abby strode out ahead, snapping pictures as she went, and Liam and I naturally fell back at a more sedate pace.

"You know a lot about the island," I said. "How often do you come here?"

"Not very," Liam answered. "Twice since I was a kid, that's all. Usually quality time with Dr. Kapoor is arranged at some neutral third location, where my mum doesn't have to see her, and Dr. Kapoor can rely on guided tours to supply quality content instead of filling the silence herself."

"I'm picking up that you're not very close," I said.

We'd stopped, and Liam put his hands in his pockets, look-ing out over the ruined buildings. "My parents split when I was young. Right after Dr. Kapoor came to work here, actually. After that, quality time required several months of notice. My grandparents—her parents—fly out to see me for months at a time and help out, but she can't be bothered. So, yes, we have issues."

"Is that why . . ." I cleared my throat and gestured generally at his wrist, suddenly embarrassed. "You didn't seem to care about hiding it, so . . ."

"This?" He laughed, pulling his sleeve up to bare the bandage.

"I didn't do this to myself. Well, I did, but it was stupidity, not intent."

"I see." My cheeks flamed. "I thought—"

"Oh, I'm horrifically depressed," he assured me cheerfully. "And intensely medicated. I'm all right just now," he added, seeing my look of alarm. "I have good days and bad ones and a lot of mediocre ones. And I overcompensate with a cheerful demeanor, or so my therapist says. It's under control, promise. I just . . . had a bad patch, recently, and got into a bit of trouble."

"Trouble that left your arm cut up?" I asked.

He winced. "Wounds inflicted by a prisoner I was retrieving from confinement."

"You staged a jailbreak?"

"I stole a falcon," he answered. "She was being used as the mascot for an amateur football team and wasn't being cared for properly, so I arranged a rescue. She did not appreciate my chivalry, however, and this was the result."

Abby chuckled. I jumped a little—I'd almost forgotten that she was there. Judging by the look Liam gave her, so had he. "You gotta ask the damsels if they *want* to be rescued," she called over her shoulder.

"Right, so when you're kidnapped I'll go ahead and wait for a signed consent form before I rescue you, then?" he called back. He sounded jokey, but there was a definite barb under the words.

"I can rescue myself, thanks," she shot back.

"Glad that's settled," I declared before *just joking* turned into *actually arguing*. Abby shook her head ruefully and ducked inside one of the buildings—the biggest one still standing.

"Sorry to pry," I added, somewhat belatedly.

"I don't mind talking about it with you. Oddly," Liam said, a little quirk in the corner of his mouth. Like I was a puzzle, but he was patient enough to hold off on solving me. It should have irritated me, but the truth was I didn't entirely hate the idea of being solved by Liam Kapoor.

"Hey, guys?" Abby called. She leaned out the door. Her eyes were wide. "You should come see this."

The building Abby beckoned us toward was larger than the others, and when I stepped past the rotting front stoop and inside, I realized why. It was a church. Small and cramped, but with vaulted ceilings, the bare rafters gave it the acoustics of a larger building. Once, eight pews had stood in two orderly rows. Now two remained in place, the others overturned and rotted apart, cast up near the door like someone had dragged them there. At the front of the room was a small wooden altar. On it was a triple-paneled wood painting, hints of paint still flecked here and there, but whatever figures had graced it were obscured completely by age.

"I didn't think Landontown would have a church," I said, looking around.

"It's older than Landontown," Liam told me. "There's never been any known Native settlement, probably because it's so inhospitable. But a group of Russian fur trappers and fishermen, plus a few Native Alaskans who'd intermarried, tried to make a go of it in the nineteenth century. Unsuccessfully, I might add. Turns out 'any source of food at all' is kind of important. Mrs. Popova's actually descended from one of those intermarried families. Landon's people restored the church for the history, but they didn't use it."

"Not for worship, at least," Abby said. I gave her a quizzical look, and she pointed past me. I turned.

It took me a moment to realize what I was looking at. Broken boards were nailed to either side of the door. Almost as if . . .

"Someone boarded up the doors," I said.

"The last transmission from Landontown said some of them had taken shelter in the church," Abby said.

Liam touched one of the pieces of splintered wood, his face troubled. "They meant shelter from a storm," he said.

"You don't board up doors just to keep out the rain." She gave him a level look.

He gave a little shake—and then snorted. I watched him push his unease away, but he didn't have a void to cast it into. It lingered, a sour note in his expression even as he dismissed her. "So which is your favorite conspiracy theory? I'm partial to 'little green men ate all the hippies,' myself," he said. She glared at him. "What do you think, Sophia? I mean, I'm not saying it was aliens . . ."

I didn't respond. There was something else by the door. Something scratched into the sill beneath the window. I trailed my fingers over the faded letters. WE ARE NOT ALONE. A declaration of faith? Or a warning? I'd listened to the supposed recording of the last transmission out of Landontown. *We thought we were alone*, the man had said.

I could hear Abby and Liam arguing behind me—Abby pointing out all the inconsistencies with the idea that a storm had obliterated Landontown to the last man, Liam responding by coming up with increasingly absurd explanations. Outside, a few wisps of mist had begun to gather low to the ground, between the buildings. A single pane of the window was still intact, speckled with dust and grit. I found myself checking my reflection instinctively.

At first, I didn't think there was anything wrong with it. No wild hair, wearing the same clothes I was, facing the proper way. And then I realized—the girl in the reflection was standing in an empty room. Liam and Abby, arguing away behind me, were nowhere to be seen.

The girl's lips moved, forming a single word: *Run.*

In the darkness behind her, a shadowed figure emerged, spreading its wings.

VIDEO EVIDENCE

Recorded by Joy Novak

AUGUST 14, 2003, 12:43 AM

*Twilight consists of three stages: civil, navigational, and astro-
nomical. At the northern latitude of Bitter Rock, the summer solstice sees only a narrow band of civil twilight and a
few scant hours of navigational twilight. The deeper darkness of astronomical twilight, much less true night, does not
return until later in the summer—true night does not return
until, in fact, this very night. Now that deepest stage of twilight has fallen. Night has not yet quite arrived, but already
this is a truer darkness than is ever experienced in the city,
with only flashlights and a flickering campfire below, and
the wheel of stars above.*

*The camera rests on a small tripod, all of the LARC research-
ers and their young tagalong in frame. Sophia curls against
her mother's side, watching the other adults with wide eyes.*

NOVAK: —for us to be out here, but not her? Sophie's been camping all her life. It'll be fine.

KAPOOR: Maybe we should take this as a sign that we should all go back.

HARDCASTLE: We don't all need to go back.

BAKER: I'm not going back, no way.

HARDCASTLE: Joy, you take her, and—

CARREAU: And what? Then we are here and we have no boat. The girl is quiet as a mouse. The number of times she's been in the room and I didn't notice until she nearly gave me a heart attack . . .

He laughs.

BAKER: We can't keep a kid around while we all get drunk.

CARREAU: So some of us will not drink. I don't drink anyway, after all.

BAKER: I thought all Frenchmen drank.

CARREAU: And yet, here I am.

NOVAK: I won't drink either. And I'll make sure she doesn't bother you.

It doesn't seem to bother Sophia that she's being discussed. She scooches closer to the camera and wets her lips, then whispers.

SOPHIA: The singing's going to start soon. Shhh. Listen.

The adults do not seem to hear.

CARREAU: And now, we wait.

HARDCASTLE: We might be able to spot a few meteors even before true dark.

CARREAU: I'm in no rush. Honestly, I am out here more for the human company than for a few fleeting lights in the sky.

BAKER: I was having fun before this turned G-rated.

She cuts a look at Sophia, who doesn't seem to notice the scru-
tiny.

HARDCASTLE: I'm sure we can manage at least PG.

He winks at Carolyn, but she's sunk solidly into her sullen
mood and only grunts.

KAPOOR: I don't think we should be here.

HARDCASTLE: Come on, Dr. Kapoor. Live a little. Break
some rules.

KAPOOR: That's not it.

She's looking up. A dim flicker, the first pale hint of the Perseid
meteor shower, glimmers behind her, but that isn't what
she's looking at.

HARDCASTLE: What is it, then?

KAPOOR: For a bunch of scientists who came out here to
stare at the sky, you're not very observant. It's August
13th—well, 14th now.

BAKER: So?

NOVAK: Oh. Oh, my God. What—

KAPOOR: Exactly.

CARREAU: I don't understand.

KAPOOR: This is the second night of the full moon.

HARDCASTLE: And?

Sophia tugs her mother's sleeve.

SOPHIA: But Momma. There isn't any moon.

One by one, the researchers look upward.

The stars begin to fall.

9

THERE WAS A buzzing deep in my bones. I spun around. Expecting, hoping, to find an empty room, and Abby and Liam looking at me with that *what's wrong with her* look I knew so well.

And there they were, startled into silence by my abrupt turn. But they seemed faded, their figures stuttering, as if under a dying bulb. And each time they dimmed, the beast in the shadows flickered more solidly into being.

A hole in the shape of a man. Six wings, outstretched so that they filled the church—so that they were *larger* than the church, the very space around it warping.

I screamed. The shadow lunged for me, past the flickering images of Abby and Liam, becoming more real as they grew less so. I threw myself backward, away from it, and hit the wall hard. I scrambled sideways, diving out the door, but my foot caught, and I spilled onto the ground, scraping my knees.

A hand grabbed my arm, yanked me around. I stared, barely comprehending, into Abby's face. Her features were blurred, streaky like looking through dirty glass. Her words distorted.

"What's wrong? Sophia, you have to tell me what's happening." Behind her, in the doorway of the church, the winged creature advanced, step by step, almost curious in its approach.

I tried to speak, gasped, tried again. "There's something there," I managed.

"There's nothing there," Liam said, bewildered. He had the radio in his hand.

"It's coming closer," I hissed, gripping Abby's arm. Her expression was focused, fierce. *Help me*, I wanted to tell her, but the words withered in my throat as my mouth turned dry with fear.

"What's happening to her?" Liam demanded.

The creature had stopped at the threshold. It watched me—I couldn't see its eyes, only that empty black, but I could feel them on me. The humming in my bones was painful now. Abby's and Liam's forms were becoming more and more indistinct.

Enough, I thought fiercely, and *shoved* the feelings out. This time, the void was waiting. It devoured my fear, devoured everything, scraping me empty to the bone. The world grew sharp edges, the clarity of a still mind. I could feel the grit of sand and stone beneath my palms, see the weathered grain of the wood planks of the church, hear the raucous calling of the terns. There was something in their calls that matched the thrum in my bones, and matched, too, the strange vibration the creature was making, almost too low to hear, a sound I could feel in my chest, rising and falling and twisting in strange notes.

"I can hear it," I said softly.

A sharp pain lanced through my arm, and I yelped, yanking it against my body.

The world shuddered, and righted itself. Liam and Abby were solid again, clear. The door of the church stood empty.

My arm was bleeding just above my wrist. My sleeve had ridden up, and there was a slice across the skin, deep enough that it throbbed. Abby had a knife in one hand, the edge stained red. "Why did you do that?" I asked—my tone slightly puzzled, detached. Abby's brow furrowed at me, and I realized that wasn't how I should sound.

"What the hell was that?" Liam asked. He quivered with unspent tension, like he wasn't sure whether to rush toward me or stay the hell away.

I was glad of the void, because I knew this part too well. The first time I lost control, it was to fear. I was five years old, and it was the first week of school. Clarissa McKenzie asked me to play with her at recess. We were dashing around the playground when I collapsed and started screaming in sheer terror.

Clarissa didn't play with me after that. That was the first time I learned that I wasn't the sort of person who got to have friends. And now Liam had seen it too. This incident wasn't the same— there wasn't a rush of emotion this time. But from his perspective, I'd freaked out over nothing.

And that would be that.

He looked at me with wide eyes, and I braced myself. "What was happening? What was in the church?" he asked.

I blinked. He hadn't said, *What's wrong with you?* "I don't know," I said, more confused than relieved. He wasn't backing away—why wasn't he backing away? Calling me nuts? Telling me to stay the hell away from him? I looked at Abby. I needed to focus. I couldn't worry about Liam.

Not yet.

"It was huge. It was—like it was made of shadows. It had wings. Six of them. But it was a person. You and Liam were getting blurry, and it was getting clearer, and there was this *sound* . . ." I faltered, unable to describe it further.

"I thought there was something wrong with my eyes," Liam said.

"You got blurry, too," Abby explained. "And kind of . . . pale? It was like you were translucent, but not to look at. It was more like it got harder to know you were there."

"Why don't you sound freaked out by that?" Liam asked with a note of panic.

She ignored him. "Did it seem like that thing was coming after you?" she asked me.

"I'm not sure," I said. "It didn't leave the church. But it was looking at me. I almost felt like it was trying to figure out who I was."

"Time out," Liam said, making a big T with his hands. "You are both acting like this is mildly upsetting but largely expected, but may I remind you that *there aren't six-winged shadow monsters*. That is not a thing that exists in this world!"

"No, not this one," Abby agreed. She stood, helping me to my feet. I had a hand around my wrist, but the bleeding had mostly stopped.

"Why *did* you cut me?" I asked.

"You were completely fixated. Sometimes things need you fo-cused on them to affect you, so I distracted you. I guess it worked." She sounded breathless, and in my hollowed-out state it took me a moment to recognize it as fear. I'd had this idea of her as implaca-ble, untroubled by strangeness, but she held on to my hand well after I'd gotten my balance back.

"What were you going to do if it hadn't?"

"Improvise," she said with a shaky laugh.

"This is not happening," Liam declared, lacing his hands on top of his head, but it was a weak protest. I bit my lip. New emo-tions were creeping in, my temporary emptiness fading.

"Liam—"

His radio crackled with static, and we all jumped. Dr. Kapoor's voice was loud and urgent: "—going on? Where are you?"

Liam fumbled the radio from his belt. "Don't tell her any-thing," Abby said urgently.

He gave her a poisonous look, but he said, "Everything's fine."

"We heard a scream. And then you weren't responding." Her voice was tight, but the relief at getting an answer was palpable.

"We didn't hear anything," Liam said. "From the radio, I mean. We were just . . ." He considered. ". . . horsing around," he finished. I raised an eyebrow and mouthed *Horsing around?* at him. He spread his hands helplessly.

"Where are you?"

"The old town," Liam said.

"I want you to get back here right away. We need to get back across the channel before the mist gets any worse," Kapoor said.

The mist? I looked around. The air was hazy. The few wisps I'd seen earlier had thickened, eddying along the ground. "Crap. Yeah. We're on our way back," Liam said.

I took one last look behind me. The church was empty, silent and still.

We are not alone, I thought, and was glad that in that moment that I could not fear.

VIDEO EVIDENCE

Recorded by Joy Novak

AUGUST 14, 2003, TIME UNKNOWN[2]

HARDCASTLE: There has to be an explanation for this. A rational—

KAPOOR: You can sit around and figure out an explanation. I'm going back to the boat, and I'm getting out of here. Joy—

NOVAK: Yeah. Sophie, we're leaving.

Her voice is tight with fear. Baker and Carreau are still looking upward in rank confusion.

CARREAU: But that was *Venus*. Venus isn't a meteor; it's not meant to fall from the sky.

NOVAK: Martin, can you help me get all of this back in the bag?

....

2 Time metadata is corrupted on all files created after 12:47 AM, the exact time of nightfall at the location in question.

KAPOOR: Don't bother. We can come back for it later if we need to.

HARDCASTLE: We don't know that there's anything to be afraid of.

KAPOOR: And that is a risk that you are welcome to take for yourself, but there is a *child* here.

CARREAU: It's the sky. How do you escape the sky?

KAPOOR: The moon was out when we set off. I remember seeing it. Maybe whatever's happening is localized. Maybe there's a goddamn good reason no one's allowed out here at night.

She grabs the camera, but doesn't seem to remember to turn it off.

KAPOOR: You'd better all come, because we've only got one boat.

She leads the march. Their flashlights provide some visibility, the beams skittering over the ground. At the crest of the hill, Hardcastle calls a halt.

HARDCASTLE: Vanya, slow down. We're going to break our necks going downhill in the dark this fast.

KAPOOR: The stars are winking out, Will.

HARDCASTLE: It's some kind of trick of the weather or—

KAPOOR: The moon is missing and the stars are going out. A lifetime of scientific pursuit has taught me skepticism, but it has also taught me that the world is full of dangerous things, and we have only learned to explain about half of them. We'll study it after everyone's safe.

BAKER: It's beautiful.

KAPOOR: Yes, the stars are falling like it's the damn apocalypse, but it's very sparkly, Carolyn.

BAKER: Not that. The singing.

The frantic activity around the makeshift camp suddenly halts as everyone freezes, listening. Novak kneels with one arm around Sophia, holding her close.

CARREAU: What language is that?

KAPOOR: I can't tell. But I feel like I can almost understand it.

They listen. To what, we cannot be certain; the microphone records only silence. Novak gasps.

CARREAU: What is it?

NOVAK: There's someone down there. Down on the beach.

Carreau steps toward the camera, and picks it up. For a few seconds it goes out of focus in the darkness, and then it snaps into night-vision mode, and he zooms in on the beach. Down below, a man stands stock-still on the shore, not far from the boat they've left moored to a huge driftwood log. His back is to them, his arms dangling inert at his sides.

NOVAK: Who is it? Someone from the town?

CARREAU: I can't tell. It almost looks like—is that an army uniform?

BAKER: Oh, shit, there's more of them.

The camera pans along the shore. At eerily precise intervals, people—men and women both—stand facing the sea, ringing the shore.

CARREAU: What are they doing?

SOPHIA: Momma, I don't want to be here.

NOVAK: I know, baby. We're going home. Just be patient.

Mist rises from the water, and swiftly gathers, hiding the strangers from view.

NOVAK: Do we go down there?

KAPOOR: I don't know. I—

In the mist, something shrieks.

10

IT WAS STRANGE to be in a place where twilight never gave way to night, only shuddered back into morning. The light through the blinds made me sleep fitfully, my dreams full of wheeling terns and Mikhail, lunging at me from out of the mist only to turn into Hardcastle and then transform into the creature from the church.

I woke to sweat-soaked sheets despite the cold. On the mainland it had been in the sixties during the day, but on the island it was a good fifteen or twenty degrees cooler—something about microclimates and ocean currents.

I stared at the wall, the scenes from the day before playing through my head again. The creature, the hum. Rushing back to the shore and piling into the *Katydid*. It seemed like the mist had been chasing us. Liam and Abby and I had no chance to talk to each other—Dr. Kapoor sent Abby back to Mrs. Popova's and assigned Lily and Kenny to teach me how to log the day's data, and then to give me an overview of the various projects they were working on.

By the time we were done it was late—and I could feel the backlash coming, the price I paid for feeding my fear to the void. Abby was now in the room Liam had occupied the night before, so I closed my own door and curled up on my bed to ride it out. I must have fallen asleep at some point because I didn't remember anything else until morning, when I woke with my head throbbing and my lip bloody where I'd bitten down on it to keep from making any noise.

A knock on the door gave me half a second's warning before Abby opened it, leaning in. She was fully dressed, her messenger bag over one shoulder. "You're late," she informed me.

I blinked groggily. "What time is . . . ?" I glanced at the clock and swore. The odd timelessness of the midnight sun had knocked my internal clock truly askew.

"This whole thing does work a lot better if the boss lady likes you," Abby said. "But you smell like dead fish and despair. Might want to hit the shower."

I made a rude gesture in her direction, scooped up my clothes, and bolted for the end of the hall. I rinsed the stale sweat from my skin and dried myself hastily, then braided my hair by touch as I hurried down the hall, Abby trailing.

I wasn't the only one, at least. I found Kenny in the kitchen, a piece of jam-slathered toast hanging from his mouth as he pulled his sweater on. "Mgrfing," he said, then took the toast out. "Good morning. Nice of you to stay behind to walk with me." He winked.

"I'm so dead," I groaned. *Not a real internship,* I reminded my-self, but I thought of Dr. Kapoor's stern gaze and hurried to lace up my boots.

"It's our lucky day. Lily messaged me. Dr. Kapoor's been in her office with Dr. Hardcastle all morning. Hasn't noticed we're missing. If we hurry, we might survive another day!"

"I'll tag along, if that's cool," Abby said. Kenny bobbed his shoulders in a shrug that was less an answer than a refusal to take responsibility.

We headed out the door together, pausing to lock up behind us. I caught a flash of my reflection in the window by the door, exhausted and tousle-haired. At least mirror-me looked as bad as real-me felt.

Lily had taken the car the assistants shared, leaving us to hoof it along the gravel road. Mrs. Popova's house was on the south-western edge of the island. In fact, given the island's hook, it was the farthest spot on the island from Belaya Skala. Which meant it was a long way from the LARC as well, and most of that uphill. I was sweating again by the time we hustled up the last stretch to the door.

Lily met us at the door. "You're in the clear," she said, and high-fived Kenny and me as we went past. She gave Abby a quiz-zical look, but she swanned past without explanation.

We shuffled into the break room, which was more of an overflow-storage room with a couple couches crammed in between the boxes. Liam was there, leaning against the counter by the coffee maker. He had his arms crossed, his body compressed with nervous energy, but when he saw me he relaxed a little. I didn't think my arrival had ever inspired that reaction in someone.

"Howdy," he said.

"Is that your attempt at an American accent?" I asked him.

"Not convincing?"

"I'd give it a solid C minus," I told him.

"That's charitable," Abby said. Liam winced theatrically.

The banter was forced, but there was a desperate release in it, like we were all grabbing at something normal.

Dr. Kapoor showed up twenty seconds later. "Morning," she said, as if unwilling to append an adjective it hadn't earned. She wasted no further time on pleasantries. "Today we are going to finish up yesterday's interrupted work. Lily, you'll be joining me for that. I think it's best if we let our intern experience some variety, and the sample room requires some attention. Kenny, you can orient Ms. Hayes before you get started for the day."

I didn't want to be stuck doing inventory and tidying—I wanted to go back to Belaya Skala. Lily caught my look and misread it. "It's much cooler than it sounds," she assured me.

"Yeah, the sample room is boss," Kenny agreed. He propped a hip against the back of the couch and folded his arms. "You'll dig it."

"Are you . . . Is that you trying to talk like the youth these days?" Lily asked him. She shook her head in mock shame, and he blushed bright red.

Dr. Kapoor wasn't done. "I've contacted Mr. Nguyen, but he is unavailable to retrieve you," she said, looking at Abby. "Dr. Hardcastle is trying to locate someone else who is able to fetch you. If he is unsuccessful, we will sacrifice the use of the *Katydid* to ferry you back tomorrow."

Abby just smiled. "That leaves me one more day to explore."

Dr. Kapoor's jaw tensed. "This island is private property," she said. "You are trespassing, and have been since you arrived. Not to mention the fact that if you were to wander off and hurt yourself, the Center could be held liable."

"Abby and I could help Sophia in the sample room," Liam suggested.

"I'd appreciate the company," I added.

"I don't know about that," Hardcastle said, striding into the room. My stomach dropped, and I took an involuntary step back.

Run, that voice in the back of my head insisted.

Hardcastle was smiling and I found myself staring at his perfect white teeth. "Vanya's a stickler for procedure. Letting civilians rifle through our old junk? Could lead to pandemonium!" He chuckled. The sound of the ocean roared in my ears. "But seriously, the insurance folks would probably rather we stick to official LARC staff only. I'm at loose ends, though—I can help you out, Sophia."

I stared at him. It felt like a fist was wrapped around my throat. I couldn't speak, and maybe that was for the best, because the only word in my mind was *no, no, no*—

"It's fine," Dr. Kapoor said abruptly. "Might as well put our guests to productive use. You were just complaining about being behind on grant writing in any case."

"True," Hardcastle said, sounding surprised. He was not used to playing bad cop, clearly.

The tension in my chest eased enough for me to breathe. To fake a smile. "Cool," I said. Too loud, too bright, but maybe they wouldn't notice.

"All right," Dr. Kapoor said. "Kenny?"

"Come, my ducklings," Kenny said, summoning us with a wave of his hands. I forced myself to walk instead of sprinting to get out of the room. Away from Hardcastle.

"Hey," Liam said softly. He snagged my elbow, and we fell a few steps back behind Kenny and Abby. "I know I'm not supposed to ask if you're okay. But. What was that with Will?"

"I don't know what you mean." I did my best to look mildly confused, but all I managed was a grimace.

"You looked like you were ready to bail out through the nearest window. Or possibly go for his throat," Liam said.

"I barely know him," I said. Not an answer. Not a lie.

He hesitated, then glanced behind us as if worried he would be overheard. "I just . . . I don't know about that guy. My mum—Shakespeare-mum, not bird-mum—doesn't like him, and I'm not sure Dr. Kapoor does either, even though she's worked with him for most of my life. Mum calls him a selfish creep. Dr. Kapoor once told me 'reliable and trustworthy are not the same thing,' and I had the odd feeling she was talking about him."

"Yikes," I said casually, as if his words weren't a dull knife digging at my insides.

"So . . . I don't know. Stay away from him, maybe."

"I can take care of myself, Liam," I said.

The look he gave me was almost sad. "Sure. Just a heads-up."

"Here we are," Kenny declared. He'd led us to a nondescript

door, fitted with a keypad. "The code's 1975," he said, punching in the numbers.

"The year the LARC was founded," I noted.

"You did your homework," he said with appreciation, and ushered us in.

The room was exactly the same dimensions as Dr. Kapoor's office, but so cramped with shelves and sets of drawers that there was almost no room to maneuver. Most of the floor space was taken up with waist-high drawer units. The back wall was floor-to-ceiling with glass cabinets, the shelves within stocked with stuffed and mounted specimens—birds, but also eggshells, drained and mounted on metal posts, feathers, feet, bones. Some of the taxidermy birds looked patchy, feathers worn away and flaking, revealing long-dead skin. And others—

On the leftmost shelf rested a bird preserved in a pose of flight, wings outstretched—but two more withered wings sprouted from its shoulders. The bones were warped, the feathers malformed so that they clumped like damp paper.

And on the next shelf, there was a chick still covered in gray down, frozen with its head tilted back, begging for food. But instead of one gaping beak, it had two, a small white one set inside the other, oddly soft-looking, like a mushroom cap.

Farther down the row, a juvenile tern perched on a driftwood branch, head cocked to the side—an eyeless head, feathers flowing seamlessly over a skull that showed no hint of even empty sockets.

"Holy crap," Abby said eloquently. Liam appeared more amused by our stunned looks than shocked, so I assumed he'd seen the birds before.

"Let me introduce you to our mutants," Kenny said cheerfully. "The red-throated tern has a very high rate of mutation. Mostly birds like these die in the shell or in their first few days, but a few of them, as you can see, persist."

"What . . ." I cleared my throat. I was a scientist, I reminded myself. Or an aspiring one, at least. Eager and intrigued. "What causes it?"

"We don't know. That's part of what we're studying," Kenny said. "My specialty is genetics. I'm trying to figure out what predisposes this species to mutation."

"What's the practical application of that?" I asked. The more I focused on the questions, the further away the encroaching fear felt. I could almost breathe normally without thinking about every breath. "Do you think it could have uses for medicine or . . . ?"

"The practical application is knowing something we didn't know yesterday. *You* should worry about the practical application of interns and wayward teens."

"'Wayward.' Good word. Better than 'nosy,'" Abby noted.

I chuckled, the sound laying uneasily over the disquiet that still buzzed in my bones. "Okay. What are we doing?"

"This place has been a dumping ground for decades. Anything damaged or worn out should be set aside—Dr. Kapoor will decide what should be saved or repaired and what should be thrown out; you just want to collect it all in one place. Which means you need a place to collect it, so . . ." He waved a hand at the tops of the drawers, which were cluttered with everything from IKEA instruction booklets to a jar of pennies to a full set of moose antlers.

"Oh, boy," I said. Liam whistled in agreement.

"Most of the drawers are labeled, but what's in them usually doesn't match. So, uh, I guess the goal is that you get everything where it belongs, and anything that doesn't have a place is set aside neatly." He scratched the back of his neck. "Good luck?"

"You know those fairy tales where a princess has to, like, sort every grain of rice and wheat by daybreak?" I asked. "This is that, but with mutant bird bones."

"Well, I don't have a band of forest creatures to help you, so Liam and Abby will have to do," Kenny replied. "Now I really need to get back to, you know . . ."

"Actual science?" I asked.

"Exactly," he said without an ounce of shame, and waved farewell. He closed the door behind him, leaving the three of us alone in a room of malformed, long-dead terns.

"Just so we're clear, this"—Abby gestured at the taxidermy birds—"is not a natural phenomenon. Right?"

"You're the expert," I replied. I peered at the cases of warped forms and suppressed a shudder.

"An expert in what, exactly?" Liam asked, his voice dangerously quiet. It was a quiet that could mutate as wildly as the birds—into panic, into revulsion, or into sheer disbelief. His face was calm, but I'd seen that calm before. Kyle Farley, ninth grade. New kid in town, didn't know the rumors. He held my hand at the movies.

Then he saw something reflected in the window beside us as we walked, and he went still like that. Quiet, like that.

I never did find out what he'd seen. He never spoke to me again.

"Don't," Abby said.

"Don't what?" Liam demanded.

"Don't ask," she replied. "You don't want to know."

"I think I deserve an answer." He was trying to sound tough, but his voice wavered, betraying his uncertainty.

"What you do or don't deserve isn't really my problem," Abby replied, the corner of her mouth hooking upward, a smile so small it meant its opposite.

"Abby," I said, intervening. "He was there yesterday. He saw."

"So forget yesterday. Both of you. Go home. Go back to your lives and be safe." She looked at me. "I promise you I'll find out what happened to your mother. I'm a professional, or as close to it as anyone can get. This doesn't need to be on your shoulders."

"*What* doesn't? What's Sophia's mother got to do with any of this?" Liam demanded.

"I'm not leaving," I told Abby. "And Liam *does* deserve to know." Or at least, I wanted him to know. Abby had known about other-worldly things for years before she ever heard my name. It was easy for her to believe me. I wanted Liam to choose to believe me.

Her lips thinned. Then she sighed, waving a hand in surrender. "Your call," she said.

I turned to Liam, and took a deep breath. "My name is Sophia Novak," I said. "And I think I'm the Girl in the Boat."

EXHIBIT F

Excerpt of a letter sent by Vanya Kapoor to Persephone Dryden

AUGUST 7, 2003

Many people think of crows and ravens as nearly the same bird, but only someone who has never seen a raven could make that mistake. The scale of them is incredible when you're used to the more familiar little tricksters. Their feathers are so black and their bodies so enormous that you imagine if they spread their wings, you would see galaxies hidden beneath them, full of nebulae and distant, cold suns.

When Joy's little girl first saw Moriarty, she ran right up to him. Joy looked panicked, and I don't blame her. He was nearly as big as the girl. But Sophie wasn't afraid at all. She is obsessed with him, and he seems to return the affection.

*But Sophie wasn't afraid at all. She is obsessed
with him, and he seems to return the affection.
He's always snapped at Liam, but he preens when
Sophie tells him he's pretty. Maybe Liam's mistake
is failing to appeal to his vanity. And it was thanks
to Moriarty that we found the girl when she went
missing last week.*

*She was up at the research center with us, and
then she wasn't. Moriarty was missing too, and
Joy and I were both frantic—her more than me, of
course, though I'll confess it was a close call. The
mist had come in hard and thick, and it was dusk.*

*It was Misha who found Sophie, thanks to
Moriarty's calling. He brought her back bundled in
his huge coat, fast asleep, and Moriarty flapped up
behind her. The bird seemed annoyed by our relief.
He seemed to say, What's the fuss? I was looking
after her.*

*Misha said he'd found Sophie down by the
water, Moriarty perched on the rocks beside her.
She was sitting with her hands on her knees,
looking straight out at the waves. Toward Belaya
Skala. She said that she'd followed a girl down to
the water and had stayed to listen to the singing.
But there are no children on Bitter Rock.*

is threatening, I stand on the porch, listening.
I can only ever steal a few minutes before Mrs.
Popova hurries out to usher me inside so she can
lock the doors for the night. But I swear last night,
when I was straining to listen in the direction of
Belaya Skala, I thought I heard it: singing, almost
inaudible over the sound of the sea.

I couldn't make out the words, but it was
beautiful. Beautiful, and oddly frightening. Or
maybe it was only a trick of the mist. That's what
they keep telling us, whenever we have questions,
whenever we see something strange. The mist plays
tricks, that's all. Now get inside, and lock your
doors.

VIDEO EVIDENCE

Recorded by Joy Novak

AUGUST 14, 2003, TIME UNKNOWN

*The shriek comes again, and is answered by something on the
other side of the island, a voice that could be human or bird.*

HARDCASTLE: We need to get somewhere safe. I—

*The cries are drowned out by a bellowing roar, echoing over
the island.*

NOVAK: The town's closest.

HARDCASTLE: Come on.

*He sets out. Kapoor begins to follow—and then Novak shouts.
Rocks skitter and scrape.*

KAPOOR: Hang on!

*The camera tumbles, coming to a rest upside down, showing
nothing but a slash of grass and gray mist. Kapoor speaks
from nearby.*

KAPOOR: I've got you. Are you all right?

NOVAK: My leg . . .

KAPOOR: Shit, that looks bad.

NOVAK: Sophie?

She seems calm at first, but her voice quickly grows panicked.

NOVAK: Sophie? Where are you? I had her—I was holding her hand and I must have let go when I fell. Where—

CARREAU: Stay calm. We will find her.

The video cuts out again. Kapoor turns it back on.

NOVAK: Does anyone see her?

HARDCASTLE: Everyone keep sounding off. Don't go too far in this mist.

BAKER: We have to keep going! We're never going to find her in this. That thing—

CARREAU: Hold on, I've got—

The video cuts again. It resumes with the view angled down-ward, as if the cameraperson has given up trying to capture anything.

HARDCASTLE: Down this way!

KAPOOR: The mist is thinner higher up. Maybe we should head that way.

HARDCASTLE: There's nothing up there but the airstrip. At least we can find some shelter if we head down.

Another unearthly shriek pierces the mist.

SOPHIA: Mama, I'm scared.

NOVAK: It's okay, sweetie. Martin's got you. I'm right here.

BAKER: I say we get out of the open.

KAPOOR: Fine. Carolyn, grab the camera so I can help with Joy.

She hands the camera off to Baker, who trains it on the mist behind them as the others start to move. A shadow shifts within the thinning mist. It seems humanoid. Baker whispers.

BAKER: What are you?

The figure shrieks and shakes, the air around it distorting, fracturing like digital glitches. Video cuts out.

When the recording resumes, the camera is lying on its side, discarded on a bench along the wall of the old chapel. Hardcastle and Carreau are struggling with a half-rotted pew, bracing it against the doors.

HARDCASTLE: That should hold.

KAPOOR: Against what? We don't know what's out there.

HARDCASTLE: Did you want to stop and find out?

NOVAK: Will you two please stop sniping at each other?

Novak sits on one of the more solid pews, her leg stretched out in front of her. Sophia sits, knees to her chest, on the floor next to her.

CARREAU: Let me look at that leg.

He steps over and carefully rolls up Novak's pants leg. She hisses, and he winces in sympathy.

CARREAU: We need to clean this and get it bandaged.

A muffled shriek sounds outside, but it seems to be coming from a distance.

BAKER: Those things aren't human. Are they?

KAPOOR: The people on the beach seemed human enough.

HARDCASTLE: But those other things in the mist . . . They didn't move right.

KAPOOR: What were they? Were they people?

SOPHIA: Not yet.

Everyone looks at her.

NOVAK: Sophie? Why did you say that? Did you see something?

Sophia buries her head in her arms, overwhelmed by the scrutiny. Hardcastle is peering out through a crack between the door and the crooked frame.

HARDCASTLE: Where's the camera?

BAKER: It's over here.

HARDCASTLE: Bring it here, will you?

She complies, and he mutters as he gets it lined up with the crack in the door. He zooms in on a distant splotch, brings it into focus.

HARDCASTLE: What the . . .

Three of the humanoid figures are walking in the middle distance, one after the other, single file. They move with an unnatural gait, sinking deeply as if their legs can't quite support them, their bodies sagging with each step before whipping upright again.

Above them, like tongues of white flame, countless birds wheel in the sky. As the procession moves out of view, Hardcastle backs away from the door.

HARDCASTLE: Where did those things come from?

NOVAK: I don't think they came from anywhere. We're the ones that came from somewhere else.

HARDCASTLE: What are you talking about?

NOVAK: This isn't the church. Not the same church, at least. Unless that was always there.

She points upward. Hardcastle lets out a whistle, then fiddles with the camera, switching the view back to normal. He points the camera upward as the others make sounds of astonishment.

The beam of the camera's light is not strong enough to illuminate more than a small patch of the ceiling at a time, but that is enough to make it clear that Joy is correct. The ramshackle appearance of the room gives way at the ceiling, which is domed and covered in a massive mural. Around the edges the figures are like those outside—gangly, walking crookedly, their eyes and mouths empty orifices that seem to blaze with light.

Within are a series of images separated by patterns like thorns and vines.

A woman in a crown stands before a pattern of waves and towers, a flooded city.

A trio of people, two women and a man, stand facing away, flanked by pine trees.

Thorny vines sprout from the shoulders of a featureless man, twining in all directions.

A white-haired woman's hands rest on the shoulders of two young women. One girl's ribs and sternum seem to shine through her skin. A goblet of red liquid hovers above them.

And at the very center, so large it dwarfs all the other figures, is a creature painted in pure matte black—not just a silhouette, but a void. Like an angel, with six wings spread from its shoulders. Its only features are its eyes—an empty white. Whatever black substance has been used to paint the thing is still wet, dripping with fat, oily drops that vanish into smoke, or rather steam, before they strike the ground.

BAKER: Where are we?

NOVAK: Better question: How do we get out?

11

"THE GIRL IN the boat," Liam repeated.

"You're saying it wrong," I told him with a faltering smile. He let out a breath and sat against the bank of drawers behind him. My smile faded. I wrapped my arms around my middle as I spoke. "My mother was here in 2003. She worked with your mom and Dr. Hardcastle. She was one of the people that supposedly died in the storm."

"And you think that whatever happened to her was, what, supernatural?" Liam asked.

"Yes."

He scrubbed his hand over his mouth, then crossed his arms. Uncrossed them. "All right."

"'All right?'" I repeated. "What does that mean?"

"It means I follow you so far," he said. "Sophia, I watched you walk into the water. And then you were right behind me, safe and dry. I saw what happened to you on Belaya Skala yesterday. Either I'm going mad, or something unnatural is happening. I mildly prefer the version of the world where I have a moderate mood disorder and there are monsters to the one where I'm hallucinating. Besides." He shrugged. "I trust you."

"Wait," Abby said. "What was that about Sophia walking into the water?"

I bit my lip. "The night you came," I said. "There was a girl in the mist. I didn't see her face, but Liam did. She looked like me." *Like my reflection,* I thought, thinking of the tangled hair and weary eyes that stared back at me so often.

"Echoes," Abby said thoughtfully.

"Say that again?" Liam replied.

Abby opened her messenger bag and pulled out a thick three-ring binder. She set it on the chest of drawers beside her and flipped it open, paging through. "Echoes are what we call doppelgangers—doubles. They can look just like a person. Sound like them. Sometimes even have the same memories. Here." She beckoned us over.

She'd flipped to what appeared to be printed still frames from a video. A girl with colorful leggings and long black hair was bent over her apparent twin—they were even wearing the same outfit. But the girl on the ground was battered and wounded, blood staining her clothes. She gaped up at the standing girl, who wore a sly little smile. *Vanessa Han and echo, Briar Glen, MA,* read the label.

"That one was on a road that didn't exist," Abby said. "One of the remnants of the old worlds I told you about."

"Are these echoes evil?" I asked.

"That one was," Abby said, tapping the picture.

"How do you fight them? A stake to the heart? Silver bullets?" I asked.

Abby regarded me with an expression that was one part approval, one part sorrow. "The other worlds are dead or dying, and things like the echoes? They're like bacteria, breeding in rotting meat. They mutate. What works once won't work again. What's true once won't be true again."

"So even if you defeated them once . . ." I started.

"They might be different here," Abby said. "There's just so much we don't know. Why the other worlds died. What the things that come from those worlds want. Whether their intrusions on our world are scattered, random incidents, or whether they add up to something."

"Like what?" Liam asked.

"That's the big question, isn't it?" Abby said. "Dr. Ashford's life's work. And mine now too, I guess. Not like I can go work retail after watching a girl dissolve into ash and getting thrown across the room by a ghost."

"That happened?" I asked her.

"Yup. Met a lovely girl named Dahut. She was possessing another girl, Becca—but we got her out. Mostly. Little bit left behind, but nothing Becca can't handle. Probably. We're keeping an eye on it."

"So is that whole binder full of supernatural stuff?" Liam asked.

"Yup," she said. The binder was huge, filled with a million

different tabs labeled in tiny, precise handwriting.

"It's very organized," I noted.

"You were expecting a scrappy, overstuffed notebook covered in manic scribbles?" she guessed. "We've got a lot of those in storage. Dr. Ashford insists on a more methodical approach." She turned the binder so I could see the labels on the tabs—everything from *Spectral phenomenon* to *Doors appearing in forests, fields, etc.* "There's an index," she told me.

"Your boss let you take this?"

"I sort of stole it. I did mention we're pissed at each other right now, right?" she said idly, but she didn't meet my eyes.

"You were talking about those things—echoes," Liam said suddenly. His arms were crossed, his gaze on the floor, but now he lifted his eyes to look at Abby. "How good are they? Could they convince you they were real?"

She frowned. "Some of them can. Why?"

He tensed his jaw. "Nothing," he said after a beat. "Look. I'm in. I'll help you."

"You don't have to," I told him. It was enough that he believed. That he wasn't running.

"I want to," he said seriously. "Just tell me where to start."

Abby sighed. "I'm not going to try to talk you out of it. Maybe Ashford could, but truth is, I hate working alone. Plus, it'll be easier getting back to Belaya Skala with the connections you two have, and that's definitely got to be our next stop."

I shook my head. "We don't have to get back to Belaya Skala— not yet, at least." I spread my hands, indicating the room around us. "We're in a room full of specimens and documents from and about Belaya Skala and Bitter Rock. We're *exactly* where we need to be. So pick a drawer. It's time to be good little worker bees."

I walked to the nearest drawer—labeled *Bones—Mounted*—and opened it with a flourish.

It was full of Tupperware.

"I think you've cracked the case," Liam deadpanned.

I threw a Tupperware lid at him.

We settled into a rhythm after a while. Empty a drawer, sort the contents—which never matched the label—move them in front of the drawer that *did* match the label, repeat. So far we had mostly managed to make the room look significantly *less* organized.

One of the cabinet drawers—one of the long, flat ones, the kind that contained maps and documents—was rusted shut. I hauled at it. Useless. It probably hadn't been opened in years.

"You need a hand?" Abby asked, looking up from a shoebox full of USB drives, which she'd been plugging into her computer one by one to check for anything interesting.

"Nope," I said through clenched teeth. I cast around for something to force it open with. I found a screwdriver and jammed it into the bent corner of the drawer. I shoved. I pulled. It creaked ominously but didn't open.

"You will not defeat me," I told the drawer sternly. It remained shut, all innocence and aluminum. I braced myself against the cabinet behind me, lifted my foot, and kicked hard at the handle of the screwdriver.

It popped open, the screwdriver pinging off to hit the wall.

"Look at the badass," Abby said. I leaned forward eagerly.

Inside I found a map showing Bitter Rock; I recognized the fat, fishhook shape immediately, along with the streets and buildings. Almost none of them had changed, although the LARC was absent from this map. There were a series of notations, X's with dates scribbled next to them, scattered throughout the islands and the surrounding waters. The note-taker had sketched a series of wobbly circles around Belaya Skala. And then around the rest of Bitter Rock. The circles expanded to contain later dates and marks, as if whatever this map was tracking was growing. The last circle was dated 1981, and it covered almost all of the island, leaving only a tiny curl of land untouched.

"Check this out," I said. I slid it across the floor toward Abby, and she scooted over to take a look. Liam crouched down next to her.

I turned back to the drawer. There was another map underneath the first, but where that one had been orderly, this one was chaos. It looked as if someone had started out drawing in the island, roughing in its topological features. And then lost their mind. There were jagged teeth scribbled along the isthmus, turning it into a grinning mouth. Eyes clustered along the hillsides. Elongated human figures that reminded me of cave paintings were scattered randomly across the page. In the center of it all, drawn with such a heavy hand it nearly blotted everything else out, was a shape that I took at first to be random scribbling. But the shape of it coalesced from the mad tangle of lines, some so ferociously drawn they'd ripped through the page.

Two wings stretched upward, two pointed down, and two

swept out to either side. They sprouted from a central body that suggested something both human and inhuman at once—a head, two arms, two legs, its eyes blank holes.

THE SIX-WING was written beneath it in shaky handwriting. And beneath: *It took them.*

My hands were trembling, my heart beating fast as a bird's in my chest, as I held the map up for the others to see. The creature from the church. The creature from my dreams.

"This is what you saw?" Abby asked, taking the map from me. I could only nod. And then I twisted back to the drawer, a metallic taste in my mouth. There had to be more here. An explanation for how the monster from my dreams was replicated in ink on a madman's map. There—something at the back of the drawer.

My hand closed around a hard object the size of my palm. A bird's skull, the bone strangely blackened, easily double the size of the others along the wall. I frowned at it. A strange sensation gnawed its way down my spine. Like a vibration, the hum of a ship's engine as you stand on the deck.

"Sophia?" Abby said.

A black liquid trickled from one gaping eye, oozing slowly down the contours of the bone. I touched it with my fingertip and found it was slippery, cold. Abby said my name again, but I heard it only distantly. Strange darts of light shivered through the air. My breath slipped from my lips in a cloud.

"It's happening a—" Liam said, but it was like listening to voices from underwater.

"What—" I began, looking up, and then the room exploded into a flurry of wings. Birds careened, screaming, around me.

Wings struck my face. Claws raked at my neck. I caught glimpses of the frantic bodies: doubled limbs, twisted spines, skulls with no eyes or too many. Birds flopped and writhed on the ground, or crashed into the walls. Screamed and screamed and screamed.

And I was alone.

"Liam! Abby!" I yelled, but they were gone. I charged for the door, the skull still clutched in one hand, and dived through. I slammed it shut behind me, putting my whole weight on it, and caught one white-winged bird. I felt the crunch and pop of its hollow ribs between the door and its frame. With the hand that clutched the skull, I shoved the twitching thing back through and latched the door. Bodies thumped against the other side, the screeching muffled now but unending.

I backed away, breath coming in short, sharp gasps that couldn't seem to fill up my lungs. My stomach lurched and roiled, all acid and revulsion. My shoulder blades smacked against the wall, and it was then I realized the hall was dark. The lights overhead were out. And there was no sign of either Liam or Abby.

I had to remind myself to breathe. Convince myself to think things through, instead of picking a direction and running until I couldn't anymore.

This wasn't right. Neither was a room full of dead birds coming violently to life. I crept forward down the hall. Ahead of me, a door banged, again and again, the seconds in between punctuated by the whistle of a strong wind. I followed the sound.

I came around the corner. The door—one of the side doors—flew open again with another bang, then rebounded to almost shut. It couldn't close all the way because someone was standing there—a man in a bright green windbreaker. The door hit his shoulders; the wind shoved it open.

I took a step closer, opening my mouth to call out to him, ask if he needed help—and the words shriveled in my throat as I drew close enough to see him in more detail.

The man's back was pulp. Blood and spurs of smashed bone. Strips of his rain shell and the T-shirt beneath stuck to the door, tacked in place by dried blood, and the flesh beneath had been beaten by the repeated slamming of the door until it was the color and texture of a rotten plum. The back of his head was caved in, glistening with brain matter and bits of skull. With each impact his lips worked to shape words, his eyes blinking hard as if trying to wake himself.

"Puh . . . puh . . . puh," he said, a moldy syllable squashed between his blistered lips.

I gave myself one quailing moment of fear, of revulsion. And then I seized my horror, my hesitation, and flung them away. I couldn't stand there and do nothing. I couldn't let fear stop me from helping someone who needed it.

I crossed the last five steps and caught the door in mid-swing. For a moment we stood there, my fingers wrapped around the edge of the door. I closed my throat up, teeth clenched. I shunted my revulsion and fear into the void, and let cold calm take its place.

I'd had to call 911 once before. Some kids had gotten drunk and wrapped their car around a telephone pole. One of them shot through the windshield like a javelin and landed on the lawn, all crooked-limbed and limp. I'd gotten to my front door in time to see his friends bailing out, running. No one else was home and there was only me, walking across the lawn with bare feet, the dew cold and the boy's blood blistering hot. The woman on the phone was the calmest person I'd ever talked to. She'd started out trying to calm me down, but quickly realized she didn't have to. She gave me directions without any frills. *Make sure his airway is clear. Put pressure around the cut on his arm. Talk to him.*

When the ambulance showed up, she told me I should consider a career as a 911 operator, that I was cool under pressure. When I told the story to my foster mother later, she gave me a look I knew well. The *is there something wrong with you?* look.

Wrong or not, it was useful. "I'm going to go get help," I said now, remembering the exact tone of voice that woman on the phone had used. "Come inside."

I put my hand on his arm. I needed to get him out of the doorway to keep him from getting hurt any more than he already was—though how he was still standing, how he was still *alive*, I had no idea.

When my hand touched his arm, his head twisted around to look at me. He was white, with a reddish beard and brown hair. He looked familiar somehow, but I didn't think he was one of the locals I'd encountered. "Puh," he said. Then, "Please. Don't. Please. Don't touch me. What are you doing? What are you—what are—"

He rushed forward, away from me, stumbling and running out of the building and toward the steep hillside on the west side of the island, only to stop, stock-still, at the top of it and fling his arms outward with a bestial howl.

Beyond him, the sky was wracked with storms. They masked the horizon as far as I could see, lightning flashing within the clouds with the quick and steady tempo of a heartbeat. The thunder rumbled and cracked like massive planks of wood splintering and straining.

The wind blasted my face. In the distance, another howling voice answered the man, and then another voice, an inhuman keening shriek that came from across the water. From Belaya Skala. The man looked back toward me with a triumphant grin. And then he stepped back, and plunged over the edge.

I raced back inside and slammed the door shut. The birds were screaming again, trapped in that room. I was still clutching the skull. I could feel that there was something carved into the dome of its head, so I forced my fingers open and read: ПОЖИРАЕТ.[3]

My bones vibrated, the harsh thrum of an engine—

I opened my eyes and stared into the shocked gaze of my reflection in the window, and the thrumming vibration slammed to a halt.

"Ms. Hayes?"

I spun with a yelp and blinked. Fluorescent light bathed the hall. No screaming birds, just the faint hum of the lights and my own scattered breathing. Dr. Hardcastle stood a few feet away, a look of caution and concern on his face. Fresh fear lurched up: *Runrunrun.*

"Are you all right?" he asked.

I cleared my throat, thinking fast. Dr. Hardcastle didn't appear aware of anything out of the ordinary. Other than me—and I couldn't afford to stand out. Which meant I had to shove my

....
3 Russian: "It devours."

fear and my confusion and my utter disorientation as deep as I possibly could as quickly as I possibly could, and never mind how much worse it would be later, and—

Smile. "You scared the crap out of me!" I declared. Just the right touch of *silly me*. Just the right shake of my head. "Oh, hey, check this out. I found it in the specimen room. I was going to ask Kenny about it, but I guess I got turned around." I held out the skull. *Get him focusing on anything except just how out of breath I am.*

"May I?" He took it from me, and I was so intent on stitching together this mask of cheer over my face that I didn't even flinch when his finger nudged against mine. "Huh. It looks like a tern, but I couldn't tell you specifically. You found it in the specimen room?"

"It was in the back of a drawer," I said.

"Part trash heap, part treasure trove. It's probably been here longer than I have, and that's saying something." He handed it back to me. "You can keep it, if you'd like."

"Really?" I didn't have to fake surprise this time.

He gave me a winning, empty smile. "Whoever it belonged to is long gone, and the LARC doesn't need it. Call it a souvenir. Since Bitter Rock doesn't have a gift shop."

I mimicked his expression, beaming vapidly at him. "Thanks," I said. "Everyone here is so great."

"We take care of each other at the LARC," he said. "Now, if you'll excuse me . . ."

"Of course." The last stitch of my mask cinched into place. My anger would wait. I would let it out later. When it was useful. Right now, I needed answers.

His footsteps faded. I put a hand on the door, but I didn't open it. I listened, straining for the sound of shrieking birds or rolling thunder. There was only silence.

I eased the door open. The sky was gray but the sun was bright even filtered through the clouds. No man, no storm, no twisted, broken birds. I let the door swing shut again, and stepped away.

"Sophia!" Liam called. He and Abby were running toward me, faces frantic with worry. I all but staggered toward them, relief hitting me hard.

"Where did you go?" Abby and I said at the same time, and stared at each other a beat.

"You disappeared," Liam said.

"So did you," I replied, a touch accusatory. But no—I was the one who had gone somewhere. I strode past them, back the way I had come. The door to the specimen room was closed. Abby and Liam trailed behind me, as if understanding that I needed to see for myself. I punched in the code and pushed open the door.

I expected chaos. I expected ruin and there wasn't any. The birds stood still in their stiff poses, stuffed and sewn up tight, watching me with glass eyes and not the slightest hint of a twitch or a cry. I looked down at the skull in my hand. And at the tacky smudge on my palm: blood, half-dried, and three bright green threads from a rain shell stuck to it. There was no sign of that black liquid.

"There was a man," I said softly. His face nagged at me. I'd seen it before. Where?

I whipped around, had to stop myself from sprinting all the way to the foyer.

"Where are you going?" Liam asked, but I shook my head, forcing them to follow. I ran to the entryway, searching the photos that hung there.

There. From last year. A man in a bright green windbreaker, standing between Kenny and Lily in front of the LARC, smiling broadly with his hands in his pockets.

I pressed my fingers against the glass beside his face. The same eyes. The same jacket. But that smile—this was a smile of joy, not that leering, twisted grin he'd flashed at me.

"Daniel Rivers?" Liam said, reading the caption over my shoulder.

"He was here," I said. "Or not here. Wherever I was. He was . . ." I swallowed, trying not to picture it. And then, my movements urgent, I stalked along the wall. 2016. 2015. Back and back. The faces changed, the numbers waxed and waned, but there was a sameness to every group. And then—

2004. 2002. "She's not here," I said. I laid my palm flat against the wall between the two photos. "2003. There's no picture."

"Maybe they took it down because of the accident," Liam said.

"You don't hide the photos of people who died tragically; you memorialize them. Make them *more* prominent," Abby replied. "Unless you're trying to hide something. Erase the fact that they were ever here."

Liam flicked his lip ring over his teeth in what I was coming to realize was a thoughtful tic. "There are other photos. And employment records," he said. "I know where they're kept. But we're not allowed in there."

"Liam Kapoor, are you suggesting a daring heist?" Abby asked. "And I thought you were such a fine young man."

"Oh, I'm trouble," Liam assured her. She snorted like she didn't believe him, and he rolled his eyes.

I could only stare at that empty spot on the wall. No wider than the gap between any of the other photos. As if the years had been folded over to make it seem like she had never existed at all. To make her vanish. "We have to find her," I said softly. I realized my error and cleared my throat. "We have to find proof that she was here," I said, correcting myself. Because that was the thing I wasn't allowed to say out loud.

If someone had lied about how she died, could they have lied about more?

How did I know that she had died at all?

It was the hope I did not dare to speak, even silently to myself: my mother might still be alive.

EXHIBIT G

Email correspondence between
Dr. Vanya Kapoor and Dr. William Hardcastle

To: Dr. Vanya Kapoor // From: Dr.
William Hardcastle // June 23, 2017
Subject: Not Again
What happened? I have about
seven messages from Rivers on my
voicemail. He's crying in some of
them. And I can't figure out what the
hell he's talking about other than
that he's quitting. In the middle of
the season, which leaves us short-
handed.

To: Dr. William Hardcastle // From:
Dr. Vanya Kapoor // June 23, 2017
It's honestly not my fault this
time. Maybe I was hard on the kid,
but it's not like that should come
as a big fucking surprise. Look, all
I know is that on Tuesday evening he
was fine and Wednesday he wouldn't

come out of his room. He wouldn't
talk to anyone and he had Nguyen
take him back to the mainland the
same day.

To: Dr. Vanya Kapoor // From: Dr.
William Hardcastle // June 23, 2017
I would say I'd call him and try to
smooth things over, but judging by
those messages, it's a lost cause.
We're just going to have to finish
the season minus one assistant. Can
you handle it?

To: Dr. William Hardcastle // From:
Dr. Vanya Kapoor // June 24, 2017
He wasn't that much help in the first
place. We can get through the next
couple of seasons without him.

To: Dr. Vanya Kapoor // From: Dr.
William Hardcastle // June 24, 2017
Hire a replacement for Rivers. If
not this season, then next season.
You need better staffing.

To: Dr. William Hardcastle // From:
Dr. Vanya Kapoor // June 25, 2017

I wouldn't need so much staffing if
you bothered to spend more time here.

To: Dr. Vanya Kapoor // From: Dr.
William Hardcastle // June 25, 2017
Someone has to secure our funding,
which isn't easy given the
eccentricities of the Center. And
you don't do public interfacing
well.
What do you think happened with
Rivers?

To: Dr. William Hardcastle // From:
Dr. Vanya Kapoor // June 26, 2017
We both know why you don't like
coming here, and it has nothing to
do with funding. Ask Rivers if you
want to know what happened.

To: Dr. Vanya Kapoor // From: Dr.
William Hardcastle // June 26, 2017
Do you think he went out in the
mist?

To: Dr. William Hardcastle // From:
Dr. Vanya Kapoor // July 1, 2017
Maybe.

To: Dr. Vanya Kapoor // From: Dr.
William Hardcastle // July 1, 2017
What do you think he saw? Do you
think he told any of the others?

To: Dr. William Hardcastle // From:
Dr. Vanya Kapoor // July 6, 2017
Leave it alone, Will. They don't
know anything, and neither do we.

12

I BARELY GOT through the rest of the day. I might not have at all if I didn't have the specimen room to lose myself in. I took things out of drawers, put other things into other drawers, and I didn't think about what I saw, didn't think about what I knew. The three of us didn't talk much, and the silence was a nervous one.

Four more hours of organization, and Dr. Kapoor rattled through to release us for the day. Liam drove Abby and me down to Mrs. Popova's. I slouched back against the seat. No storms on the horizon. No murderous malformed birds, no wounded men with sickly smiles. But I didn't feel safe for an instant.

I'd told Abby and Liam an abbreviated version of what had happened, my voice low in case Kenny or Hardcastle walked by, but I repeated it in excruciating detail once we were tucked away in my room. Abby and I sat on the bed, while Liam folded himself down onto the floor in front of the door in a pose that made him look particularly gangly. Abby took the skull from me, slipping on a pair of leather gloves first, and examined it carefully.

"Pozhirayet," she read. "The inscription. It means 'it devours.'"

"You speak Russian?" I asked her.

"I have a knack for languages, and everything's useful in our line of work. Only real job where fluency in Latin can save your life." She pulled her laptop out of her bag and tapped away at the keyboard.

"What are you looking for now?"

"Your mutilated man," she said. "Daniel Rivers. Age twenty-eight. Lives in Colorado. Lists a PhD from UC Berkeley, but he works at a ski resort." She spun the laptop around so I could see the Facebook page she'd pulled up. Liam craned his neck to get a look.

I stared at the dates under the photos. Three days ago, two weeks ago, a month ago. He'd shaved off his beard, but it was him. "I don't understand. I *saw* him."

"And Liam saw you, down by the beach," Abby pointed out.

"The man I saw wasn't Daniel Rivers," I said, realization dawning. "It was an echo?"

"That's my guess," she said.

"This is fucked-up," Liam muttered. We looked at him, and he crossed his arms. "I just feel like someone should say that periodically, to remind us. Abby's acting like this is normal. But it isn't. It's fucked-up."

"Fucked-up *is* normal for me," Abby said.

"We need to get to those records," Abby muttered.

Then the ground lurched beneath me. Cold shivers ran down my back, and my stomach churned.

Backlash.

"I'll—I have to—I need a shower," I managed, and turned abruptly, marching into the hall. I ignored Liam's puzzled response, not even registering his words. I was almost running by the time I reached the bathroom, and I had to try three times to throw the lock. I turned the shower on full blast and sank to my knees, biting my sleeve to stifle the moan that escaped my lips.

No. No. No, I thought, and my mind filled with the image of Daniel Rivers's broken flesh. Of wings and claws. Of William Hardcastle, his empty smile, his hand outstretched.

No. No. No—and I realized I was saying it, too, bent to the floor, my words soft and my lips pressed almost to the tile.

There was nothing to do but endure.

INTERVIEW

SOPHIA NOVAK

SEPTEMBER 2, 2018

ASHFORD: It's interesting to me, Ms. Novak, that you are so concerned about what I did and did not tell Abby. Given how much you concealed from her and Mr. Kapoor yourself.

SOPHIA: What do you mean?

ASHFORD: You doled out information so carefully. You knew that Abby was investigating your mother's disappearance, yet you did not tell her about your reflection until she noticed it herself. Nor did you tell her about the girl that you and Mr. Kapoor saw on the beach the night she arrived—not until Mr. Kapoor mentioned it himself.

SOPHIA: I wasn't trying to deceive her.

Ashford leans back in his chair, considering her.

ASHFORD: Is that so? But you didn't tell them about this emotional backlash you experienced either. Why?

SOPHIA: Isn't that obvious?

ASHFORD: Please. Assume I'm ignorant.

Sophia looks down at her hands, fingers laced, palms spread.

SOPHIA: It took me years to learn how to tell when the backlash was coming. And even then, sometimes there was no warning at all. It came sometimes without me pushing away emotion to trigger it. Over time, I learned how to ride it out without hurting myself—or anyone else. But by then, I'd been to too many psychiatrists to count. Been fed drugs that made me sleep and shake and even have a seizure once but never helped. Lost every friend I managed to make. Do you know what it's like to have people look at you like you aren't even human?

Her eyes burn with intensity.

SOPHIA: Do you know what it's like to wonder if they're right?

13

TWILIGHT CAST EVERYTHING in an eerie gray when we met
Liam by the LARC, but if anything, Abby seemed more at ease
than in the daylight. "Got us a key?" she demanded.

Liam produced a key ring. "I have to get these back into Dr.
Kapoor's coat pocket before morning or we'll all be strung up for
the birds," he warned. "And be careful. Mikhail's around here
somewhere."

"Is he dangerous?" Abby asked.

Liam looked troubled. "He was weird with Sophia," he said.
"And I've heard Dr. Kapoor tell Hardcastle something about not
wanting to run into the warden while she was alone."

"If she's afraid of him, why employ him?" Abby wondered
aloud, but Liam didn't have an answer. She glanced over at me.
"You going to be all right?"

I'd told them my sudden exit was indigestion. I didn't think either of them believed me—but I'd heard Liam mutter something about a panic attack to Abby, and even that was better than the truth. Normal people had panic attacks. They didn't have whatever it was that I did.

"Ready to go find some answers?"

"I'd settle for knowing what questions I should be asking," I said.

She grimaced. "Sounds like something my boss would say."

Inside, our shoes squeaked on the tiles. Good thing there was no one here to notice. "This way," Liam said, stepping into the lead after shutting the door behind us. He brushed past Abby, and she stepped back with an annoyed look. Some people were like oil and water, and I was starting to suspect these were two of them. But I didn't need them to be friends.

The light through the windows made it unnecessary to even turn on the lights. "I'm not used to this sneaking-around-before-dark thing," Abby murmured as she walked beside me.

"Maybe we should have waited for the mist," Liam said.

"You mean do the one thing that you're warned not to from the moment you step on Bitter Rock?" I asked.

"Yeah, that," Liam said with a little laugh.

"In my experience, there are three reasons for a rule like that," Abby said. "One, everyone's hiding something. Two, something supernatural is going to eat you if you disobey."

"And three?" Liam asked.

"They don't want you falling and breaking your neck with zero visibility, a bunch of sharp rocks, and no hospital in reach except by airlift," Abby said.

"Fair. This is it," Liam added, pointing at the door to the records room.

I knew the LARC kept paper records because I'd filled out a bunch on the first day. The internship was unpaid, which meant I didn't have to add social security fraud to my résumé, but I'd had to supply a fair bit of personal info, most of which I'd made up on the spot.

The door was locked—with a standard lock rather than a keypad this time—and Liam spent several minutes trying various keys from the big ring before Abby jimmied it with a department store gift card ("More flex than a credit card, so it works better," she explained). When she flicked on the light inside, I let out a breath. I don't know what I had expected. Shadows and cobwebs, padlocks, *something*. Instead there was an orderly bank of filing cabinets against one wall. Metal shelving on the opposite side held boxes labeled in neat handwriting.

"Here we go: 'Employment Records, Archived,'" Abby said, indicating the farthest file cabinet. "You want these, or the boxes?"

"Those're all just old office supplies and that sort of thing," Liam said. "No one stores anything important in here."

"It's not like they're going to write 'Damning Evidence' on the side," Abby pointed out.

"I'll take the files," I said. I wanted to be the one to find my mother's file. To see her name. That belonged to me.

I opened the first cabinet, and Liam went to the opposite end of the row. I trailed my fingers over the tabs of the files, my eyes skipping over strangers' names. I opened the next drawer and the next. Nothing. No *Novak, Joy* waiting for me to find. As if she had been snipped out of the history of the LARC entirely.

"She's not here," I said. I hadn't meant to whisper, but it was as if there was a weight bearing down on me, diminishing even my voice. "Maybe—" Maybe I'd been wrong. But I knew she'd been here. There was the photo. There was the bird. There was the damn story—*The Girl in the Boat*, my existence reduced to a catchy title.

"Look at this." I wasn't sure if Abby hadn't heard, or if she just didn't know how to respond. Her voice was as blunt and forceful as always, not a hint of softness or consideration in it, but I was glad; the first time I caught a whiff of pity off her, I knew I'd stop trusting her.

She held out a large glossy photo print for Liam and me to inspect. I recognized the format immediately: a group photo in front of the LARC building, just like the ones in the foyer out front. This one was marked 2003. There were seven people, and I read their names one by one. *Dr. Damien Breckenridge. Dr. Helen Whitcomb. Dr. William Hardcastle. Dr. Vanya Kapoor. Carolyn Baker. Martin Carreau. Joy Novak.*

She was here. "Where was it?" I asked, failing to disguise the shaking in my voice.

"In a box labeled 'Reimbursement Receipts 2005–2007,'" she said.

"Misfiled?" I asked.

"Not a chance," Liam replied. "That's my mother's handwriting. And she does not misfile things."

Abby grunted. "I'll take your word for it. There's some other stuff in there, but I think we should take it with us. We've been here long enough." She took off the empty backpack she'd been carrying for this purpose. Just as she unzipped it, something clattered down the hall. We froze.

"Goddammit!" croaked a familiar voice. "Hello, hello, hello."

I relaxed. "Moriarty," I said.

Liam shook his head ruefully. "He's likely picked the lock on his cage again, the little bastard. We can't just leave him wandering the halls—last time he managed to injure himself."

"I'll pack up here; you two corral the bird," Abby suggested. "We can meet up outside."

"Don't forget to lock the door behind you," Liam said, and she waved a dismissive hand at him, turning back to the mislabeled box.

We exited the file room and looked in the direction I thought the sound had come from. With all the echoing it was hard to be sure—but then Moriarty gave a gurgling chuckle, settling any confusion. "Silly bird," I murmured, and we headed down the hall.

"What do you think of her?" Liam asked as we walked.

"Who, Abby?" I shrugged. "She's smart. Seems like she knows what she's doing."

"Just remember that you don't have any reason to trust her," Liam said.

"And what reason do I have to trust you, Liam Kapoor?" I asked.

"My good looks and ravishing accent," he replied. I shook my head, chuckling, but there was a strain in his voice.

"Are you all right?" I asked him. "I know this is a lot."

"That's a hard question to answer, for me. Even in the most normal of times," he confessed. "I often find that the moment I think the answer is yes, I'm about to fall into a hole again. All of this . . . It's almost pleasant to have something to be afraid and angry about that's real, and not just a chemical imbalance trying to mess with me."

"I think I know what you mean," I replied. "It's not quite the same, but knowing that this is real, and that I haven't been imagining it all my life? It's weirdly a relief."

"Three cheers for objectively real horrors," Liam said wryly. This time neither of us laughed.

Moriarty was near the bathrooms, perched on the top of one of the ubiquitous stacks of plastic tubs and cardboard boxes that migrated around the LARC like glaciers of clutter.

Moriarty croaked and examined us with one black eye. "You're not supposed to be out here," I told him. He made another guttural caw.

"Come on, bird," Liam said. "Let's get you back to—"

Moriarty gave Liam a withering look, spread his wings, and launched himself down the hall. I threw myself back, avoiding the storm of black feathers and flashing talons. He didn't get far before he thumped down on the ground, hopping along at a surprisingly fast gait.

"At least he's heading in the right direction," Liam said. "Maybe we can herd him." We hustled along after the bird.

My foot slipped in a wet patch, nearly making me fall. Water had pooled on the floor. Random drips and patches of wet—and others that weren't so random. Bare footprints traced a path along the hallway before vanishing. Moriarty crouched at the end of the trail, his wings hunched, his pupils narrowed to pinpricks.

"Liam," I whispered, goosebumps prickling up my arms. "I don't think we're alone here."

"Hello, little bird," Moriarty said, but with the odd angle of his head, I couldn't tell if he was looking at me or at my reflection in the window beside us. Liam motioned for me to stay still, and he crept around the other side of the bird. Then—

"Damn it, Moriarty," a familiar voice said from around the corner, and Liam and I looked at each other in horror. Dr. Kapoor was here. What was she doing here in the middle of the night?

"I thought you put a combination lock on the cage," Dr. Hardcastle said.

"Clearly that isn't a foolproof solution," she snapped back. "I'll get him. You work on getting that equipment fixed. We can't afford for it to fail with the way the mist's been acting up."

"Normal seasonal variation," Hardcastle replied, sounding exasperated. They were getting close. They were going to come around the corner and find us. Liam's face was a mirror of my own dread. We were on opposite sides of the hallway from where Hardcastle and Kapoor's voices were coming. *Go*, I mouthed. I moved backward as quickly as I could without making a sound. I reached for the nearest door—*Please be open, please be open.*

It was. I slipped inside and shut the door slowly behind me, hoping Liam had found someplace to hide.

Only then did I get a look at the room I was in—and I frowned, puzzled. The room was filled with audio equipment, enough to stock a recording studio. There was a bank of monitors and computers that looked like they had enough computing power to put a man on Mars, and printouts strewn around or tacked up on the walls with what looked like sound waves and—satellite imagery? They were of the island, and the mist.

A window stretched along one side of the room, and on the other side was a shadowed chamber. I could make out several microphones, and something else—a birdcage, covered in a white cloth. A recording booth? Hardcastle was studying bird calls, but this seemed like overkill. I crept toward the window, the glass throwing back my dim reflection.

And then a footstep sounded outside the room. Hardcastle.

Something shifted at the corner of my vision. A trick of the light, but my eyes went to my reflection, wild-haired and waifish in the dim light, features indistinct. I touched the sleek braid that hung over my shoulder; my reflection mimicked the movement—but she didn't have a braid, just that wild tangle of hair.

She crooked her finger toward me.

The reflected room around her was dark, the angles of the walls and ceiling barely perceptible. The doorknob began to turn.

"Little bird, little bird," Moriarty croaked in the distance. I lifted my hand tentatively toward the reflection.

The door swung open. I spun around, trying to form a plausible excuse.

A hand grabbed my wrist and yanked hard.

VIDEO EVIDENCE

Recorded by Joy Novak

AUGUST 14, 2003, TIME UNKNOWN

The camera switches on, then off, then on again. It focuses on floorboards, then spins to look up at Sophia Novak's face. She squints in the bright light and shifts it quickly away, training it instead on the adults, who are clustered together near the other side of the room. Joy Novak still has her bandaged leg stretched out on a pew.

HARDCASTLE: We can't stay here. We need to leave as soon as it gets light out.

NOVAK: When is that going to be? Night was only supposed to last an hour. It's been at least twice that long.

HARDCASTLE: Morning has to come eventually.

NOVAK: I wouldn't put much faith in natural laws here, Will.

KAPOOR: So then we don't wait. We find a way out now.

CARREAU: What does that mean? Out? How do we do that?

KAPOOR: Obviously, I don't know. But I refuse to believe that there is no way back to—what, our world? Our reality?

CARREAU: A way out of the mist.

Novak cocks her head to the side.

NOVAK: That singing is starting again.

The others seem to hear it as well, but the camera picks up nothing but the faint sound of wind between the gaps in the walls.

CARREAU: It doesn't sound threatening.

KAPOOR: What, that doesn't creep you out?

CARREAU: Unsettling, yes. Threatening, perhaps not. I think we should investigate.

KAPOOR: I agree. We need to know more, and we aren't going to learn it hiding in here.

NOVAK: It isn't safe out there. Sophie—

KAPOOR: No, of course you'll stay. Two of us should go see what we can find, and someone able-bodied should stay behind with you. Bar the door behind us.

CARREAU: It sounds as if you have already decided you will be one of those to go.

KAPOOR: I couldn't stand waiting while you two went without me.

HARDCASTLE: You might have control issues, Vanya.

KAPOOR: Massive ones. So which of you wants to come?

BAKER: No way.

HARDCASTLE: I'll go.

Kapoor nods.

KAPOOR: A quick scouting trip to start. Twenty minutes, just to get the lay of the land and see if those things are still out there. We'll head toward the beach for now. See if there's a way to the shore and off this damn island.

Various sounds of agreement go around the group. Neither Kapoor nor Hardcastle look thrilled to be leaving their questionable sanctuary, but for each of them, the presence of the other guarantees that they will not want to be the first to express reluctance or fear. Kapoor and Hardcastle lift aside the pew and open the door cautiously.

KAPOOR: Got your flashlight?

HARDCASTLE: Yeah. Kind of feels like lighting up a neon sign that says 'Here's dinner.'

KAPOOR: A scouting trip isn't much good if we can't see anything.

She switches on her own flashlight, takes a deep breath, and steps out. Hardcastle is only a second behind her. The others watch as they recede into the mist. After they have vanished, Baker and Carreau drag the pew back in front of the doors.

The camera continues to record sporadically, cutting out at random intervals, but for the next several segments of salvageable footage there is little activity. Eventually, Novak rises from her seat and walks tenderly, testing her leg. Carreau sits on the floor near the door, glancing at his watch from time to time.

CARREAU: That can't be right.

NOVAK: What can't?

She approaches him. Sophia zooms in so close on her mother that every tremor of her hands makes the view bounce dizzyingly.

CARREAU: I don't think the night is still here because the sun has somehow changed its course. Time is behaving oddly. Look.

He unstraps his watch and hands it to her.

NOVAK: I don't see what—

She glances up, then back at it.

NOVAK: Huh. It went back a few seconds.

CARREAU: I am reminded of saccadic masking. If you look away from a clock and then back to it, the second hand seems to tick slowly the first time. An illusion, your brain's attempt to fill in the moment of blurred vision when your eyes were moving.

NOVAK: Time isn't passing. But our minds are filling it in?

CARREAU: Or this place is. We are not built to process a world without time. How does that even work? How can we breathe and think and progress if the world is temporally static?

Any further discussion is interrupted by shouting. Hardcastle's and Kapoor's voices are raised and urgent.

HARDCASTLE: Open up!

He hammers against the door. Novak and Carreau rush to it, hauling aside the pew that blocks it. Kapoor and Hardcastle spill through the door and slam it shut behind them, prompting a frantic knot of activity as they get the pew back in place.

NOVAK: What happened? Will, where did that gun come from?

Hardcastle doesn't look at her. He's staring at Baker, who stands in front of the altar, looking a bit dazed. He does, indeed, have a handgun—a revolver—at his side.

Then he steps forward, and points it at Baker.

14

I YELPED. IT was like shouting into a damp blanket—the sound hit the air and died.

There was no hand on my wrist. No one to have grabbed it. Just an empty room. Except it wasn't the same room.

The long window was cracked and caked with grime. The cage within was torn open, as if the bars had been wrenched outward with great force. The equipment was old, broken, dented.

I gulped down my fear—not pushing it away, not yet, knowing it would keep me sharp before it overwhelmed me—and walked to the door. As I had expected, Hardcastle was gone. And the hall beyond was as changed as the room.

The doors were in the same places, but they were wrong—one hanging crookedly from a broken hinge, another swollen and rotting, covered in green-black mold. Water dripped from the ceiling. The window beside me was cracked and beyond it was only mist that seeped in through the shattered windows, spilling like a thick carpet over the pitted tiles.

"Where am I?" I whispered. This wasn't the LARC, but it wasn't where I'd found Rivers either.

A faint scratching came from behind me. I whirled around. A hand, slender and pale, reached around from behind the corner, the nails scratching at the wall. It withdrew, and wet footsteps, the slap of bare feet against the tile, sounded a retreat.

"Wait," I called. A drop of water splashed onto the back of my hand. I ran after the footsteps.

I rounded the corner. The mist was thicker here, coiling in the air. The other girl stood at the end of the hall, half-shrouded. She wore a long-sleeved gray shirt, soaked and sticking to her skin, and a heavy skirt that dripped water from the hem. I couldn't see her face through the mist.

"Who are you?" I asked, but I already knew: the girl in the mirror. The reason my reflection was wrong.

"Who are you?" she whispered. Her voice was hoarse, a croak as garbled as Moriarty's.

"I'm Sophia," I said.

"I'm Sophia," she echoed, cocking her head to the side.

"Are you . . . me?" I asked. My legs felt weak. I still couldn't see her face.

"I . . ." she began. And then she shuddered. "Don't let them find you," she said, low and urgent—and then she turned and fled.

I plunged after her. "Wait!" I called. The word crumpled as

soon as it left my lips. No echoes in this place; the air was too thick. I had the sensation of being inside some great beast's throat. With every step the mist curdled around me, growing denser.

The walls fell away around me. I stumbled to a stop under open sky. It was as if something had torn the front half of the LARC away, leaving only rubble, twisted rebar, and wiring tangling like snakes. The mist spilled across the island. It wasn't night, exactly. The breaks in the clouds showed a glimpse of a sky without sun-light—but without stars either, and instead a strange ridged and whorled texture that reminded me of glass left long under the waves, until the shape of it was nearly lost.

"Wait," I said again, my voice thin, but she was gone.

I made my way down the path. If this island was like Bitter Rock, that's where shelter would be. And it did have the island's shape—though the road beneath my feet wasn't gravel, but some kind of solid stone, as if it had formed naturally. Instead of the speckling of white and yellow flowers beside the road, the flow-ers were fleshy things, a deep and glistening purple-red like liver meat.

I wasn't alone. There was someone out in the empty field past the road, the dim light reducing them to a silhouette. Not the girl—not my half-wild twin. It was a man. Or at least I thought it was a man. Hunched over, moving at a lurching gait.

I hesitated at the edge of the road. Nothing here had tried to hurt me—not yet, at least. Not even the dark angel in the church. And if there was someone here who could answer my questions, I had to risk it. I stepped forward. It was like stepping into emptiness, though the ground remained solid beneath my feet. I had no tether, nothing to hold on to, nothing to hold me back. Only the thrumming need. *Forward. Find the answers. Find* her.

The man stood with one knee knocked inward, one shoulder hunched so far forward I didn't see how he managed to balance. He stood utterly still, his back to me, the only motion the wind tugging at his wild, ash-blond curls.

His knee wasn't just bent inward oddly; it was broken. The foot twisted inward until it was completely perpendicular to the other. His clothes hung in shreds. I thought for a moment his skin was blistered, but as I drew closer I made out the craggy edges of rocks that seemed to be growing out of his skin, the smallest the size of a thumbnail, the largest as big around as a fist, lodged at the base of his neck.

His shoulder jerked. His head turned toward me, and I started to take a step back. He rotated, his bad leg collapsing, his weight flinging the other way to keep some semblance of balance. Rocking back and forth unsteadily, he regarded me from behind a ragged net of salt-rimed hair. The rocks were embedded in his cheeks. No, not rocks—barnacles.

He took a lurching step toward me and spoke rapidly in what might have been Russian.

"Von otsyuda!" he said, and repeated it, over and over. "Von! Von!"

He reached for me, but his leg gave out and he collapsed onto the ground, grasping for my ankle. I stumbled back. He screamed a bloodcurdling sound, high-pitched and tortured. He clawed his way across the grass toward me, and distantly, something—someone—answered his scream.

I ran. At first I sprinted back the way I had come, but the road was no longer empty—there was someone there, a figure standing on the road. Man or woman, I couldn't tell, but they were coming toward me with long, purposeful strides. I turned, scrambling down the face of the hill instead. Pebbles shot out from under my feet, making a sound like rain. I had to get to safety. I had to get help. But where either of those things were, I had no idea.

I chanced a look behind me, slowing so I didn't trip and send myself on a neck-snapping journey down the hill. My eyes scuttered over the dark and the mist, finding no purchase—but then the figure on the road moved. It was still coming for me. It let out a sound between a howl and a scream, and broke into a loping run.

I pelted down the hill so fast I almost overbalanced myself. I hit the base of the slope hard enough that pain lanced through my shins, but I didn't break stride. I'd angled away from the road, heading toward the inward curve of the island. There: A house. Not Mrs. Popova's. This must be where Mikhail's house was, if it matched the real world.

I ran up on the nearest porch and hammered on the door. No answer. I tried the knob, and it turned. The door swung inward—but it was more like folding it inward on a seam, no hinges at its edge. I stared in from the doorway.

It was like a patchwork room. Parts of the walls were wood paneling. But there were gaps of bare, utterly featureless wall too. The rest of the room was the same way: a kitchen table set with a dinner of roast chicken and carrots—the far end of which ended abruptly, held up by gray, stony spikes instead of wooden legs. A door opened into another room, but there was only a crooked sliver of the room visible beyond and then—nothing. Solid, blank gray.

I stepped back, and back again. From here, all I could see through the widows was the normal-looking room, because that was all there was. There was only what you could see from the windows, as if it was a diorama created by someone who had never ventured inside. I backed away, swallowing hard and battling panic.

The ground thrummed. I could feel it through the soles of my feet, and the windowpanes rattled with it.

My pursuer was running down the street toward me. He passed through the oily circle of light beneath one of the lanterns, and I recognized him with a startled jerk. Bristling beard, huge shoulders. Mikhail.

I couldn't outrun him, but I sprinted away, hoping the distance between us would buy me some time to find safety, find help. But I didn't make it far. Two houses down, a buckle in the pavement caught the toe of my shoe and I sprawled forward, hands scraping painfully against the ground, and then the footsteps were on me. Blunt fingers dug into my arms. I screamed in raw terror as he flipped me onto my back, the bulk, the sheer weight of him seeming to crush all coherent thought from me.

A meaty hand closed around my throat. I couldn't breathe. My limbs smacked against the implacable mass of his body. His breath washed over me. It was hot and stank of low tide: fish rot

and brine. Spots of color burst in my vision. The strength leached
out of me quicker than I could have imagined possible and then—

A horrible cawing screech and a flurry of black feathers sig-
naled my rescue. The man reared back, letting out a wordless
bellow and swiping at the air, but his avian attacker was already
wheeling away into the sky, screaming right back at him. Moriarty. I didn't waste the time it bought me. I scrambled upright,
my limbs sluggish and my breath seeming to ooze back into my
body reluctantly. My vision slewed over the landscape, searching
for something, anything to tell me which way to run, and caught
against the pale figure at the end of the road, standing in the center of a yellowed patch of light, mist coiling around her knees.
The girl.

She beckoned. I went to her. I glanced back once to see Moriarty still harassing the giant, diving at him and then flapping
wildly to gain altitude and avoid the swipes of those massive
hands. Then I had reached the light, and the girl.

There were no shadows now to hide her. She had my face.
Thinner than mine, cheeks sunken, rings around her eyes nearly
as deep as bruises, but she could have been my twin. She put out
her hand. The fingers were rough with calluses and scars, healed-
over cuts and fresh ones. Grime caked the creases of her palm.

Apprehension skittered over my skin, like a creature with too
many legs. Her fingers twitched. Waiting. I looked back. Moriarty
flew high, free of the man's grasping hands, and the man's attention turned to me once more.

I took her hand.

She spun at once, pulling me with her. Off the road and away from the house, running straight for the rocks and the water. She didn't head down toward the pebbled beach but out along a spit of tumbled boulders, black and scabbed over with barnacles and mussels. If I slipped, they'd tear my skin open.

The man had slowed, forced to clamber over the rocks and far less nimble than we were. But he was still coming. I looked at my twin. She pressed a finger to her lips, dropping my hand. She fell back a step and I had to pivot to still face her.

"Do you remember?" she asked.

"Remember what?" I replied helplessly. He was coming. We didn't have time to chat.

She shook her head sadly. "Listen," she said, and she grabbed both my hands.

The hum in my bones, the sound I had almost stopped noticing, swelled and swelled, growing so loud it made my teeth ache and my skull feel like it was splitting. I opened my mouth to scream, but the sound that came out was something else entirely—a sound like the clamor of birds.

My feet went out from under me on the slippery rocks, and then I was falling. Light and dark broke around me, warring for dominance, and then I hit something—hard—and the darkness won.

15

I WOKE UP warm, which was the only good thing about my circumstances. My eyes felt crusty, and the idea of opening them
was exhausting, so I took an inventory of myself instead. What
I had: pain, a lot of it, shooting in jagged pulses from the back of
my skull to the base of my spine. What I didn't have: clothes. My
bra and underpants were still on, wet but warm, but the rest of
my skin was in direct contact with whatever rough, woven blanket was covering me.

A blanket seemed good. People generally didn't cover you
nicely with warm blankets when they were intent on bludgeon-
ing you to death.

I couldn't hear anything but the omnipresent ocean. It was
muffled—I was obviously indoors—but close. I could smell it, the
salty tang of the ocean air, but that was everywhere on Bitter
Rock. Along with the ocean was the smell of woodsmoke.

Nothing for it. I forced my eyes open and found myself staring up at the wooden beams of a ceiling. Not very informative. I pushed myself cautiously upright. My head throbbed and my back gave a spasm of protest, but nothing seemed broken and I didn't immediately pass out, which I assumed were good signs.

The room I was in was tiny and wood paneled. The smell of the blankets told me the narrow bed hadn't been used in a long time. There were clothes folded at the end of the bed. An old, soft gray sweater, a long brown skirt, socks that looked bulky and wonderfully warm. I pulled them on eagerly. I felt a bit braver with something between me and the outside world, even if it was just wool. By the time I was done getting dressed, my aches and pains were working themselves loose. My fingers found a hole in the cuff as I stole my way to the door.

Unlocked. I let out a breath, tension easing out of me. The room beyond wasn't as cramped as the bedroom, but it was built on about the same scale, woodstove and table and fireplace crammed together. My clothes were draped over a rack near the woodstove. A heavy coat hung on a peg by the front door, and blue curtains covered the windows, blocking the light so only the glow of the fireplace illuminated the interior. There were only three doors: one to the outside, one open and leading to a tiny bathroom, the last to my right. Another bedroom, maybe.

How had I gotten here? I'd dreamed— No. My mind grabbed at that nearly sane explanation, but I shoved it away. It hadn't been a dream.

I moved farther into the room, and my gaze snagged against something on the mantel. Small shapes, arranged haphazardly. I had to draw close in the dim light before I could be sure what they were.

They were birds. Two dozen, maybe, none of them with a wingspan bigger than my palm, carved out of pale wood, their throats painted with a single red patch. Terns. Some had their wings stretched to the sky, others pointing straight up, still others tucked neatly at their sides. I reached out, running one tentative finger along the proud crown of one bird's head. Like my mother's and Abby's, they were simple, but something in the pose of each one gave it a spark of life. No two were exactly the same.

There was only one place left to explore. I crossed to the closed door. It wasn't latched, and I pushed it lightly with my fingertips. It swung inward with only the whisper of a creak.

It was another bedroom, and it wasn't empty. A man stood with his back to me—a massive man, shirtless, the whole of his back covered in a blue-black tattoo: a snarling bear, claws raised to swipe and rend. He had a shirt in his hand, clearly in the middle of changing. A floorboard creaked under my foot, and he turned.

And then I screamed. It was *him*. Mikhail.

I jerked back, hitting the stone mantel. One of the wooden birds clattered to the ground. Mikhail held up those giant hands. "Ne boysya," he said. "It's okay."

I looked at him. Really looked at him.

This wasn't the man who had attacked me. He looked nearly the same—graying, curly hair, thick limbs, bristling beard. But his eye—the man who'd attacked me had two bright, angry eyes. Mikhail had only one clear eye, the other scarred over, pale and sightless. The way the other man had held himself, it was like he was all body, all meat and momentum. This man hunched, like he was used to intimidating people by his sheer size and he didn't like it.

"Please," he said. His accent was thick, his voice pleading. "I won't hurt you."

"Okay," I said. It wasn't much, but he looked relieved, almost like he was the one who'd had cause to be afraid. He lurched, and I startled, but he only grabbed one of the kitchen chairs and pushed it toward me.

"Please, sit. You are tired," he said.

I didn't move. "What's out there? What were those things?"

"They are—" He gestured, swiping his hand in the air over his face. "Gosti. The Visitors. Not usually so dangerous in the daytime, but . . ." He shrugged. "Not always."

"I saw you," I said. "You attacked me."

He shook his head. "No. That was not me. They look like us, but they are hollow."

"He—" I put a hand to my throat. It was tender where he'd choked me. I flinched at even the light brush of my fingers across it. I'd been lucky.

"Prosti menya," he said. I stared at him blankly, too weary to ask what it meant. He let out a sigh and picked up his shirt from where it had fallen, pulling it on.

"How did I get here?" I asked instead.

"I found you. In the water," he said. "Just there." He pointed toward the back wall of the cabin, which faced the sea.

I must have lost consciousness when I fell. I was lucky I hadn't drowned.

A memory shimmered below the surface of my mind like a pale fish beneath the water—a hand in mine, walking down toward a rocky beach. But not the same beach. Not the same hand—or was it? I shook my head to clear it. "What is going *on* here?" I asked, more plaintively than I meant to. "Who are you? What was that place? What are those *things*?"

He stopped me, holding up his hand. "This is no way to talk. I will make tea. You sit, rest. Then ask your questions." He gestured to the small kitchen table. I considered. He wasn't the man who'd attacked me, but they shared the same face, and the most primal part of me refused to let go of my fear. And even if that had not been true, he was a strange man and he'd taken me here, alone and vulnerable.

A glass lantern hung from the wall on a hook, the smudges on the interior suggesting it wasn't just decorative. I stared at the miniaturized reflection in its surface.

The man in the reflection wasn't Mikhail. It was the other one. He had his back to us, and twitches of movement rippled over his body, his limbs, his head jerking an inch to either direction every second or two.

"What do you see?" Mikhail asked with interest.

"Nothing," I said. I sat down in the chair heavily. "I think I'd like that tea."

Mikhail spoke as he filled the kettle and set it on the heat. "You have figured out by now that there is something evil on these islands."

"The Visitors?" I asked.

Mikhail shook his head. "The Visitors belong to it. They merely do as it says."

"It. You mean the Six-Wing," I said.

"Yes. The Six-Wing cannot leave the other world," he said. "The echo world. The Visitors, though, they can slip out."

"They come when there's mist," I said.

"Hm. No. The mist comes with them," he said. "They are stronger at night. In the dark months. But they come in daylight too."

"That's why no one's allowed here after the summer," I guessed. "During the summer, there's no night."

He nodded. "It is why you must not go out in the mist, or in the night. Sometimes, nothing. You come home, all is well. Sometimes, you do not come home. Sometimes, someone comes home, and it looks like you, and it sounds like you, and it is not you." He leaned forward, his voice urgent. "You must not trust them. Not even for a moment. Some of them are like animals, worse than animals. They will tear you apart the moment they see you. But others, they have learned to smile. To say, 'It is all right. Come closer. It is only me, your old friend.' But you do not trust anyone you meet in the mist. You do not trust a knock on the door. You do not trust the voice you hear, calling for help."

"Do you . . ." I swallowed. "Do you know what happened to Joy Novak?"

Something like surprise and something like regret flashed through his eyes. "I know they took her," he said. "I was only there at the end. The bird people had gone to Belaya Skala. It was not allowed, but smart men are sometimes the greatest fools."

I blinked a moment, thinking he meant some kind of bird-person monsters I had yet to encounter, but then I realized he must mean the ornithologists—the LARC staff. "What do you mean, 'at the end'?" I asked. "What happened at the end?"

"I found you," he said, as if it was obvious. "I found you in the boat, Sophia. You were all alone, and the others were gone."

I went still. The fisherman in the story—it was Mikhail? "I need to know," I said. "I need to know what happened to my mother."

Mikhail scowled. "You should not be asking these questions. Your mother would want you safe. And you are not safe here. What you can see can also see you. The island has not noticed you yet, but it will. You should go. Leave this place, and stay safe."

"I have to find her," I said quietly.

"The people who vanish here do not come back," he replied. His voice was gentle.

"I did."

He looked at me a long moment. And then he sighed. "If you won't leave, I will tell you only to be careful. Do not trust a familiar face just because it is familiar. Some of them have learned to walk outside the mist."

I knew I would get no more from him. Not now, at least. "Thank you," I said. "For saving me. Twice, I guess. And for the clothes. Who . . . whose are they, anyway?"

"They belonged to my wife," he said.

"Does she live here?" I asked.

"Oh, no. She left a long time ago," he replied. "But sometimes I still see her. And I lock the door."

VIDEO EVIDENCE

Recorded by Joy Novak

AUGUST 14, 2003, TIME UNKNOWN

Hardcastle's gun is aimed straight at Baker's heart. Carreau steps in front of Baker immediately, holding out a restraining hand.

CARREAU: Put that down. What are you doing?

Novak takes the camera from Sophia and trains it on Hardcastle.

HARDCASTLE: Put that away.

NOVAK: No. Whatever happens here, it happens on camera.

He gives her an angry look.

HARDCASTLE: See this?

He reaches over to Vanya and yanks on her collar. She jerks away angrily, but not before the movement reveals a necklace of darkening bruises around her throat.

HARDCASTLE: She did that.

NOVAK: That's impossible. She was with us the whole time.

CARREAU: The door was barred. She could not have gotten out.

BAKER: I haven't done anything. I don't even know what's happening, please . . .

HARDCASTLE: She was out there. She was crying. We went to help her, but she sounded crazy. Babbling nonsense. We started to bring her back and she went along at first, but then she attacked Vanya. She would have killed her if I hadn't—

KAPOOR: Will. They're obviously not the same person. I mean, they are, but—

Novak's hands are shaking, and so is the camera. Sophia whimpers beside her, clearly terrified.

CARREAU: Where did you get that gun, Will?

Hardcastle looks down at the revolver.

HARDCASTLE: I don't know.

KAPOOR: You said you found it.

HARDCASTLE: I don't actually remember picking it up. Did you see me pick it up?

Kapoor shakes her head. Hardcastle swears.

HARDCASTLE: What the hell is happening?

NOVAK: I'll tell you what isn't happening. No one is shooting anyone else. Put that thing away.

Hardcastle hesitates.

NOVAK: She was with us the whole time, Will.

He grunts. Reluctantly, he tucks the revolver into his belt. Baker lets out a sob of relief, digging her fingers into her hair.

Something bangs against the back wall. Everyone jumps; Baker scurries away from the altar. The bang comes again, and then comes a croaking, groaning voice, each syllable strained and stretched.

[UNKNOWN]: He waits.

Another bang. Another, each at a different point along the wall. The thuds come faster and faster until they're like hail, striking at the roof and the sides of the building. The wood creaks and cracks. Sophia is screaming. They all draw back, away from the cacophony.

A huge crack spreads across the roof, splitting the mural in two. The walls bulge inward, splinters of wood flying under the unseen onslaught.

KAPOOR: It's going to come down! We have to get out of here.

Novak reaches for Sophia. Carreau picks her up instead.

CARREAU: I've got her. Don't worry.

The camera dangles by its strap from Novak's wrist as she helps with the effort to unblock the door. The pew falls to the ground, momentarily drowning out the ferocious noise around them, and they scramble outside.

HARDCASTLE: Jesus Christ.

Novak gets a good distance away before she turns and, with shaking hands, lifts the camera to capture the sight before them. A roiling mass of terns fills the sky. One by one they plunge from the swirling cloud and plummet, striking full-force against the church. Black sludge drips from the walls, the roof, as the birds lose cohesion in death, reverting to that strange liquid.

All at once, the building collapses. The birds cease their assault, but continue to swarm up above. Their silence is somehow obscene.

Lightning flashes in the distance, illuminating a six-winged shadow.

HARDCASTLE: The bunker. We can take shelter in the bunker. Come on. Run!

Baker grabs Novak's arm to help her, and they flee.

16

MIKHAIL GAVE ME tea, but no more answers. I couldn't tell whether he'd told me all he knew, or whether he thought he could protect me by staying silent. Either way, I left as soon as my clothes were some semblance of dry.

We were supposed to be at the LARC at seven thirty a.m. My shoes were still soggy, but I shoved them on anyway and jogged for Mrs. Popova's. I hoped that I could sneak in without being noticed. I went around the back and was relieved to find the door open. That would put me at the end of the hall, and hopefully people were still scraping together breakfast in the kitchen and hadn't thought to try to rouse me yet.

I crept toward my room, but urgent voices to the right, coming from Abby's room, stopped me. Abby was saying something I couldn't make out, and then Liam's voice cut through.

"Bullshit. We can't just sit here and do nothing while—"

"Keep your voice down, will you?" Abby hiss-whispered. "Do

you want the whole house to hear you? There's nothing we *can* do. We don't know where she is. If she's even alive."

I opened the door. They both jumped, Abby reaching for something at her belt—a knife, probably—and while her hand paused when she saw it was me, she didn't entirely relax.

Liam, though, just about collapsed with relief. He crashed into me with a hug, and if I stiffened up for a moment, it was a brief moment. I hugged him back, taking more pleasure than I cared to admit from holding his slender body, the very *boy* scent of him. Human and normal and cute and clever and a million things that weren't monsters in the mist.

"Missed you too," I said, before the moment could get too intense.

"Where were you?" Liam demanded. "We couldn't find you anywhere."

"Second verse, same as the first," I said.

"A little bit louder and a little bit worse?" Abby supplied.

"Pretty much. It was that other place—only it was different this time, and . . ." I trailed off, gave them a questioning look. "How did you get away from Dr. Kapoor and Dr. Hardcastle?"

Liam's cheeks flamed. "Uh. We didn't, exactly. They saw me."

"How are you not locked in your room for the rest of your natural life?" I asked.

"We sort of . . ." He looked at Abby helplessly, and she rolled her eyes.

"Liam was just showing his new girlfriend around, to impress her," she said. "We're dating now. Whee."

I might have been jealous if they weren't so obviously horrified by the necessary deception.

"It's just a cover," Liam said. "I'm not—"

"I get it," I said. "It was smart."

"Okay, enough with the tedious romantic subplot. What happened to you?" Abby asked. Lily walked past in the hall, and we fell silent.

"Let's take a walk," I suggested. We headed out to the beach and wandered down it in the pale morning light. I told them what had happened, every step of it. The other island, the strangers, my flight down the hill, the half-formed house. And then I got to Mikhail.

"What do you think?" I asked Abby when I was done.

"About what?" She tucked her hair behind her ear, a losing battle against the wind.

"Mikhail. What he said."

"I think he was telling you as little as he could," she said. "He's hiding something."

"You don't know that," Liam said.

"No. She's right," I said. I didn't want her to be. Mikhail had helped me. He'd been kind, and wounded, and lost. But he knew more than he'd said, I was certain. "But it doesn't matter."

"It doesn't?" Abby asked with a skeptical arch to her eyebrow.

"No. Because whatever he is or isn't telling us, we know the important thing. What happened to my mother—to me—happened on Belaya Skala. I've crossed over to that other world twice, but never on the headland. We need to get over there if we're going to find the truth."

"You want to go back to that place?" Liam asked.

"If it gets me answers," I said.

"You shouldn't go alone," Abby said.

"I can't ask you both to risk yourselves for me," I said. "Especially you, Liam. Abby has her own reasons, but you . . ."

He hadn't looked at me yet. "I'm not exactly doing it for you," he said. He swallowed. "I want to help you, but it's not just that."

"What, then?" I asked.

"That summer, the summer of the Girl in the Boat, something changed," Liam said. "I was really young, but I remember how close Dr. Kapoor and I were. She's the one that convinced Mum to have a kid in the first place. But after that summer, she never had time for me. She barely spoke to me at all, or looked at Mum, except when they were fighting. And then she left and came back here. And it was a relief, because it felt like we'd been living with a stranger." His voice was raw and thick with bitterness.

Abby looked away, clearly uncomfortable, but on impulse I reached out and grabbed Liam's hand. He didn't meet my eyes, but he squeezed my hand and took a deep breath. And then he continued.

"I've always thought that she just realized she wasn't cut out to be a mother. But it wasn't just me—she used to be incredibly close with her parents, but she hardly ever sees them now. And with all of this, I just . . ." He faltered, then set his jaw and looked straight at me. "What if we *were* living with a stranger? What if she isn't here because of the bloody birds?"

"What are you saying?" I asked.

"What Mikhail said. Sometimes people come out of the mist, and they look the same, and they sound the same, but it's not them." Liam asked. His eyes were dark, intense, and fixed on me. "What if what came out of the mist isn't my mother at all?"

VIDEO EVIDENCE

Recorded by Joy Novak

AUGUST 14, 2003, TIME UNKNOWN

The group calls out to keep track of each other in the mist. No-vak and Baker are together still, falling behind as Novak's injury slows her. The occasional glimpses of the landscape ahead of them show the others as indistinct silhouettes in the mist, sometimes nearly vanishing completely.

BAKER: Come on. Come on.

NOVAK: Just go.

BAKER: I'm not fucking leaving you. I'll get stuck babysitting your kid. I hate kids.

She grunts, tripping over something.

BAKER: What—

She lets out a gulping sob. A woman lies sprawled on the ground in the graceless pose of the dead, one leg bent so far her foot is near the middle of the back, her head tipped up and mouth open in an expression of guileless surprise. She wears the same green jacket and black T-shirt as Baker. She wears the same face as well. There is a hole in her flesh just below her collarbone. The ground beneath her is soaked with blood.

Novak's voice is quiet.

NOVAK: Just keep moving.

But Baker seems not to hear. She creeps forward, her breath uneven, and bends over, reaching a trembling hand toward the shoulder of her double. Her fingers have almost brushed the body's shoulder when it twitches. Baker stumbles away with a stifled scream as the woman rolls awkwardly forward, then flops to the ground. Her jaw works once, twice. She blinks her eyes. They snap over to Baker.

BAKER [2]: Wh . . . wh . . .

It's not clear if she's trying to say something, or merely aping speech. The sound is wet and slurred. She rolls again, this time more successfully. Her hand closes around Baker's ankle. Baker screams and kicks, but the woman's grip is implacable.

BAKER: Help! Help!

She falls over backward. Her double claws toward her across the ground, still forcing out those gasping syllables. Novak seems frozen. And then, dropping the camera to dangle by its strap, she lunges forward. She grabs a rock from the ground the size of two closed fists. She brings it down. The camera strikes the ground as she does. The lens fractures. Someone—Baker or her double—screams. Novak slams the rock down again.

NOVAK: Shh. You're all right. Caro.

BAKER: I know her.

NOVAK: She looks like you.

BAKER: You don't understand. I know her.

NOVAK: You're not making sense. Stand up, Caro. We have to catch up with the others.

She seems as disturbed by the fact that they haven't appeared as by the body at their feet. She clears her throat, checks the camera. She murmurs to herself.

NOVAK: No one's going to believe this if we don't . . .

She doesn't finish the thought. She wipes off the lens as best she can, though there is nothing to do for the crack now running through the image, and helps Baker to her feet. Baker is weeping, but she follows placidly enough as Novak leads her.

NOVAK: Don't tell anyone what happened. Just say you fell.

BAKER: Why?

NOVAK: Because we're almost at the bunker. And the bunker is higher on the slope than the village, and toward the north bluff.

BAKER: Why does that matter?

NOVAK: Vanya and Will were supposed to head toward the beach. They didn't say anything about coming up here.

17

WE WALKED BACK to Mrs. Popova's together. It was early enough that we were the only ones up. "Do you get used to this?" Liam asked Abby. "Does it ever stop feeling like you're dreaming and you'll wake up at any minute?"

"It does. But then you miss when it felt like that," Abby said. "When it still felt like there was a chance it could all be undone." She was thinking of her sister, I was sure.

"It doesn't feel like I'm dreaming," I said. "It feels like I'm awake for the first time in my life. When I'm in that other place—it's like when there's a loud fan running, and you've stopped noticing that it's there, until suddenly someone turns it off."

"Does that worry you?" Abby asked.

"Of course it does," I said with a laugh. "Who feels relaxed on Spooky Echo Island?"

"It's not actually that weird, necessarily," Abby said slowly.

"How is that not weird?" I asked.

"There are certain people who have a connection to the other worlds," Abby said. She rubbed her thumb along her jaw thoughtfully. "They're special. Different. My sister was like that. She'd get feelings about things that turned out to be true, and she could see things that even Ashford couldn't. Ashford thinks that's why . . ."

"Why she's a ghost?" I asked.

Liam's eyes widened, and he opened his mouth as if to ask a question, but then he just shook his head and fell silent. Maybe he'd used up his budget of weird.

"Not just a ghost. She's different now too," Abby said. "She doesn't act like she should. She sent me here, and that's just not something ghosts do. If you're attuned to the world that's intruding on Bitter Rock, it could be why you could see the Six-Wing. And why you have some kind of connection to your echo."

I felt an odd flutter of hope. Could that be it? I had some strange bond with my echo, and she had caused all the strange things in my life? I wasn't a freak. It wasn't my fault. It was hers.

"What if she has some hold on you?" Liam asked. We'd stopped at the head of the long driveway down to Mrs. Popova's, and he turned so that we were all facing each other. "If you're connected to your echo, you're connected to the Six-Wing."

"It *is* worrying," Abby said. "But listen. This is what I do, remember? Most of the time, I'm only there for the aftermath, when it's too late to do anything. But this time, I can help. I'll keep you both breathing, I promise."

Liam scoffed slightly, but I could tell that he was relieved to hear it—and trying not to show that he was relieved. Oil and water, but I was glad that both of them were here. Glad not to be alone.

"We'll get through this," I said.

"If something happens to me, I'm sure Dr. Kapoor will cover it up for you," Liam said wryly.

"Well, if I die, gather up all of my stuff and send it to Dr. Andrew Ashford," Abby said. "He's the only person left in the world who would care what happened to me."

"I'd care," I said.

The corner of her mouth twitched. "You've known me a day, Sophia Novak."

"And I already like you better than anyone back home," I said. "I'm not big on friends."

"Aw. I like you too," she said.

"Just to be clear," Liam said, "I might be fake-dating you, but I don't like you."

"Oh, no. Totally hate your guts. Glad it's mutual," Abby responded, and they gave each other a fist bump. I rolled my eyes, and Abby laughed. "I should get back to my room. I still haven't gone through that stuff from the LARC."

"I'll help. I've still got time before Dr. Kapoor needs me up at the Center," I said. "Liam?"

"I'd better get back into my bed before Dr. Kapoor figures out I'm not in it."

"Sweet dreams, *sweetie*," Abby replied, and waggled her fingers at him. Then she hooked her arm through mine and pulled me off down the driveway. I twisted around to mouth *sorry* at him, but he just chuckled ruefully. Abby jostled me a little. "Be careful," she said.

"What, with Liam?"

"Not just with Liam. With making friends. Especially with people like me."

"And what kind of person are you?" I asked.

She was quiet a minute, like she couldn't decide if it was a good idea to explain. When she did speak, her tone was serious, her words slow and careful. "I'm like you," she said. "So focused on the prize I don't care about the risk that it puts me in. Or puts other people in. We get killed. And we get people killed."

"No one's going to die because of me," I said dismissively.

"Just be careful. Like I said." She didn't say anything more on the subject, but I couldn't stop the words from looping in my mind, again and again. Echo and warning.

Inside, we ditched our boots and padded past Lily, who stood staring at the brewing coffeepot with furious intensity, and Kenny, sprawled on the couch in the living room with his phone on his chest and his eyes closed.

Abby had stowed the backpack of looted evidence under her bed. She set it on the bed and pulled out a stack of files, a bunch of loose papers, and a folded map. I grabbed the map.

It reminded me of the one I'd found in the specimen room—marks and dates around the area. But that one hadn't been updated since the eighties. This one had dates up to last summer, and the dots had short phrases next to them as well as dates.

Oct. 17, 2015—cruise passenger reports cabin flooding, men screaming. No water found.

Nov. 3, 2014—crew member on fishing vessel reported lost at sea. Storm confirmed by weather service, likely unrelated.

There were no lines drawn on this one, but the dates on the map painted their own picture. The echo world's impact was still spreading, year by year. Winter by winter, I realized, examining the dates more closely. The summer dates never exceeded the range of the previous winter. It was in the darkness that its influence grew. I turned my attention to the other papers. What had fallen into the category of "worth hiding"?

There was data on the terns—notes on their mutations. *Seven human teeth found growing in chest cavity,* I read, and shuddered. These were the ones too strange to preserve or explain. There were weather reports and reports on currents, which I couldn't make heads or tails of, and a number of photocopied documents in Russian that I set aside. Someone would be able to translate them for me.

I was moving a manila envelope—this one actually full of receipts for reimbursement—when something made me pause. I hefted it. The weight was wrong. Unbalanced. What . . . ?

I peered inside and let out a sound of satisfaction. An SD card was taped against the side of the envelope. The irregular shape of the receipts inside meant you'd never know it was there unless you actually looked in. I peeled it free and showed it to Abby. But Abby wasn't paying attention. She was staring at something she'd pulled from one of the other envelopes—a photograph.

"That doesn't make any sense," she said. She looked up. Her expression was lost.

"What doesn't?"

She held the photo out. I recognized the backdrop immediately as Landontown on Belaya Skala, though the buildings were newer, freshly painted. It was a group shot: men with long hair in corduroy pants, women with high-waisted jeans with bell-bottoms, quintessential 1970s styles, the date confirmed by the fuzzy numbers in the bottom corner: *July 1973*. They looked out of place on the rugged island. There were four women and five men. I recognized the one at the center, a man with gleaming, intense eyes and the kind of face I could imagine people following all the way to the middle of nowhere to start a new society.

"It's Cole Landon," I said. And the woman beside him with frothy blonde hair was his wife.

"Not him. Them," she said. She pointed at a man and a boy of maybe thirteen standing beside Landon. The man had a hand on the boy's shoulder; both were smiling. Father and son, I thought; they had the same bold features and nearly black hair.

"What about them?" I asked.

"That's my grandpa," she said, pointing to the older man. "And that's my dad."

"Are you sure?" I asked.

"I'm sure. I've seen lots of pictures. My dad was really proud of his family—they're sort of old money, big on legacy, you know? I grew up in a house that had a name and a dumbwaiter. He wanted us to know where we came from. But why would he be here?"

"I don't know. But I bet it's why Miranda sent you here," I said. "To find out." Not to help me. I'd started to think of Abby as *mine*, my protector, my friend. But this wasn't just about me.

"It was in an envelope with this," she said. She had a USB drive in her other hand.

"What do you think's on it?" I asked.

"I don't know," she said. For once, she didn't take the lead. She only stared at the photo and the drive, as if she wasn't sure she wanted whatever answers were waiting.

I took the drive from her. She almost looked like she wanted to stop me. "We have to find out," I told her, and plugged it into the laptop.

EXHIBIT H

Video recorded by unknown Landontown resident

SUMMER 1973, EXACT DATE AND TIME UNKNOWN

The image is grainy. A group of people sit within a poorly lit room—the church on Belaya Skala. Cole Landon stands at the front.

LANDON: Are we all here? Wonderful. As you no doubt have heard, we have special guests tonight. I'd like you all to welcome James Ryder and his son, Jimmy.

The gathered assembly claps and lets out a chorus of friendly welcomes. A man at the front, the elder James Ryder, stands and waves as he steps up to join Landon.

RYDER: When Cole first approached me, I knew he had something exciting on his hands. He'd heard about my interests and my expertise and thought I might be interested in helping to put this project together. Well, I'll tell you, I was more than interested.

He chuckles, and Landon grins.

RYDER: You're all aware of what we're trying to accomplish. This place is a nexus. We don't know why, but we know that *here* one of the great gates is opening. Seven worlds, friends, besides our own. Seven worlds filled with wonders. And one of them?

He pauses for dramatic effect.

RYDER: One of them is waiting just . . . out . . . of sight.

He holds up a hand, as if he can almost touch that other world.

RYDER: Once, the secrets of these worlds belonged to mankind. Once, the Eidolons, those glorious kings and queens, shared their knowledge and their power with the kingdoms of earth. The Eidolons have been trapped. But you . . . *you* are going to be the first to bring *back* one of the eidolons: the Seraph.

A murmur, worshipful, goes around the gathering.

LANDON: It's not too late to stay, James.

Ryder chuckles.

RYDER: Would that I could. The Seraph is a being of beauty and immense power, but my heart has always yearned to serve another of its kin. The—

The tape abruptly runs out.

INTERVIEW

Dr. Vanya Kapoor

JULY 3, 2004

*Dr. Kapoor and Dr. Andrew Ashford sit across from one an-
other at a table in the LARC break room. Ashford is smok-
ing, and his eyes are dark with shadows. Both he and Dr.
Kapoor look more than just fourteen years younger than
present day—their faces unlined, hair free of gray, a sharp-
ness to their eyes that age and the burdens of their lives have
dulled.*

KAPOOR: You've seen everything now. Did you find what
you wanted to?

ASHFORD: What I wanted to? No. But answers, nonetheless.

KAPOOR: And what about my answers? I think I deserve an
explanation.

ASHFORD: Just one?

He laughs. The sound is hollow. He stubs out the cigarette.

KAPOOR: Let's start with what the hell an Eidolon is.

ASHFORD: A king. Or a god. Or a demon. It depends on your point of view. There were seven. Seven kings of seven worlds. Long ago, long before the founding of Rome, the boundaries between their worlds and ours were thin. There were roads between them that you could simply walk down. The Eidolons demanded worship and tribute and sacrifice, and loosed horrors on humanity. Plagues. Monsters. Slaughter. And then they fell.

KAPOOR: How?

ASHFORD: There are many theories, but none of them is likelier than the next. Maybe some kind of disease. Or some kind of metaphysical change, like a natural—supernatural—disaster. Or else humanity fought back and won. Whatever it was, the seven worlds were broken. What remains of them now is to their original state what a rotting corpse is to a man. The Eidolons sealed away inside of them, behind what we call gates. Not literal gates, but metaphysical barriers, preventing them from entering our world.

KAPOOR: And if they open?

Ashford grimaces.

ASHFORD: Then surely these benevolent gods shall shower us with blessings. That's what Landon thought.

KAPOOR: And this Ryder guy.

Ashford makes a noncommittal sound.

ASHFORD: Each world, each gate, is different. But in all cases, to open them requires people of our world who are in some way attuned to the one you are trying to reach. That attunement may be intrinsic, a matter of birth, or it may be manufactured by ritual or other unknown processes.

KAPOOR: It sounds almost scientific.

ASHFORD: We do our best to contain this madness with sterile words and rules, but the truth is, it's a wilderness of ruin. As soon as you find a rule, you discover a situation where it doesn't apply. Still. It gives us a framework. A way to comprehend the unknowable. But sometimes I wonder if that is more dangerous than accepting the wilderness.

KAPOOR: What do you mean?

ASHFORD: The men on the *Krachka* found something in the ocean. They should have cast it back, but they were *curious*. They kept it, and it wrecked them on the rocks and made these islands its home. The military thought to contain it in that bunker, guard and study it. Landon thought to worship it. All of them seeking a kind of understanding. But if they had only understood its one desire, they would have left it alone.

KAPOOR: Its desire. The Six-Wing wants to be free.

ASHFORD: Yes. But what you encountered wasn't the Six-Wing.

KAPOOR: No? Because I counted. There were definitely six wings.

ASHFORD: Let me be more accurate: the Eidolon that Landon was trying to free is the Seraph. The Six-Wing is *not* the Seraph. Not an Eidolon. The worlds you wandered through were echoes, layered over each other, creating a bridge between the Seraph's world and ours. And the creature that inhabited them was an echo too. The Six-Wing, as you call it, is the echo of the Eidolon called the Seraph.

KAPOOR: How can you be sure?

ASHFORD: If you had met the true Seraph, you would not have made it out.

KAPOOR: Not all of us did.

ASHFORD: Even the echo of a god is a dangerous thing.

18

A KNOCK ON the door made us jump. Abby tossed a throw blanket over the papers and shut her laptop as the door opened. It was Lily.

"We're heading out," she informed us. "And Liam is here, looking for Abby."

"Right," Abby said dully. "Be right there." She palmed the USB drive and the SD card, which I'd set down on the bedspread. She put both in her bag, along with her laptop—more of her habit of keeping all the evidence with her at all times, and I didn't blame her. With everything that was going on, I wouldn't be surprised to find Dr. Kapoor or even Mrs. Popova going through our things.

She grabbed her bag. "I'll see you, Hayes." Her voice was tight. We needed to talk about what we'd seen on that drive. *She* needed to talk—needed to get it out, the confusion and the betrayal, before it festered like a wound. Her grandfather had been here, had been *involved*. And her boss, the man who'd taken care of her for years, had known.

At least my foster parents hadn't known they were keeping secrets from me.

"See you," I said, because Lily was there and we had no choice but to let silence win. Abby gave me a weak wave, looking more like she was walking to the guillotine than to meet up with her supposed boyfriend, and headed out.

"Liam and her?" Lily said when she was gone. She scrunched up her nose. "Okay, I guess."

"Don't ask me, I'm new here," I said. "I'm going to change my clothes really quick and I'll meet you at the car."

"Better not be late again. We won't get lucky twice," she told me. I gave her a mock-salute, forcing every bit of false cheer into it, and she headed down the hall.

I quickly gathered up the documents and stuffed them between the mattress and the box spring. As hiding places went, it was a bit cliché, but it would do in a pinch.

I bolted to my own room to quickly change. I didn't have time to shower, and my skin felt gritty, but there was nothing for it. At least I could pull on fresh clothes. I also hadn't slept, unless you counted being unconscious for a couple hours, and my body was starting to catch up with that fact. Today was going to be brutal.

I skidded into the kitchen to discover Lily ready to go, boots on and travel mug in hand, but Kenny was still snoring on the couch.

"Uh—are we going to be late?" I asked tentatively. Fifteen minutes to the hour of doom.

"Don't worry, I've got this," Lily said. She walked to the foot of the couch, took a deep breath, and shouted, "KENNETH!"

Kenny bolted upright, somehow managed to catch his phone, and started yanking on his boots.

"Thirty seconds," Lily told him, and headed for the door. She gestured for me to follow her. By the time we reached the porch, Kenny was right behind us, even if he was hopping on one foot while he tugged the other boot on.

I was glad it wasn't a long ride up the hill to the LARC, because the whole time my leg was bouncing, and I chewed on my lip. Lily and Kenny were so normal. They had no idea what was going on, and that felt more alien than the place in the mist.

We caught up to Liam and Abby, who were sitting in the Jeep, talking. I wondered if Abby was catching him up on what we'd seen, and then realized that of course she was—I was the one who kept secrets. Liam caught my eye and waved. I could tell just by that glance that he felt the same sense of dislocation I did.

I got out of the car quickly, thinking I would go walk with Abby and Liam, but they split off as soon as they were inside the door, heading for Dr. Kapoor's office while the rest of us were meant to go gather, as was customary, in the break room. It would have been weird to try to follow, but I chewed my lip until it hurt, wishing we could stick together.

Dr. Hardcastle was already in the break room. I felt like I'd been run over by a truck last night—not too far off from the truth—but he looked immaculate. You'd never know he'd been up in the middle of the night.

"Good morning, everyone," he said cheerfully. He had a very

particular brand of male authority: polished, a kind of folksiness that only underscored that he was the one in charge. "Dr. Kapoor will be here in a moment, but I wanted to take the opportunity to catch up. Everyone was so busy yesterday, I feel like we hardly saw each other. Sophie."

I jerked, my cheeks flushing as he turned his gaze on me. "Sophia," I said.

"What's that?"

"I go by Sophia," I told him.

"Right," he said. I searched his face for some hint that it hadn't just been a mistake. I went by Sophie when I was here as a child—did he know? But if he did, he didn't let it slip in his expression. "You've been doing good work. I admit I've been very curious about you."

"Oh?" I said.

He smiled. "Why don't you tell me a bit about yourself? Since I didn't have the advantage of a long correspondence to get to know you, the way Vanya did."

All the careful lies I'd practiced about Sophia Hayes, lover of birds and northern climes, fled. My mouth was dry. I couldn't think of anything to say.

"Is something wrong?" he asked.

Why did he affect me this way? "No," I stammered. "It's just—"

"Everyone here? Good," Dr. Kapoor said, striding in. Dr. Hardcastle half turned with a frown.

"Ms. Hayes was just going to tell us a bit about herself," he said.

"Another time," she said briskly. "The water's going to be foul midmorning, so we shouldn't dawdle on the crossing. Ms. Clark and Mr. Lee will be on Belaya Skala, Ms. Hayes in the specimen room. Dr. Hardcastle and I will be handling some administrative matters here."

I couldn't stop the muffled squawk of protest that came out of my mouth. Dr. Kapoor gave me a measured look. "Yes, Ms. Hayes? Do you object to your task?"

"Of course I do," I said. "I came here to learn, not declutter. I barely got to watch you work yesterday. And no offense to Liam, but I didn't come here to hang out with him either."

"She came hundreds of miles and, by God, she wants to count some birds," Lily said, obviously amused. "She can tag along with Kenny and me. We'll make sure she doesn't count a bunch of pebbles as chicks and bump our babies off the endangered species list."

Dr. Kapoor hadn't spoken. Her steady gaze made the hair on the back of my neck prickle. *Just strict? Or is there another reason you make me uneasy?*

"Very well," she said. "Get your gear together, Ms. Hayes."

"Yes, ma'am," I said. I'd expected to get chewed out, but then it occurred to me that letting me onto Belaya Skala might not be an act of consideration and charity, given what lurked there.

"Now, if you'll excuse me. Moriarty got out last night, and I need to check on his well-being," she said, and turned away. I felt a stab of guilt. After Moriarty had helped me, I hadn't checked on him to see if he got back all right. I didn't know how he'd gotten into that place at all, let alone returned.

"Let's head out. We're playing catch-up from yesterday," Lily said. She and Kenny started bustling about to gather up supplies.

Dr. Hardcastle gave us an officious nod before wandering off to parts unknown.

We walked down to the beach together. Lily and Kenny kept up a sort of slow-motion conversation about nothing in particular. We'd just secured the last of the gear when Liam and Abby appeared, jogging across the beach.

"Wait up," Liam called. Lily straightened, a frown ghosting across her features. She was the hard target here, I knew. Kenny would go with whatever we said.

"What's up?" she asked, addressing Liam but looking at Abby with a jaundiced eye.

"Abby and I are going to tag along," Liam said. "I checked it out with Dr. Kapoor, she said it's all right." He wasn't nearly as good a liar as I was. His throat kind of wobbled when he spoke, and he didn't know what to do with his hands. Abby clearly had the same opinion of his skills, but she was working gamely to keep it off her face.

"Uh. Really?" Lily asked. "Why exactly?"

"Because . . ." Liam flushed a little. "I invited her. She wanted to see the island again, and I promised I'd show her. Like . . ."

"A date?" Lily said.

Abby, to her credit, looked only briefly bemused before carefully constructing an expression of faint embarrassment, complete with a little shy smile. "Shy" suited her about as well as lying suited Liam, but most people, I knew, see what they expect to.

"I thought that you and—" Kenny started, his thumb starting to point in my direction, but Lily stepped on his foot.

"Are you sure you have permission?" she asked.

I laughed. "I've been here for two days and I know no one in their right mind would piss off Dr. Kapoor for the chance to show a girl some birds and rocks," I said. "And Liam's no rebel."

Here's the funny thing about lying: the substance of the lie often doesn't matter nearly as much as the conviction. So ignore the fact that Liam Kapoor was out here in the first place for breaking rules—breaking *laws*, in fact. I sounded sure, and more than that I made it sound like anyone who disagreed wasn't *in on it*. And people will do just about anything to make you think they're "in," because being "out" scares the crap out of us.

"Fine," Lily said. "Just don't flirt in front of me. I'm entirely too cynical for teenage love."

"Aren't you, like, twenty-three?" Kenny asked.

"Yes, but I tested out of my teenage years and went straight to middle age," Lily replied.

I reminded myself that this did not make me jealous or upset at all, and got into the boat, busying myself in the front so I didn't have to watch Liam help Abby in. They sat together on the back bench as we skidded across the water and past the jagged bridge of rock toward the headland. The tide was low, baring masses of barnacles like tumors on the rocks. At low tide you might be able to inch your way along the base of the rocks to Belaya Skala, but one slip and those barnacles would slice you to ribbons before you plunged into the cold, rough water. Kenny kept the boat well clear of them.

When we reached land, Liam held out a hand to help Abby out, but she hopped to the shore herself without even glancing at him.

We stole a moment to ourselves while Lily and Kenny fiddled

with the gear that was too expensive for the grubby hands of mere interns. "Okay. We're here," I said. "Now what?"

Abby didn't answer. She was looking out across the island, as if searching for something.

"Abby?" I said. She jerked.

"Sorry," she said. She bit her lip. "The bunker. We need to see the bunker. On the video, Ashford . . ." She stopped. Took a sharp breath. Then pressed on. "Ashford said that the military brought something there to study it. Right? So maybe there are records down there."

"Or the Six-Wing is down there, getting ready to eat us," Liam said.

"That's a risk we're just going to have to take," Abby replied, tone flat.

"Hey, intern. Time to earn your keep," Lily called. I turned reluctantly.

"We'll be fine. Just gathering intel," Abby said.

"Be careful," I said. Because that look in her eye wasn't a *keen on self-preservation* kind of look.

"Don't worry. I'll look after mop top," she said, and ruffled Liam's hair. He ducked out of reach.

"We're going to go for a walk," Liam said, covering his reaction with a wave.

"Have fun canoodling," Kenny called back.

They headed up the hill together. Abby glanced back and gave me a wave that was one part charade and one part reassurance. She had this handled, that wave said.

I wished I believed her. But I could see the hurt and uncertainty roiling behind her eyes, and I knew that however confident the Abby of yesterday had been, today was different.

Lily trusted me only marginally more than Dr. Kapoor did, but Kenny convinced her to let me man the massive binoculars. It was actually kind of fun, if I ignored the anxiety gnawing its way through my small intestine. The chicks liked to clump up into indistinct masses like wadded-up cotton balls. I had to check and double-check that I'd counted all the eyes, beaks, and black legs properly, and more than once I *did* almost count a pebble.

"So is this all you do?" I ask. "Count birds?"

"When they're a little bit older, the parents get less testy and we start being able to go in to do some more direct observations, tag them, that sort of thing," Kenny said.

"Tag them?"

"ID tags, mostly, but we're currently trying to solve the mystery of their migration pattern," Kenny said. "We've got these little GPS doohickeys we've been attaching for a couple years, but the failure rate's pretty high."

"How high?"

"One hundred percent," Lily said blandly.

"So you don't know where they migrate to?" I asked, finding myself getting kind of into the question, despite my previous interest in birds being limited to avoiding getting pooped on.

"Sort of?" Was Lily's answer. "They've been observed down south—South America, Chile mostly, and South Africa. But only individually. Which could be because there aren't many of them, or could be because they're gathering somewhere else we haven't found yet."

"And you do the bird calls with Hardcastle," I said casually.

"Yeah, though honestly, I'm not convinced of the value," Lily replied. "It's not a funded project, just his pet thing. Him and Kapoor. I've heard them play the tapes after hours sometimes." She kept talking, but I was listening to something else entirely.

Music. It wasn't *singing*, not precisely. More like humming that might break into song at any moment. *Almost* words, but almost tuneless enough to dismiss as the hum of some machine.

"Do you hear that?" I asked.

"Oh, the music?" Kenny asked. "Kinda freaky, but it's just the wind in the rocks."

"That's not wind," I said. "Wind whistles. It doesn't hum."

"Careful," Lily warned. "This far out from civilization, it's really easy to scare yourself. People have had nervous breakdowns working at the LARC, and it's not *entirely* Dr. Kapoor that causes them. This guy Rivers, he—"

"Can you try Liam on the radio?" I asked, worry squirming through me. I shouldn't have let them go off without me.

Lily hesitated. "Look, if there *is* something going on between you and Liam and Abby, I don't want to get into the middle of it."

"It's not that. I swear," I said. "I'm just worried about them. Please."

She stared hard at me, analyzing my face. The trouble with lying all the time is that when you're telling the truth, you still have to fake it, because you're so used to training your expression into something other than what you feel. Those are the moments that trip me up. But she grabbed the yellow plastic walkie-talkie from her belt.

"Liam, this is Lily. Just checking in. Over." Silence. She frowned. "Liam, stop making out and answer, over."

More silence.

"They're probably just dicking around," she muttered. "Liam, answer the damn radio."

And then—a burst of sound. Static, a metallic rattle, and a swell of that not-quite-song, and then an electronic squeal and silence. We all stared at the radio.

I started sprinting up the hill.

"Wait! Where are you going?" Lily called.

"I'm just going to go check on them. You stay here," I hollered back, hoping she'd follow my advice. I glanced over my shoulder long enough to see the two of them looking at each other like they were trying to decide which would get them in more trouble if they abandoned it—the equipment or the intern. I didn't wait for them to decide.

But then Lily puffed uphill behind me. "Hold up," she said.

"You should go back to work. I'll find them," I said.

"If something's wrong, I should help," Lily said. "I have first aid training, if anyone's hurt." The way she said it sounded more like *if anyone's done something stupid.*

There was no reasonable way to put her off. "They were going to the bunker," I said.

"The bunker? It's welded shut," she said. "To keep people from blundering in and getting tetanus or bubonic plague or something." Her tone suggested that "people" absolutely included idiotic lovestruck teenagers. She sighed. "Let's go, then."

I let her lead the way. She was in much better shape than me, with a runner's quads and sure steps. The exertion made me pant, so out of breath my vision seemed to shimmer.

"I thought you said it was welded shut," I said as we came into view of the bunker. The door hung wide open. The music, I realized, had stopped abruptly as we came into view. The first staccato thrill of apprehension tapped its way down my spine.

"There's no way they went in there," Lily said. "I *swear* it was welded shut."

"It's not shut anymore," I said. "And look." There was a muddy footprint with a waffle tread on the concrete pad in front of the door.

"Shit," Lily said. She cupped her hands around her mouth. "Liam! Abby!"

The only reply was the dull plink of water in the dim interior.

Lily swore again and grabbed her radio. "Kenny, they're in the bunker. I'm going to go down there to check it out." She looked at me. "The intern's coming back your way."

"I'm coming with you," I said. She took her thumb off the button. We squared up with glares and tight jaws. She was treating me like a child, but she was the one stumbling into things she didn't understand. My anger was a hot coal and I clenched my hands tight around it, savoring the burn. "You're not my boss and you're not my parent. You don't get to tell me what to do."

"I outrank you or whatever," Lily said. Twenty-three wasn't much older than eighteen, though. We glared at each other, and Lily was the one who broke. "Update. Intern's coming with me,"

Lily said into the radio. "If you don't hear from us in ten minutes, radio the LARC for some help. Over." She cast me one last glare. "Stay close and stay behind me. If a wall collapsed on them or something, it might not be safe for us either."

I didn't tell her that a collapsed wall was the least of our worries.

She hadn't seem to notice that Kenny never replied. I let her take the lead. She unclipped a flashlight from her well-stocked belt as she did. All the LARC employees carried them, just in case the mist rolled in unexpectedly. It was easier to find each other when you had beacons on hand. I hadn't brought mine, though. It was in one of the dry bags on the beach. Stupid.

Lily swept the light over the interior cautiously. Concrete, and lots of it, covered in water stains and black mold. The passage led straight back with doors to either side. The end of the passage was heaped with junk. The door to the right was ajar but couldn't be opened any further. Rusted hinges and a pile of detritus on the other side kept it too narrow for even a kid to squeeze through. The door on the left, though, was off its hinges, lying on the damp floor.

"How big is this place?" I asked.

"It can't be that big," Lily said. "No more than a few rooms. They must not be in here."

"We need to check," I insisted.

She was shaking her head, and she made a reluctant sound in the back of her throat. I knew what she was feeling because I felt it too. Like the rush of beetles away from a light. A skittering and chittering in the air that you couldn't hear but you could feel—

something here, something *wrong*, but nothing that you could put words to.

To her credit, she gritted her teeth and walked farther in. Our steps had an odd, crumpled quality to them, as if the walls were drinking in the sound. Beyond the downed door was a low-ceilinged room. Ancient tables and chairs moldered, some knocked over, others sagging in place. Another door stood open at the end of the room, leading to a storage closet. Near it, a metal staircase led downward.

"They must have gone down," I said. I stepped toward the stairs, but that insect-crawling feeling intensified until I could swear I should have seen them scurrying over my limbs.

"We shouldn't be here," Lily said.

"It's okay. Give me the flashlight. I'll go."

For a moment, she seemed tempted. Then she muttered, "You're just a kid." She took a deep breath and stalked past me. I followed.

Lily shone the flashlight down the stairwell. The steps were rusted. They didn't look very safe, but we were going to have to go down. Because there was another footprint at the top of the stairs, right where we were standing. The same waffle print as the one out front. Except this one wasn't made of mud. It was blood. Blood was smeared on the wall leading down, too, and glistened on the rusting metal steps.

"We should go get help," Lily said.

A bang reverberated through the bunker as the door to the outside slammed shut.

PART THREE

CERTAIN FATHOMS IN THE EARTH

VIDEO EVIDENCE

Recorded by Abigail Ryder

JUNE 30, 2018, 8:16 AM

The camera switches on, focusing on the hillside and the empty, cloudless sky. It pans around slowly until it reaches Liam Kapoor.

LIAM: So. Care to take a romantic jaunt into the bowels of the earth?

ABBY: Let's agree, right now, that we are not going to try to keep up that ridiculous lie when we don't absolutely have to.

LIAM: If it makes you feel any better, I regret it deeply.

Abby snorts.

ABBY: If all my relationships are lies, at least I'm in on this one.

LIAM: You're talking about your boss. Dr. Ashford.

ABBY: He always told us that he was hunting the creature

that killed our parents, but he didn't know why it came after us. He claimed he had no idea who we were. But that video was from fourteen years ago, so not only was my grandfather—and my father—somehow aware of the supernatural, Ashford knew it. Long before he ever showed up at our house.

LIAM: You'd think between the three of us we could scrape up a functioning parental figure.

ABBY: What about "Shakespeare mum"?

LIAM: Okay, fair point, that's one. Still a pathetic average.

Liam huffs a bit as they reach the site of the bunker. The door is shut and covered in a mottled layer of rust.

LIAM: And here we are. The forbidden bunker.

ABBY: Does it open?

LIAM: You know, I don't know. I've honestly never been tempted to explore it.

There's a beat as they stare at each other.

LIAM: Oh, I'm sorry. You want me to go first. I suppose it's the gentlemanly thing to get eaten first.

ABBY: It's less about you getting eaten before me, and more that when you get eaten I need to capture it on camera.

LIAM: That's much better. Very reassuring.

He walks up to the door and hauls on it. The metal squeaks, but there's no appreciable movement.

ABBY: Hold on, I'll help

She sets the camera down on a rock—it is already mounted on a small tripod—and makes sure it's trained on the door. Together, they strain to pull on the handle, but other than a slightly louder squeal, this produces no result.

LIAM: Ah. Damn. Look, it's been welded shut. We'll never get that open.

Abby runs a finger along the welded seam. It's hardly precision work, but it is thorough.

ABBY: That's a lot of effort to protect some empty rooms. Considering the only people who come here are, theoretically, trained professionals.

LIAM: Yes, but they're also field scientists.

ABBY: Which means what?

LIAM: Field scientists are particularly noted for their tendency to do questionable things in pursuit of discovery. The things they will lick in the name of science would astound you.

ABBY: Wait. Hush.

She holds up a finger, tilting her head toward the door in concentration. Liam looks confused but complies. His eyes widen. He presses his ear to the door.

LIAM: It's coming from in there.

Abby glances around, chewing on her lip.

ABBY: Maybe there's another way in.

Liam shakes his head.

LIAM: Just the one entrance.

ABBY: That you know of. We should check anyway. Geography is negotiable under these circumstances.

LIAM: You sound like you're quoting someone.

ABBY: Ashford.

LIAM: Ah.

She clears her throat and looks away.

ABBY: That damn music. I—

LIAM: Something just moved down there.

He points. Abby squints in the direction he indicates, down the slope.

ABBY: I don't see anything. Wait. What is that?

LIAM: It's a bird. I think it's hurt. Look at the way it's moving.

He moves toward it.

ABBY: Hold on. Where do you think you're going?

LIAM: They're endangered. The LARC does rehab too. If it's hurt, I'll have to call the others to come collect it.

He strides off.

Grumbling, she follows him. Their footsteps fade as they move off-screen.[4]

ABBY: So? Is it [hurt]?

LIAM: [Indistinct]

ABBY: What are you doing? [Indistinct]

The microphone picks up a new sound, a strange, discordant humming.

The door swings open.

Beyond is darkness; the camera, adjusted for the bright daylight, shows only flat black. And yet something moves within. The image is too grainy to make out any detail. In one frame it seems as if it might be a person; in another, it seems to expand, as if many wings are unfurling around it.

---

4 Note: Audio has been enhanced in order to transcribe this section. A greater degree of error may be present than usual; where dialog is indistinct, a best guess has been supplied.

The shape recedes; the strange humming swells.

LIAM: We need [to go/to know].

ABBY: What's that on your hands? Where's the bird? Liam—

LIAM: It's [near/here].

ABBY: Liam, look at me. Damn it.

Several seconds pass. Then Liam walks back into frame. He walks steadily, eyes fixed ahead, hands by his sides. Something black and viscous drips from his fingers, the substance coating his right hand all the way to the wrist.

Abby follows at a wary distance. When she sees the open door, she lets out a hiss between her teeth. Liam never breaks his stride as he heads in.

ABBY: All right, then. We're doing this.

She picks up the camera and follows.

19

WE RAN FOR the door together, the flashlight beam bouncing over toppled tables and chairs and casting crazed shadows on the walls. I skidded around the corner first. The door was shut tight. I walked up to it and shoved with a shaking hand. It didn't budge.

"Let me try," Lily said. I knew it wouldn't work, but I stepped aside. As she pushed and strained, I wandered back toward the other room. There were drips of something on the floor I hadn't noticed before. Not blood, I thought, kneeling.

The flashlight beam fell across me as Lily abandoned her efforts, and I touched a finger to the black blot. It had the texture of motor oil, slippery and thick. I rubbed it between my thumb and the pad of my finger. A thin tongue of smoky black rose up, and it vanished, boiling off into the air. I smelled something sharp and astringent, like cleaning fluid. The same liquid that had oozed from the bird skull.

"It won't open," Lily said unnecessarily.

"Only one way to go, then," I said. Of course we would go down. It was as inescapable as gravity. "Give me the flashlight. I'll go first." This time there was no protest. She handed the flashlight over. I hoped it had fresh batteries.

I walked with steady purpose to the top of the stairs. More black drips on the ground; I'd gone right past them before. The bloodstains were still there. If they were bleeding, I thought grimly, at least they were alive.

The first step creaked alarmingly under my foot as I descended, but the stairway held. I eased myself down. There were ten steps before a landing, more metal bolted into the concrete shaft. I stopped there and shone the light down the next expanse of stairs, leaning out over the rail a bit to see how far down I could see. Two more flights before the next level. The bottom was concrete, but I couldn't make it out well from this distance.

"Why would they come down here?" Lily asked, barely above a whisper. Her voice seemed to breed in the shadows, hushed echoes swarming down the stairwell ahead of us.

"They were invited," I said. She stared at me. I stared back. I had no idea why I'd said that. "Ask me another question," I suggested, curious.

"What's down there?" she asked.

"A crack in the world," I answered automatically.

"You're fucking with me," she said. I shook my head, unable to speak through the fear closing up my throat. Why had I said that? It was like someone else was answering with my voice. "Where are Abby and Liam?"

"The memory room," I replied.

"This is a weird prank to pull," Lily said. "For the record, you have succeeded in freaking me out, and it's cool if you stop anytime."

I let that hang. It wouldn't do any good to argue with her. If thinking it was a prank let her hold herself together, it was for the best. I had no such illusions to fall back on.

I reached the bottom of the steps. Another metal door blocked the way forward, another bloody footprint staining the ground in front of it, but at least it wasn't more stairs.

"What do you think is on the other side of that door?" Lily asked. I stepped forward to answer her by hauling open the door.

The room beyond was circular, and large enough that the flashlight only reached the middle. But that was enough to illuminate Liam, sitting cross-legged with his back to us, shoulders hunched and head low.

The floor sloped toward a drain in the center of the room, and Liam sat beside it. I approached, flashlight shaking. Lily stayed right at my elbow, her breath loud in my ear. Liam was holding something cradled in his lap. I edged around him.

It was a bird. A tern, or part of one—one white wing, a quivering side, a neck bent violently to the left and single eye pinning and flaring. But the rest of it was gone, body giving way to viscous black that dripped between Liam's fingers, over his forearms, as the bird shuddered and strained and shook.

"Shh," Liam crooned to the bird. "Shh, it's all right."

Its wing extended, fluttering, the movements like the spasms of dying muscles. Lily swore under her breath. I choked back a sour taste in my throat. The drips of black liquid slid down the sloped floor and into the drain. The bird tried to lift its head, but it no longer had the right muscles in its neck, and it flopped down again. A gurgling sound came from its throat. It sounded of drowning.

"Put that down," I said.

"It's hurt," Liam said.

"There's something really wrong with it, Liam. You need to put it down," I said. "Liam, where's Abby?"

"She left on wings of shadow. Two and two and two," he said, singsong. "Hush, hush." His thumb stroked the side of the bird's neck.

I put my hand on his forearm, above the dripping black. "Liam. *Liam*. Let go of the—"

"No!" he shouted. His hands closed around the bird, clenching, fingers digging into the feathered chest. There was a sound like paper crumpling. Black liquid burst from the bird's skin where Liam's fingers dug in, and the bird thrashed and came apart in his hands, stringy tendons stretching like taffy, feathers turning black and bubbling into smoke, and then the bird was gone and all that was left was the black liquid sliding down his skin, running down the drain.

Lily screamed. Maybe I did, too, but that was nothing next to the desolate sound that ripped free of Liam's throat. He dropped down and clawed at the drain as if he could stop the flow of the liquid, as if he could bring the bird back, and then he sobbed, hands limp on his knees. I pulled him against me, holding tight as his shoulders shook with his ragged gasps of breath. He was cold to the touch. I think I said something, but I don't remember what it was, soothing nothings that he probably couldn't understand anyway. But after a few minutes or a few seconds—you lose track of time during moments like this—he pulled away from me. His hand went to his temple. He drew in a breath and let it out in a rush.

"Hey," I said softly. "You back with us?"

He swallowed. "I'm sorry," he whispered. "I'm here."

"What happened?" I asked. "Where's Abby?"

His eyebrows drew together, a look of intense concentration on his face as he tried to string together fragmented memories into narrative. "I can't— There were wings. So many wings. And there was the voice. Singing. It said . . . It said one of us could stay. It said choose. I wanted to go, but she stopped me." He looked away, an expression of shame passing over his face.

"Who took her?" I asked. "Was it the big man, Mikhail's double?"

But he only pointed behind me. Behind Lily. We looked at each other and turned slowly.

The wall behind us was covered in strange designs. Someone had taken paint to the concrete walls and turned them into a chaotic mass of handprints, spirals, random phrases, people rendered like cave painting stick figures. White Vs with flecks of red, terns, wheeled about. All of the paintings were layered, one thing painted over another until you could hardly see an inch of concrete or pick out one figure from another.

But in the center, stretching from floor to ceiling and snaking out to the sides, was a massive human figure—mostly human. Arms outstretched as if in benediction, face black and blank except for two empty holes where their eyes ought to be. Huge wings, six of them, emerged from the figure's shoulders—they were the wings of a tern, angular and elegant. The wings were not solid, not like the central figure. They were made of overlapping letters, words written in overlapping lines until most were incomprehensible. Here and there I picked out meaning.

six-wing—song—it brings the mist—little bird—warden—she dreams—she drowns—

The words dripped from the wings, turning into rambling, mad sentences, braided together in overlapping strands like a woven rope, hardly any more comprehensible.

Seven kings seven kingdoms seven gates seven worlds—
—drowned beneath the sea but the road still—
—went to meet the bramble man and—
—lacuna house, and time twists—
—six wings, the dreamer—
—the girl and the ghost—

I followed the rambling thread of them, gliding through snatches of what might have been poetry or prophecy or prayers— and then, there, in the intersection of two threads, was a house. There was nothing terribly remarkable about it. A single story, a bay window in the front, a tree beside it. Nothing remarkable except that I knew it. It was the house I'd lived in after my mother died, my first foster home. The one that lasted the longest before they realized something was wrong with the lost little girl they'd wanted to love.

It couldn't be. No one on this island could know what it looked like. But it was.

"We need to get out of here," Lily said.

My mouth was so dry my tongue stuck to the roof of my mouth. "We need to find Abby," I said, though it felt as if my voice was coming from very far away.

I followed the course of the ropes of words with my flashlight. Opposite the image of the Six-Wing, on the far right from where we'd entered, the words formed an arch above a doorway, a black gap in the wall, leading on. Leading deeper. Another bloody footprint stained the ground just in front of it. Liam wasn't hurt. That meant that Abby must be. "There," I said.

"You heard Liam. She said not to," Lily replied. Her voice was frail. She was holding up pretty well, but things were still skating along the edge of the possible. It would get worse if we went deeper. I knew it. Lily knew it.

"There's only one way she could have gone," I said. I tore my eyes away from the painting. My mother, the house, my double. This place was focused on me in a way I didn't understand. I couldn't escape its gravity, but maybe Lily could. "Wait here with Liam. I'll go."

I bent, fetching Liam's flashlight from where it lay on the ground. I handed it over.

"I shouldn't let you go," Lily said. Guilt in her voice.

"You wouldn't be able to stop me." I turned toward the black

hole. Lily made a noise in a final protest, but I knew she was relieved to be staying behind.

I approached the darkened doorway. The edges were rough.
They hadn't been part of the bunker, I thought, but chiseled out
of the wall after it was built. The space beyond was more tunnel
than hallway, the walls rough and rocky. Natural caves beneath
the island, maybe? But it seemed too straight for that, and while the
rock wasn't smooth like a manmade tunnel would be, it had odd
marks, almost ripples, that seemed too regular to be random.

Something had carved this, I thought, but not a human something.

I walked forward cautiously. The tunnel narrowed, almost
scraping my shoulders, and the ceiling was only a few inches over
my head. My breath filled the space until it seemed it was the tunnel itself that was breathing. The walls cinched in, and now my
shoulders did bump against the damp rock, and I realized what
the ripples reminded me of—the ridges of a trachea.

Soon I was moving sideways, and every breath was cool and
wet and tasted of silt. The flashlight beam struck stone ahead and
stopped. No more dark corridor, only a final narrowing of gray
rock with a crack the width of my hand running through it.

"Come on, Abby. Where are you?" I whispered. No answer.
I growled in frustration and slammed my hand against the wall
beside me, only succeeding in scraping the side of my fist. I forced
my way forward to the crack.

"Abby!" I called. She had come this way so there had to be a
way through. And maybe there was, in that other place. "Abby,
can you hear me?"

There was a breeze through the crack, faint as a sigh. I could sense the void on the other side, the emptiness of another tunnel, maybe even a cavern. Nothing and nothing and nothing answered, and then at once there was an eye, pressed to the other side, glistening in the thin sliver of light from the flashlight. I let out a startled scream and jerked back, forgetting the cramped quarters. My back smacked against the wall.

"Sophia?" It was Abby. I steadied myself and leaned close to the crack again.

"Are you all right?" I asked. "Liam wasn't making a lot of sense. He said something took you."

"It's coming back," she whispered. "I got away, but I don't know how long I can hide," she said. She made a gulping sound of fear and animal distress. "I hear it. Please—"

She reached for me through the crack, and I reached for her, as if I could pull her through, as if I could save her. But it was so narrow I could barely fit my hand through. She looked over her shoulder and her eyes widened. "No, no, no," she said, in prayer and panic. I thrust my hand farther in, wriggling to try to eke out one more centimeter, and she did the same, frantic.

Our fingertips touched for one instant. I shoved forward, and my hand closed over hers. If only I could hold on to her. If only—

Something pressed into my palm. The sharp wooden wings of a bird, and with it something smooth and plastic. She closed my fingers over it. "So he knows," she said. "Don't let me be another mystery to haunt him, Sophia. Don't let him follow."

She meant Dr. Ashford, I realized. The man who'd protected

her for years. Raised her. And if I didn't get this out of here, he would never know what had happened to her.

"Next time you see me, don't trust me," she whispered.

"Abby—"

"Sophia. Run."

The tunnel echoed with the sound of wings. Abby snatched her hand away.

"Abby!" I called, jamming my flashlight against the crack, but I couldn't make out anything but emptiness beyond. Emptiness, but not silence. In the deep, in the dark, someone was singing.

20

I RAN BACK through the tunnel and squeezed my way free into the circular room, half fearing that the others would be gone, but Lily was kneeling at Liam's side and looked up as I stumbled in. "Did you find her?" she asked.

My breath came too fast. My fear was turning to panic, the useful edge of adrenaline giving way to a frantic confusion that would only get me killed. But the void was waiting. I focused inward, feeling my breath expand my lungs, letting it out—and letting the fear go with it, into the darkness of the void. It drank up my fear, leaving me steady again.

"We have to go. Now," I said, smooth as glass. I looked down at my hand, closed in a fist around the thing Abby had given me along with the bird. I eased my fingers open to find an SD card. Not the one we'd found earlier—this was different. From Abby's camera? "Liam, can you walk?"

But he was staring at the wall, eyes unfocused. His lips moved, and he was mumbling something, but it was impossible to make out.

The music was getting louder. It was like a hundred voices, all overlapping over each other, but it was somehow only one voice at the same time. A language I knew and didn't know. I kept catching the edge of understanding and then losing my grip on it.

"We have to go," I said again, shaking Liam's shoulder.

"I've got him," Lily assured me. She got her arm under Liam's and hauled him to his feet, surprisingly strong for her size. We shambled to the stairs, cajoling Liam into moving at every step. And at every step, I waited for the sound of wings. We reached the first landing, and I turned, shining my flashlight back toward the black mouth of the tunnel.

It had gotten wider, and there were people in it. The beam didn't reach far enough to illuminate their faces, but their silhouettes were crowded together, watching.

I didn't look back again. Not until the top of the stairs, and then only fleetingly, and all I saw was the wild leap of shadows as the flashlight beam raked across the stairwell. Then we were back in the main room of the bunker, and Lily paused to catch her breath. Liam pulled away from her, stumbling and catching himself on one of the tables.

"You all right?" I asked. He shook his head, which was its own kind of progress. "We need to keep moving. Fast."

"The door is stuck closed," Lily reminded me. I ducked out from under Liam's arm anyway and jogged toward the entrance. Had the walls been striped with that much mold before, glistening and black, shot through with silvery lichen?

The door hung open, and beyond was only gray. The mist. Lightning flashed sporadically in the sky, but no thunder to follow it. The flashes illuminated shapes in the air, strange and twisting things far above.

"We're on the wrong island," I said dully.

"Sophia!" Lily yelled. I twisted to look behind me, back toward the stairwell. Mold crawled from the stairwell, creeping its way along the walls, and among it bloomed strange mushrooms that looked like teeth. A sound rose up from the stairwell, a dusty, thrashing sound, and the soft percussion of feathers striking stone.

Liam stood rooted in place. Lily grabbed one of his arms, I grabbed the other, and we pulled him with us. Lily was muttering, eyes wide, keeping herself from total panic with visible effort.

Before, the mist's landscape matched the real one. I'd tumbled in through a reflection and escaped—how? I didn't have time to stop and ponder.

"Follow me," I said. "Stay close." Anywhere was better than staying put.

Liam moved to follow without prompting, blinking as if coming awake, but Lily kept close to him just the same. I set out for the beach where we'd left the boat. The ground shifted, the grass thinning as we came toward the rockier shore. I followed the slope and the sound of the water, and tried not to think about what might be chasing us. I reached the edge of the shore and there, as if waiting for us, was a boat. A skiff. Larger than the *Katydid*, though not by much. I couldn't read the name on the side; black mold covered it, swallowing half the hull, the seats, and wrapping across the lettering so only a hint of an *R* was visible.

"That's not our boat," Liam said, voice full of confusion. It was the first time he'd spoken since we left the bunker.

Lily looked at him, then back at me. "So should we take it? Sophia?"

I heard her, but the words didn't register as my pulse thudded in my ears. I tasted salt on the back of my tongue.

"Sophia? What's wrong?"

I wasn't sure. I only knew that the sight of that boat shattered the calm I'd constructed. My throat constricted around my breath. "We can't," I said. "We can't I can't don't—don't—" I stuttered over the word, not knowing what I meant to say, what I *was* saying. There was a roaring in my ears like the rush of water.

A hand in mine, the hillside falling away before us, the shore waiting

The wood beneath me, splintering, worn gray

Water sloshing in the bottom of the boat

Screaming, shouting voices

Hands on me, tangling in my hair, shoving me pulling me forcing me deep

Water in my mouth, water in my eyes, the harsh salt sting of it

"Sophia." Lily was holding my arms, looking into my face. "Listen to me. Listen to my voice. You're having a panic attack."

I wasn't having a panic attack. I didn't panic. When I was afraid, I sent my fear away, and this was something else—this was dying. I couldn't breathe, I couldn't think, I felt like I was collapsing inward, like my heart would beat so hard it would burst.

"Focus on breathing slowly. You're okay." Lily gripped my

hands, and I focused on those two points of pressure. Her hands were warm and callused and strong.

Breathing. I could do that. I could breathe. Breathe air, not water. Focus on the ground beneath me, not the heaving of a boat or the endless dark of the ocean.

"You're here. Now. With us," Lily said. "And I need you to tell us what to do, so I need you to *be* here. Understand?"

I did. I nodded. The fist around my throat hadn't released, but it eased, and whatever flood of memories had dragged me under was a formless trickle now.

"Good. Good?"

"I'm good," I confirmed, only somewhat untruthfully, and Lily gave a wry sort of chuckle. She let go of my hands with one final squeeze and stepped back a bit.

"I was worried I was going to have to drag both of you around, and I'm not feeling exactly with it myself," she said, and then paused. "I don't think anything followed us from the bunker. We don't have to rush down to the shore. We can take our time and be—"

A mass of darkness hurtled from the mist and slammed into her.

At first my mind could only process it in pieces. The dark sweep of wings. The emptiness at the core of it. The fingers, too long and with too many joints, wrapped around Lily's neck as it held her up. She thrashed, legs kicking, clawing at the hand that gripped her throat. It lifted her close to its face, and her eyes grew dark with its reflection.

And then—a crack. Her head twisted to the side. It cast her

away like a bit of trash, whatever it was searching for not found.

I reached out, as if I could still do something. As if there were anything left of Lily to save but bones and blood. Liam made a sound, the start of a scream, and the creature turned toward us, eyeless, featureless, yet somehow staring directly at us. And there was that sound. The hum, the vibration in my bones. And there was the song—wordless and yet full of words, many voices and one voice all at once, and I could also hear how the thrum in my bones matched the song. And how the song matched the crying of the birds who flocked this island. Who vanished without a trace.

Ravens, I thought, are excellent mimics. And Moriarty had slipped into the echo world and back to save me. Had he mimicked the terns? Is that how he'd slipped from one world to the next? Echoes were sound, after all, and this place was a kind of echo.

Hardcastle and Kapoor were studying the birds' cries. That's what all of that fancy audio equipment was for. Crafting sounds to match the songs of the birds. The song of the Six-Wing. Maybe they were searching for a certain sound, a certain song, that could carry them between the worlds.

And I'd heard something, *felt* something, when I slipped from the echo back into the real world. That song was in me. If I was right, if I could use it—

The Six-Wing started toward us. I grabbed Liam's hand, held it tight, and focused on that vibration. It wasn't something I *felt*, it was something in me, something emanating from my body. It was *mine* and I seized it, changed it, acting on instinct. *Get me away from here. Get me out*, I thought, and the hum grew higher-pitched, sliding out of synch with that hideous song, and then—

The mist rushed away like a sigh, and the Six-Wing with it.

I sank to my knees with a cry of relief. Liam reeled back, staggering in a quick circle. No dark angel, no mist. Just the island, and the bright white, perfect wings of birds gliding and wheeling above us, calling contentedly to one another.

"Are we out?" Liam said. "Did we get out of that place?"

"Yes," I said. "Look around."

"But how can you be sure?" he demanded. I opened my mouth to answer and realized I didn't *have* an answer. Except that I could feel it—hear it—in my bones.

"We're safe," I told him, which wasn't exactly true. "We got out. And there's the boat."

I pointed down the slope. The other skiff was gone, the LARC boat in its place. And Kenny stood on the beach beside it, equipment heaped next to him, speaking into a radio. I'd lost its match somewhere along the way. But he spotted us and waved frantically.

Liam was staring at a patch of hillside. The place where Lily had fallen. He walked toward it.

"She's not there," I said softly, but if he heard me, he didn't respond. I followed, trailing behind him. He crouched down and pressed his hand against the smooth hillside.

Liam looked up at me. "How are you not . . . ?" he asked. He gestured around him, but I knew what he meant.

How was I not a complete mess? How was I not paralyzed with fear and confusion and the utter wreck that reality had become?

"There's nothing we can do now."

"Don't you at least feel bad?" Liam demanded, rising suddenly. I took a step back, startled. "Doesn't it bother you? She died right in front of you and you're acting like you don't even care."

"Of course I care," I said. And I did. But it was knowledge, not emotion. I *knew* that Lily shouldn't be dead, that it was tragic, that I wished I could have done anything to help her. I just didn't hurt yet.

That would come later.

"You're not acting like you care. Fuck! I can barely breathe. I want to scream. I want to tear my bloody skin off because this feeling hurts so fucking much and you're standing there cool as a fucking cucumber!"

I stared at him. His face was reddened with anger. Maybe most of it wasn't really meant for me, but some of it was, and maybe I deserved it.

"Hey!" Kenny was calling to us from down below. I turned away from Liam and headed toward the boat, my cheeks hot. He thought I was a monster, then. He wouldn't be the first.

I was halfway down before I heard Liam following. If he wanted to avoid me, he'd have a hard time. Wasn't like the boat was that big. Unless he wanted to stay here by himself.

"Yeah, I've got Liam and Sophia here," Kenny said into the radio.

"Are they all right?" Dr. Kapoor's voice was crisp, efficient, without undue emotion. Maybe she and I actually had something in common. The thought struck me as funny—odd things often did when I was emptied out like this. I had the sense not to laugh.

"They look okay," Kenny said uncertainly. "Hey, where's Lily and Abby?"

"They're not coming," I said. Kenny's finger was still on the button; Dr. Kapoor had heard me.

There was a long moment of silence. Then, "Mr. Lee, bring my son and Ms. Hayes back immediately."

Liam didn't seem to hear. He stared at me with a look I knew well. Like there was something wrong with me. Like my calm, my ability to push away any inconvenient emotion, was freakish.

Like I wasn't a person at all.

VIDEO EVIDENCE

Recorded by Joy Novak

AUGUST 14, 2003

Novak and Baker draw closer to the others. Martin sees them first and lets out a sound of relief.

CARREAU: There you are! We thought we lost you.

BAKER: Didn't you hear me calling for help?

Hardcastle looks disturbed.

HARDCASTLE: We didn't hear anything. What happened?

BAKER: I—

She glances at Novak.

BAKER: I fell and panicked, that's all.

SOPHIA: Mama!

She squirms out of Carreau's grasp and runs to her mother, who holds her tight. Hardcastle clears his throat and gestures toward the bunker door, which is open.

HARDCASTLE: Nothing in there I can see. It should be safe.

KAPOOR: Should be?

HARDCASTLE: Might be. Better than staying out here.

He waits, shrugs, and heads inside when no one else takes the lead. The others trail after with varying levels of reluctance. Novak remains outside a moment longer.

SOPHIA: Mama? Is it safe?

NOVAK: I don't know, sweetie. But I promise I will keep you safe. I will not let anything happen to you. No matter what.

She starts to lead Sophia inside, and then she stops.

CARREAU: Joy?

NOVAK: I thought I heard something.

SOPHIA: Mama, something's out there.

Her voice is soft and trembling.

NOVAK: Get inside with Martin, Sophie.

SOPHIA: Mama, I'm scared.

Novak steps out into the mist cautiously. Now the microphone picks up what she hears: a faint whimpering. She takes another step, and another.

A small figure stumbles out of the mist. Her knees are muddy, her hands scraped from a fall. Tear tracks line her cheeks. Novak lets out a low moan as her daughter lurches toward her.

SOPHIA [?]: Mama, I'm scared. I got lost and I couldn't find you. Mama?

Novak turns slowly. Looks at the Sophia in the doorway to the bunker, clinging to Carreau's leg. Then back to the girl, wide-eyed and trembling, who reaches for her.

SOPHIA [?]: Mama?

21

KENNY ONLY ASKED what had happened once, and when he didn't get an answer he didn't press. Maybe the looks on our faces were grim enough he didn't want the answers. By the time we got back to the dock, Dr. Kapoor and Dr. Hardcastle were waiting for us. When they asked what had happened, silence wasn't an option.

Liam cleared his throat, but I stepped forward. I gave them a sanitized version: we went to find Liam and Abby, Lily went in, when she didn't come out, I'd gone in and found only Liam, insensible.

I'd composed the lie on the way over. People disappeared on this island. Trying to come up with a logical explanation for what had happened, saying that I'd seen them die or something—that would just lead to more questions I couldn't answer. But the inexplicable? The people here were used to not digging too deeply.

"You're hurt?" Dr. Kapoor asked Liam with brusque concern.

"No, I just—I had a panic attack or something. I don't remember anything between going into the bunker and leaving with Sophia."

"Going into the bunker that's supposed to be welded shut because it's dangerous and unstable, you mean," Dr. Kapoor said. "A room might have collapsed. The two of them might have fallen. We'll need to go and look for them. I'll handle that. Kenny, drive Liam home and then take yourself and Ms. Hayes back to Mrs. Popova's."

"I can help look for them," Kenny objected.

"We will handle this," Dr. Hardcastle said, not a drop of his usual friendliness in his tone. He was looking over at the island, and I couldn't read his expression. Dr. Kapoor, though—that look was fury, pure and incandescent. Did she know what had happened? Was she part of it?

I allowed myself to be bustled along. Kenny was full of concern and trying desperately not to demand details from me.

Dr. Kapoor must have called ahead, because Mrs. Popova was waiting for us on the porch.

"You'll be all right, yeah?" Kenny asked, parking the car without turning off the engine. I nodded. "I need to get back. In case they need my help to search," he said.

"You're a good friend, Kenny," I told him. "You're a good person." I didn't lie and tell him that everything would be all right.

"Thanks," he said, distracted, I don't think he'd actually heard me. I curled my hands slowly into fists. I'd never had to use the void so frequently before. The backlash was already threatening, like a migraine aura at the edge of my vision.

One step at a time, I told myself, and made my way stiffly toward Mrs. Popova. She took a look at my face and clucked her tongue softly.

"You look exhausted," she said.

"I'm fine," I told her, but my voice broke. I gulped down a breath and looked away. I just needed to get inside. I just needed—

"Oh, you poor lamb," she said, and the next thing I knew I was sobbing.

"I'm sorry," I choked out.

"Don't be absurd. You cry all you must," she told me. "There are things worth crying over. You'll be made of steel again in the morning, but for now you weep. Come inside, and I'll make some cocoa for you." She rubbed my arms briskly.

I wished I could have pulled it together then, in the face of her generosity, but it only made me cry harder. She installed me at the kitchen table and didn't ask a single question. By the time the cocoa was gone, so were my tears, leaving behind a headache and a pile of tissues she wordlessly swept into the trash bin.

"Get some rest," she suggested. I liked her way of taking care of people—nothing particularly maternal in it, just a gentle efficiency that recognized comfort alongside hunger and cold, a practical matter to be tended to. "And make sure you stay in. Mist tonight." She rose. All the warmth went out of me.

Mrs. Popova lived on the island. She'd lived on the island for ages. Which meant she knew. Knew that it wasn't safe to go out in the mist, and not just because you couldn't see where you were going. No wonder she hadn't asked me any questions. She either didn't want the answers, or she had them already.

I mumbled something that might have been "thank you" and stumbled back to my room. After dumping my bag on the bed, I went over to the small desk where I'd left my laptop. I turned it on and fumbled in my jacket pocket for the SD card Abby had handed me.

I wiped a bit of grit off the memory card and slid it into the slot. Video files popped up—Abby's files, dozens of them since she'd arrived on the island. The last one was from the exact time she went into the bunker.

I started to press play, then stopped. There was someone else who needed to see this. Or maybe it was that I knew he'd want to see it, and that I could use it to make him see *me*.

I checked the time. Still an hour before the mist was expected to roll in. A light rain had started up, a thin layer of gray clouds rolling over the sky. I packed up my laptop and hurried out of the house, shutting the door lightly behind me so that I wouldn't disturb Mrs. Popova.

Dr. Kapoor's house was on the inward curve of the island, facing Belaya Skala. It took me only a few minutes to get there, crunching over the gravel road and weaving around potholes. I walked up to front door and knocked.

I had to wait a long time before Liam appeared, his hair and clothes rumpled. He'd showered and changed, at least, but his eyes looked hollow. As soon as he saw who was at the door, he started to close it.

"Wait," I said. I stuck out my hand, catching the door. "We need to talk."

"We really don't," Liam said.

"I know you're angry with me. Just let me explain."

"Explain how you're a sociopath? Or possibly a robot?" he asked.

I glared at him. "We're in this together whether we like each other or not," I said. "And I have Abby's camera. If you want to know what happened to you two, you'd better let me in."

He stared at me for the space of three quick heartbeats, then simply turned and walked inside, leaving the door open. I followed him in, shutting the door behind me. And, after a moment's consideration, doing up all three heavy locks.

Liam's room was at the back of the house. There was just enough space for a small desk, a bookshelf, and a bed. In typical teenage fashion, he hadn't unpacked, and a large suitcase filled with unevenly folded clothes sat crammed in the corner. A few books—science fiction, mostly—were stacked on top of the bookshelf, but the only other hint of personalization was a line of collected objects on the windowsill—seashells, stones, and yet another little carving, this one of a deer. Mikhail's work.

Liam had sat on the bed, hands laced around one knee. "All right," he said. "Let's see it."

I took out the laptop. "You're sure you want to?" I asked.

"Don't you?"

"Yeah. I'd rather know. But it should be your choice."

"I want to see," he insisted.

I sat beside him and started the video.

VIDEO EVIDENCE

Recorded by Abigail Ryder

JUNE 30, 2018, 8:22 AM

Abby's breath is loud as she follows Liam into the bunker. The change in light is too much for the camera, and the scene goes dark for a moment until she switches the settings. Now the scene is lit in eerie shades of green. Liam has paused in the middle of the main room, head cocked to the side as if listening to the music that emanates from somewhere below.

ABBY: Liam appears to be under some kind of compulsion or other effect.

Ms. Ryder is clearly trying to remain professional, but it is impossible to forget in this moment, with her voice vulnerably raw, that she is still only seventeen.

ABBY: His hand is coated with a substance—I can't see what it is. I'm going to try to snap him out of it.

She approaches cautiously.

ABBY: Liam? Can you hear me?

She mutters something unintelligible, then reaches for his shoulder.

ABBY: Liam, you need to—

Her fingertips brush his shirt. He jerks, turning on her, and backhands her. We cannot see the impact, but Abby—and the camera—fall backward. Abby swears loudly.

ABBY: My arm—damn it, I'm bleeding. A lot. Shit.

She doesn't sound frightened yet, just angry. The camera, resting on the ground, is trained on her as she examines the outside of her upper arm, where a piece of metal has ripped open a nasty gouge. Blood flows freely from the wound. She covers it with her palm and looks up, presumably at Liam.

ABBY: Liam. Snap out of it.

LIAM: He's waiting. We have to go.

ABBY: Who's waiting?

LIAM: The lord with six wings. The prince of many voices. The one who is shattered.

ABBY: Oh, in that case, no problem.

Liam crouches in front of her. His eyes reflect oddly in the camera's night vision. He speaks patiently, as if explaining to a child.

LIAM: He witnessed the destruction of the kingdom, and he will witness its rebirth.

ABBY: No offense, Liam, but what the f—

LIAM: We have to go. The Six-Wing is waiting. He will test us. He will discover if we are the ones who are awaited.

ABBY: And if we aren't what he's looking for?

LIAM: Don't worry. We can still serve.

He stands. Closes his eyes, listening with an expression of pure bliss.

LIAM: He's close. We must go to meet him.

He sets off swiftly, moving out of frame, but the microphone picks up the metallic creak of the stairs as he descends. Abby collects herself, swearing under her breath.

ABBY: Run or follow? Should probably run.

She stares after him.

ABBY: Not letting him die.

She picks up the camera and takes off after Liam.[5]

Video flickers. Abby moves awkwardly, bracing herself sometimes against the wall and leaving streaks of blood. As she descends, the video begins to glitch, lines crawling across the screen. The singing is louder down here. As Abby comes around the bend of one of the landings, there appears to be a visual distortion in the shadows near the ceiling. However, closer inspection reveals that it is the movement of mold, growing unnaturally fast across the ceiling.

Picture and audio cut out; camera records only black for several seconds. Then disconnected audio:

ABBY: This doesn't make any sense. How deep does this go? This has to be at least sev—

The calling of birds drowns out her voice.

Video resumes. Hundreds of birds hurtle through the air, their bodies so dense it's impossible to tell whether they're indoors

....

5 Note: Remaining video and audio is heavily corrupted. Auditory and visual distortion is heavy, and the camera ceases to record any information in increasing intervals. The following segments are those that contain decipherable information.

or outdoors. Their cries are deafening, the crack of their wings like a storm.

More blackness. Then three seconds of video. Played frame by frame, it shows a shadowy, winged form. It judders, flickering, the image sometimes doubling as if two figures stand there—or three. And then they collapse together again, wings quivering.

Another gap. When video resumes, the ground is littered with birds that seem to be in various states of dissolution, bodies collapsing into the same thick liquid that coats Liam's hand. He stands in the middle of the round room.

ABBY: No. Take me. Let him go.

The camera jerks backward. Video blinks out, then resumes. The camera rests on the ground, pointed so that only a rough stone wall is in view.

[UNKNOWN]: No. I won't let you.

There is a hissing, rustling sound in response, almost like words.

Video cuts out a final time.

22

LIAM LOOKED QUEASY. We sat side by side on his bed, not quite touching, the last frame of the video paused on the screen. "It's like trying to remember a dream," he said. "I recognize it, but I don't remember it. All I remember is—it felt like I was in an empty room, and the room kept getting smaller. Like I was being bricked up in my own mind."

"That sounds terrifying."

"It wasn't fear I felt."

"What did you feel?" I asked, looking at him. He flicked his lip ring against his teeth and thought a moment before answering.

"Despair," Liam said at last. "It's not the first time I've felt that way. Like *me* was being compressed, cleaned up like so much clutter. But this time it was all at once, and it wasn't my own mind doing it to me." His hands were slack in his lap now, his gaze fixed on a knot in the wood paneling on the far wall. I touched his forearm gently. He jerked it away. "You wouldn't understand."

"You're not the first person that's called me a sociopath," I told him. The words were like fingers pressed against a bruise, a hurt I didn't often admit aloud. "When I start to get too frightened or sad or anything, I just—push it away. Don't feel it. It's useful. It means that I can just do what I need to do without freezing up or getting weepy. Would it help Lily if I'd fallen apart? Would it have helped us get out of there alive?"

"It would let me know you were human," Liam said. "You ought to feel *something*."

"I do," I snapped. I shut the laptop with more force than I should have and shoved it back into my bag. "I feel horrible. Is that what you want me to say? I just . . ."

"Bottle it up?" Liam offered.

I frowned, thinking it through. I'd never had to describe it to someone before. "Not really. More like—step outside of it."

"I think you might be describing dissociation," Liam said. "Not exactly healthy."

"It is when it keeps you from getting killed," I pointed out. I kept my grip on the strap of my bag, expecting him at any moment to tell me to leave. I was already angry at him for it, scraping together rage so that I wouldn't have to wallow in the disappointment of yet another rejection.

"Fair point," he said instead. The fight went out of me. I slumped back, and we sat in weary silence for a while. Then he said, "That was the most horrible thing I've ever seen."

"Me too. Obviously."

"How do you live with a thing like that in your head?" he

asked. He looked me in the eye at last, and his expression was one of utter sorrow. "We can't even tell anyone what really happened."

"We just have each other."

"I'm sorry I called you a sociopath," he said.

"Sometimes I worry that it's true," I admitted.

"I'm pretty sure that a real sociopath wouldn't be bothered by being a sociopath," Liam said. I chuckled wryly, and then was surprised when he slid his hand over mine. "At least you were useful. I just stood there like a lump."

"It happened too fast for anyone to stop it," I said.

"I know. I know, but . . ."

"It doesn't make it better," I whispered. I leaned against him, and he put an arm around me, his cheek against my brow. I don't know how long we stayed like that, taking comfort from each other's presence. I listened to the sound of his heartbeat, felt the rise and fall of his chest. I let the moments and the minutes slip away.

I wanted to stay like that forever, suspended between moments, far from the mist.

The mist. I jerked upright and twisted to look out the window over the bed. The air was already growing hazy.

"I thought I had more time," I said, standing. "It was supposed to be another hour."

"The weather doesn't follow a set schedule even in normal places," Liam pointed out, still sitting at the edge of the bed.

"Maybe if I hurry—"

"You don't need to." He put his hand on my hip. "You can stay. Until the mist is gone." He eased me toward him with the lightest of pressure until I stood directly in front of him, too close to simply be friendly.

His eyes weren't perfectly brown, I realized; they were ringed with amber, so bright it was almost gold. It matched the faint golden highlights in his wind-tousled curls, the kind of unruly that models spent hours to achieve. It was made to run your hands through. He was skinny, but I liked skinny. And I liked his sharp features, his smooth brown skin, the one dark freckle right next to the corner of his eye.

Before I could overthink it, I kissed him. His lips were warm, and he kissed me back without any hesitation. I slid closer, and his hand moved higher on my hip, the other brushing back my hair, which had started to come free of its braid. I matched his movements carefully as he deepened the kiss.

He pulled away slightly. A flash of doubt went through me, but he stroked his thumb along my jaw. "It's okay to feel this," he whispered. "Don't push it away."

He was right. I'd been stepping outside myself. Managing the moment from a remove, the way I always did. "I'll try," I promised, and let my emotions rush in.

We lay together for a long time, fully clothed and without having ventured too far past simple kissing. The narrow confines of the bed made for a kind of default intimacy that was pleasant, though, his arms around me, my head nestled against his chest. We talked, but not about Bitter Rock or the mist. He told me about his mother—Dr. Kapoor's ex.

He said that at first people always thought they were strikingly similar. They were both women, both academics, both dedicated to their research and their fields, and both always seemed to be smarter than anyone else in the room. But spend any real time with them and it became obvious that they were actually complete opposites. He called his British mother *ethereal* and *romantic*, and I could imagine how odd that would be against the sharp practicality of Dr. Kapoor.

"She always seems a million miles away," Liam said. "And Dr. Kapoor is more, like, *intensely* present. Like she redirects gravity with the sheer force of her personality."

"And you really think she might be one of those echoes," I said. "But in the video with Ashford, it didn't seem like she was in on any of it."

"So she was lying. Or she didn't know."

"An echo is a weaker version of the original. Fading," I said. "Dr. Kapoor doesn't seem like a pale imitation of anyone."

"I suppose."

"You almost sound disappointed."

"I'm trying to decide which is worse—my mum being replaced by an evil twin, or my real mum covering up what's going on here." He nodded toward the window. "The mist is gone."

I sat up, disentangling myself from him, and saw that he was right, though the sky was slate-gray, thick clouds dimming the light. "I should probably go."

"Knowing Dr. Kapoor, she's not going to let a few disappearances get in the way of a full day's work," Liam said.

"I'd almost forgotten I'm doing an internship," I said.

"Well, you haven't actually managed a full day's work without being set upon by the supernatural," Liam pointed out. He tucked a strand of hair behind my ear. "Your hair's all mussed," he said.

I felt along my braid. It had come loose, snarling out from the careful plaiting. I made a face and combed it out, letting the hair spill in waves over my shoulders.

"You look quite wild," Liam said. "Like a mermaid or something."

"The kind that's friends with lobsters?"

"The kind that lures ships onto the rocks, maybe," Liam said.

"I'll take that as a compliment."

"Oh, you should," he assured me. He kissed me lightly, and somehow this time it was a bit awkward. Like we needed to practice saying goodbye. "Be safe."

"I can promise careful. I can't promise safe."

"Let's be honest. We're talking about you. You can't promise careful either," he said. "I should walk you back."

"And then you walk home on your own, and I worry about you," I said. "Vicious cycle."

"You aren't the worrying sort like I am," Liam said. It was true, and he smiled a little to show that he didn't think that was a bad thing, exactly. I cared what happened to him, but I didn't fret the same way.

"Fine," I agreed. "My white knight."

"Just give me a sec to find socks," he said, looking dubiously at his luggage. I snorted and stepped out into the hall. I padded toward the front door and had just reached the middle of the hallway when Dr. Kapoor appeared, stepping out from the kitchen. She saw me and froze.

"You shouldn't be here," she snapped. I blinked, unsure what I'd done to earn quite so pointed a response. "I told you not to let anyone see you right now. You—" She stopped. Looked at me again, more focused this time. My stomach dropped.

Liam emerged. "Found 'em," he declared, waving his socks aloft. "Oh, sorry, didn't realize you were home. I— What's wrong?"

"You thought I was her," I said wonderingly. With my hair a mess, with dark hollows around my eyes from lack of sleep and crying—I might have mistaken myself as well.

Liam's gaze switched swiftly between the two of us. It would have been comical if the moment hadn't been so tense.

"You know about—?" Dr. Kapoor whispered, but she didn't finish. Didn't want to be the first to say it outright, I guess, in case she was wrong.

"The girl that looks like me," I said.

"Then it is true," Liam said. He sounded sick. "You're . . . you're one of them."

Dr. Kapoor looked baffled. "Don't be absurd. Of course I'm not—no." Outside, a car door slammed. She glanced behind her, then fixed me with that intense glare. "You should leave here. It was a mistake letting you come. I thought . . . But it was a mistake."

I stepped toward her. "I need to know what happened. What's happening here."

"No, you do not, Ms. Novak," Dr. Kapoor said. She knew who

I was. She'd known all along. "Trust me. Those answers aren't worth the price that comes with them."

"What price? What is this place? What are those *things*? The girl who looks like me, is she—"

Dr. Kapoor made a harsh, almost amused sound in the back of her throat. Her voice was pitiless. "The girl who looks like you. Or is it the other way around?"

VIDEO EVIDENCE

Recorded by Joy Novak

AUGUST 14, 2003, TIME UNKNOWN

The second Sophia stands trembling in the mist, her arms wrapped around herself. Novak makes a sound, not quite a word, a soft "ah" repeated.

HARDCASTLE: Joy, get away from that thing.

SOPHIA: Mama? Who is she?

SOPHIA [2]: Mama, who's that girl? Why does she look like me? Mama, I'm cold.

NOVAK: Right. Okay. Okay.

She steps forward and lifts the mud-stained Sophia into her arms. She begins walking back toward the bunker, limping heavily.

BAKER: Don't let that thing in here!

NOVAK: She's just a child.

HARDCASTLE: That thing that attacked us looked just like Carolyn.

CARREAU: She weighs twelve kilos. I think we can defend ourselves.

HARDCASTLE: No. Joy, think about your daughter.

NOVAK: I am. I am bringing her in out of the cold, where it's safe.

HARDCASTLE: What—

KAPOOR: She got lost, Will. None of us was with her. She could have— We don't know which one is real.

BAKER: Oh, shit.

NOVAK: Move out of my way, Will.

BAKER: No. No way. We can't—

Carreau shoulders past Hardcastle, opening enough of a gap for Novak to squeeze through. She walks gingerly to the other end of the hall and sets the second Sophia down near the wall.

NOVAK: Stay there, sweetie.

She sets the camera down on a chair that has been left in the hallway. She gives it a short, steady look, and adjusts it fractionally so that it is trained on the people in the hall.

CARREAU: Get that door closed.

BAKER: You want to shut it in with us?

NOVAK: Stop saying "it."

Sophia—the first Sophia—has backed up against the wall, staring at her double wide-eyed. The new Sophia tugs on Novak's sleeve.

SOPHIA [2]: Mama, who is that?

NOVAK: That's—you're—

Baker suddenly lunges for Sophia. She grabs the girl by the arm, shakes her.

BAKER: Which one are you? Which one?

She seizes the girl's chin as Novak yells and lunges forward. Sophia shrieks and struggles. Novak cries out in pain and her leg gives out, spilling her onto the concrete floor. Carreau grabs Baker's arm, trying to pry her free, but she's still shaking the little girl, yelling.

BAKER: Which—which—little crawling thing, little sneak, little thief, little stray.

She twists Sophia's arm. Sophia howls in pain.

KAPOOR: Caro!

BAKER: We have to know!

Sophia jerks free of her grip and pelts to her mother, who gathers her close and whispers to her. The girl retreats farther, joining the second Sophia. The girls whisper.

SOPHIA [2]: Who are you?

SOPHIA: I'm Sophie.

SOPHIA [2]: *I'm* Sophie.

SOPHIA: Oh. Me too.

Hardcastle has his hands raised, palms out, separating Novak and Baker.

HARDCASTLE: We can't lose our heads here. Calm down, Carolyn.

BAKER: That other me attacked us. That thing is going to do the same.

KAPOOR: Attacked us?

NOVAK: Caro . . .

BAKER: We saw her. We saw her out there and she wasn't
dead. You didn't manage to kill her, Will, but that's okay,
Joy took care of it for you.

She laughs hysterically.

SOPHIA [2]: I'm scared.

SOPHIA: Me too.

Sophia holds out her hand. Her double takes it.

CARREAU: I thought you said you went—uh. To the . . .

He clears his throat, a rather liquid sound.

CARREAU: You said you went toward the beach.

KAPOOR: We did.

HARDCASTLE: That's what we were going to do.

KAPOOR: That's what we did.

NOVAK: You still haven't explained where you got the gun.

HARDCASTLE: I don't know. I don't remember. We were
down by the beach and we saw Carolyn. She attacked us.
Maybe she had the gun?

KAPOOR: No, you picked it up— Where did you pick it up?
It was . . .

*She frowns and walks toward the doorway leading to the con-
trol room of the bunker.*

KAPOOR: We were here.

HARDCASTLE: That doesn't make any sense.

KAPOOR: Something is messing with our memory.

BAKER: It's them. It's their fault. It's all going wrong because of them. What are you? Why won't you listen? Just

listen to him, little devil, little rebel, little sneak, little thief, little—lit—lit—tell—tell me—

Her jaw works side to side in abrupt movements. She chokes, coughs.

BAKER: No nonono. This one's not lasting. Oh, God— What's wrong with me?

KAPOOR: Oh, my God. She's . . .

NOVAK: No. She can't be. That would mean— But I—

Baker's head lolls forward, then snaps up.

BAKER: No, I'm fine. Fine. Fine fellow. Fellows. Fellowship. Ships. Ships on the ocean, all of us drifting. Listen. Listen.

She laughs again—and then lunges for Hardcastle with a shriek. She claws at his chest while Kapoor and Novak try to pull her off.

The newly arrived Sophia looks at the other girl and tugs her hand.

SOPHIA [2]: Come on.

She tugs Sophia toward the open door on the left. With a toddler's impulsiveness, Sophia grabs the camera, hugging it against her chest as the two girls scurry away from the violent scene playing out before them.

23

I STARED AT Dr. Kapoor, thoughts wheeling through my head, my careful emotional remove fracturing. Footsteps came up the walk. Dr. Kapoor stepped closer and dropped her voice to an angry hiss. "Go home, Ms. Novak. Go home, and never think of this place again."

The front door opened, and William Hardcastle stepped in. Dr. Kapoor gave me a look—a warning look. And a frightened one. *Don't*, she mouthed.

William Hardcastle smiled. "Sophia," he said in surprise. "I didn't expect to see you here. Ms. Hayes, I'm sorry for everything that's happening."

His voice echoed in my mind. In my memory. *I'm sorry.*

My eyes dropped to his hands, hanging easily by his sides. They were large hands. *Spade-like*, I thought. Strong hands with blunt fingers and light brown freckling across the backs. I knew those hands. I was sure of it now.

I'm sorry, he'd said.

They'd been holding me under the water, the day I drowned.

He was still talking, but all I heard were those two words. Those words, and the hollow sound of water closing over my head. He was sorry. He was so sorry for all of this. His regret was suffocating, and I could only pray that the emptiness of my eyes, my inability to speak, could be excused by the circumstances. Two people missing. Maybe dead.

"I know that this is a difficult situation, but we're going to do everything we can to find Lily and Ms. Ryder," he said.

I tried to push my fear, my shock away. I needed that numbness. I needed that distance and coldness, but it wouldn't come, because the cold was the water and the water was all around me, it was in my mouth and it was dragging at my limbs and I couldn't breathe.

"Thank you," I managed, a whisper that left my throat raw.

He smiled. It made his blue eyes look flat.

"Liam, why don't you walk Ms. Hayes back to Mrs. Popova's?" Dr. Kapoor said pointedly.

"Right," Liam said. Anger hummed below the syllable, and for a moment I feared that he would lash out. If he demanded answers from his mother now, Dr. Hardcastle would realize we knew the truth—or part of the truth, at least. And he would be able to put together who I was.

I took Liam's hand to pull him away, and to anchor myself. I had to get out of there, and only my grip on him kept me from running as fast as I could.

I drew him along down the road. We bypassed the car by unspoken agreement. Tension jangled in the air between us. Liam said my name. He sounded concerned. The worrier of the two of us. At least he'd kept it together. Not like me. Not this time.

"Sophia, slow down."

I realized I was walking so fast that Liam could barely keep up. I halted abruptly. Whatever brief respite I'd earned myself was gone now, my fear tangling around me once more.

The wind stirred my hair, whipping stray strands across my face. I clawed them back behind my ears. There was something wrong with me. Or something wrong with the air. I couldn't get a deep enough breath.

"You're panicking again," Liam said quietly. He started to reach for me.

"Touch me and I'm going to fucking lose it," I warned him. I shut my eyes, but it didn't help. I saw the water. Saw the boat. Saw Hardcastle's hand around my wrist, holding so tight it hurt— saw Lily's hands, closed over mine in comfort.

I saw her broken on the ground, and I saw the yawning black of the ocean.

I turned on my heel and strode off the road. We were in a gap between the houses, just a spit of rock and sand and driftwood. It was too gray and nondescript to be beautiful.

I walked all the way to the edge of the water and two steps farther. Liam called after me again, and I wondered if he thought I would keep walking, the way she had, walk all the way into the sea and let the waves fold over me. It was an efficient way of vanishing.

But I stopped with cold water lapping over my shoes, up to my ankles. It rushed out and I sank a centimeter into the sand as the water drew away the ground I rested on.

The girl who looks like me. Or is it the other way around?

"Tell me I'm real," I whispered.

"Of course you're real," Liam said.

I looked back at him. Salt spray pricked my cheeks. "Am I? Or am I one of them? Just an echo? What if she's the one that's real?"

"You're nothing like those things. What you told me about Mikhail's echo and that other one—"

"But she's not like that either," I said. "She's . . . strange. But that doesn't mean anything, not if she grew up in that place. What if I'm not me at all? What if I'm the monster who stole a girl's life?"

"You're not a monster," Liam said firmly.

"Maybe that's why I don't feel things properly," I said. "Maybe that's why it takes so long for emotions to catch up with me."

"Or maybe it's a natural fucking response to trauma," Liam said. "Something happened to you here. And you don't even know what it is so that you can deal with it. I was a complete shit to call you a sociopath, Sophia, especially when I've had enough therapy to have my own PhD by now. You're real. You're human. You're *you*."

"I'm not even sure what that means." I let out my breath, long and slow, and looked out over the water. Dr. Kapoor had chosen a house that faced Belaya Skala. The window of her bedroom, I realized, looked right out at the headland. "They know," I said. "They know about this place."

"You mean Dr. Kapoor and Hardcastle?" Liam asked.

"I mean all of them. Your mom. Hardcastle. Mrs. Popova. Everyone here knows. They know that Lily isn't missing, that she hasn't fallen down and passed out behind a rock or drowned in the ocean. They know the island took her. Is there even going to be a search? Or will they just send a boat over and wait on the shore long enough to make us think they tried?"

Liam didn't answer. I crouched, letting the waves run over my hands. Foam flecked my wrists. Even in the summer, the water was shockingly cold. It had been cold then too. "Hardcastle was there," I said. "I don't remember much, but I remember him. There was a boat, and the waves, and he grabbed my wrist and . . ."

I shuddered. My hands were going numb in the cold water, and I let that numbness seep through me. I wouldn't be afraid. I wouldn't give anyone my fear.

"No one is going to know the truth about what happened to Lily and Abby," Liam said. "They're going to think it was some freak accident."

"So no one's going to know it was our fault," I said. "Lily wouldn't have been in danger if it weren't for us."

"It's not our fault," Liam said. "It's that fucking island's fault."

From here, it just looked like a lump of rock. Barren and inert. "I don't understand," I whispered. "What *is* that place? Why is it here? Why does anyone stay?"

"You think Dr. Kapoor will tell us?" Liam asked doubtfully.

"I doubt it," I said. "But she sure as hell knows more than we do. She knows the other me. She . . ." I frowned. "Those shells and things on your windowsill. Are they yours?"

"No. I'm not really the collecting type," Liam said.

"But could they be from when you were a kid? Something you left there years ago?"

"Definitely not."

"And there's no way that Dr. Kapoor has a random shell collection," I said. He snorted in amused agreement. She hadn't been surprised to see me—the echo-me—in the house. She'd been annoyed, but not surprised. "She lets my echo stay there. She must. Which means those things belong to my echo."

Including the deer, carved so carefully. One of Mikhail's. If he'd given it to her, it meant he knew too. He didn't recognize me when I arrived because he knew me as a child. He recognized me because he knew *her*. He hadn't told me everything.

I straightened up. Salt water dripped from my fingertips, and I felt nothing. All my fear and anger and grief were on some other shore. Maybe I wasn't human. But maybe it was better not to be.

"I know what we need to do next," I said, and started back toward the road.

VIDEO EVIDENCE

Recorded by Joy Novak

AUGUST 14, 2003, TIME UNKNOWN

The camera turns on in night mode. The exterior light is not on, but a flashlight lying on the floor provides some minimal illumination. The camera rests at floor level as well, underneath the wire frame of a bed. It shifts slightly, scraping against the concrete floor.

SOPHIA: Shh.[6]

Someone enters the room. A man's boots pass in front of the camera. One foot drags slightly.

CARREAU: Sophie? It's okay. You know me. I'm your friend. I want to help. Please.

The camera turns, shifting so that both girls are visible. Sophia and her echo—whichever is which—lie on their stomachs

---

6 It is not always possible to tell which child is which, particularly after sections of corrupted video. Our best efforts have been made to identify the girls consistently, but errors may remain.

---

beneath the bed, holding each other's hands tightly. The So-phia who was holding the camera puts a finger to her lips and shakes her head. The Sophia farther from the camera bites her lip and presses a hand over her mouth, as if trying not to whimper.

CARREAU: Sophie. Sophie. Sososososososo—

His foot taps rapidly, the nervous drumming of a rabbit against the dusty ground.

CARREAU: Sloppy work.

He walks out of the room. In the distance, muffled, come three rapid gunshots and screaming.

Approximately five minutes pass with the camera on the ground beneath the bed, the two girls, holding each other's hands, breathing in ragged, staggered rhythm. The shouting has stopped. Footsteps sound in the hall outside; Joy enters, recognizable by the bright blue laces on her boots.

NOVAK: Sophie?

The girls clamber out, one after the other.

SOPHIA: We got scared.

SOPHIA [2]: We hided.

NOVAK: It's okay now.

The lie is a flimsy one, and even the girls seem to know it.

SOPHIA: What happened?

NOVAK: Um. Carolyn, she was . . . sick. She had to go away.

SOPHIA: She tried to hurt me. I have a ouch.

She holds out her arm for the requisite kiss. Novak rolls up the girl's sleeve. The imprint of fingers is visible on Sophia's skin. Novak, struggling to maintain an unworried smile, plants a kiss on the girl's arm.

NOVAK: Okay, kiddos. Come with me. Everything's going to be okay.

She puts force behind the words, as if her determination will make it true. Together, each girl holding one of Novak's hands, they walk through the hallway and into the control room. The camera dangles by its strap from Sophia's hand. It captures a few frames of the door, closed, and of the wide pool of blood on the concrete floor in the hallway.

In the control room, Hardcastle and Kapoor sit in dilapidated chairs. Martin leans against a table. He smiles at the Sophias and taps a finger to his lips; no one else appears to notice.

HARDCASTLE: You found them. Good.

NOVAK: If anyone tries to touch either one of them—

HARDCASTLE: You've made yourself clear.

KAPOOR: No one's doing anything until we figure out which one of them is which.

Novak looks down and notices the camera. She takes it from Sophia and positions it.

KAPOOR: Carolyn seemed to, I don't know, glitch out or something.

NOVAK: What about the other one?

She sounds queasy.

KAPOOR: The other . . . the one outside.

NOVAK: If this was the copy, the one out there was the real Carolyn. But you said that she attacked you.

KAPOOR: She did. She came out of nowhere, screaming at us.

NOVAK: What was she screaming?

KAPOOR: She . . . I don't remember. She was asking something. Where something was.

HARDCASTLE: Where did you take them.

His voice is monotone, his gaze distant. He shakes his head a little, eyes focusing.

HARDCASTLE: That was it, wasn't it? She was asking where we took them. Took who, though? And how did she end up near here?

KAPOOR: We were heading for the beach. I remember that. And we weren't gone that long.

NOVAK: We don't know how long you were gone. None of our watches work here.

KAPOOR: The camera . . . ?

NOVAK: I checked the display. It's stuck on 12:47, and the recording light flickers on and off. There's no way to be sure how much of an interval might be missing. I thought you were gone about fifteen minutes, but it might have been longer.

KAPOOR: It would be easier to think if it weren't for that damn singing.

NOVAK: Where is that coming from, anyway? Is it even singing? I can't quite make it out.

Carreau hums, as if to match something he hears. The microphone picks up no such music.

SOPHIA [2]: Oh! I like the singing. I heared it before. But then I got lost.

Novak has gone very still.

NOVAK: Sophie? Sweetie?

She limps over to the left-hand Sophia and takes her by the shoulders.

NOVAK: When did you get lost, Sophie?

SOPHIA [2]: I know I'm not supposed to.

NOVAK: Not supposed to what?

SOPHIA [2]: Not supposed to go out when it's misty. But I wanted to see the beach. And then whoosh!

She waves her hands in front of her eyes.

SOPHIA [2]: Can't see anything! Aaahh! Sploosh, fall in the water. And then I'm cold.

SOPHIA: But then there's a shadow. It's standing up, not on the ground. I not seen a shadow stand up before. So cool.

The adults gape as the two girls trade off seamlessly.

SOPHIA [2]: So I touch it! And then I sleep. And I wake up a differenter place.

SOPHIA: And I look and I look and I look for you but I not find you.

NOVAK: You— The day you got lost. But you came back. Mikhail brought you back.

SOPHIA [2]: Mikhail! The big man. I like him.

SOPHIA: He carry me back.

SOPHIA [2]: Mor-arty come too.

NOVAK: Which one of you . . . Who came back? Did you? Did Mikhail carry you?

She looks at the left-hand Sophia, who looks confused.

SOPHIA [2]: Why you sad, Mama?

KAPOOR: Their clothes.

Novak understands. The girls are wearing matching sneakers, mud-stained, and jeans close enough not to be easily distinguished. Their jackets, too, are identical, but Novak carefully unzips each one and looks at the shirts beneath. One girl wears a black T-shirt with a cartoon dog printed on the chest; the other's shirt is gray and striped, long-sleeved. One of those sleeves is still slightly rucked up where Novak moved it to examine her bruises.

KAPOOR: Which one was she wearing today?

Novak's eyes flicker over the girls. She wets her lips.

NOVAK: I—I'm not sure.

HARDCASTLE: Wait. Let's be clear here. You're saying that Sophie was copied—swapped—days ago? Back when she went missing?

NOVAK: We don't know that. You heard them. It's like they're sharing memories.

HARDCASTLE: It sure as hell sounded like that was what happened. So which one did we bring over with us? Because that's the double.

NOVAK: I don't know, Will. I can't be sure.

She keeps her back to him and her head down. She zips the girls' jackets back up, adjusts their collars. Tugs Sophia [2]'s sleeve down more firmly toward her wrist.

Carreau has been humming softly. Kapoor glares at him.

HARDCASTLE: It's bad enough having to listen to it. Do you have to sing along?

SOPHIA: It's coming from down.

KAPOOR: She's right. It's coming from below us. I'm going to check it out.

HARDCASTLE: No one goes off alone.

KAPOOR: Then come with me.

NOVAK: No. If we go anywhere, we all go together. No more being out of each other's sight. Period.

Hardcastle nods.

HARDCASTLE: Bring the camera. Our memories aren't reliable. Maybe it can help.

24

WE WALKED TO Mikhail's house. We weren't his only visitors, it turned out. Mrs. Popova's truck was out front. *They know each other*, I thought, and then realized how ridiculous that was.

They were arguing inside, but I didn't understand the language—Russian, I assumed. When the front step creaked beneath me, the voices ceased. Instead of knocking, I cleared my throat. "Mikhail?" I called.

Clomping footsteps, and then the door opened. "You should not be here," he said. Mrs. Popova stood behind him, face pinched in a displeased expression and sweater wrapped tight around herself.

"You didn't tell us everything," I said.

"Yes. Because I want you to leave. Go away and be safe," Mikhail said, scowling at us.

"Let them in, Misha," Mrs. Popova said. "They aren't going to let go of this, and the girl deserves the truth. Don't you think?"

"Truth is overrated," Mikhail muttered, but he waved us in. I stopped in the middle of the room and stared down the two adults.

"You knew about her. Both of you. She has one of Mikhail's carvings. You gave it to her, didn't you?" I held out my own carving, the little tern with its upward-swept wings. Mikhail took it from me gingerly, turning it over in his hands. "You gave this one to my mother. You gave others to the echo."

"Sophie," he said.

"What?"

"That's what she calls herself," Mrs. Popova said. "Not Sophia, Sophie. You left. She didn't. Of course we know about her." She waved at the table. "Sit down."

I glanced at Liam, but he seemed to be happy letting me take the lead. I had imagined this as more of an interrogation, but I took the offered chair and Mrs. Popova folded her hands on the tabletop.

"Ask what you need to ask," she said.

"What is Sophie?" I asked. "Is she like the other echoes?"

"No. She's different, but we don't know why."

"We take care of her," Mikhail added.

"Who's we?" I asked. "Dr. Hardcastle too?"

He shook his head sharply. "No. He does not know she is here. Maria and Vanya and I, we watch over her."

"He did something," I said. "I can almost remember, but . . ." I shook my head.

"It seems so," Mrs. Popova said. "We don't know what it is,

but Vanya does. She's the one that told us we had to be careful to hide her from Dr. Hardcastle."

"That's why he didn't know me," I said. "But you did. Why didn't you say anything?"

"We weren't certain what you wanted," Mrs. Popova said. "Or what would happen when you came."

"What *is* this place?" I demanded.

"A barren hunk of rock where a few fools tried to turn desolation into abundance and failed," Mrs. Popova said. "This place had always been empty, because there was nothing here. No food, no warmth, no hope. Only evil."

"The evil in this place wasn't here until we brought it," Mikhail rumbled.

"Who's 'we'?" I asked.

"The *Krachka*," he said. "A fishing ship. There were seven of us. One day the nets dragged something up from the ocean that we didn't understand. It was like a piece of broken glass the size of a man's chest. From every angle, it looked different. Like it was flat, but you could never find the edge. It was held in a box covered in strange writing, wrapped with chains."

"The *Krachka* crashed like a hundred and fifty years ago," Liam said. Mikhail fixed him with a look.

"Hush. I am not finished. We started to hear things. Singing. When we looked at the glass, we saw the Six-Wing, the angel. I knew it was something wicked. Something that should be destroyed. But others seemed to worship it. They wanted to free it. I tried to stop them, so they tied me up in the hold, but I broke free. Ran the ship onto the rocks. That was when I lost my eye."

He took a shuddering breath, as if the pain still lived in him.

"Things got a bit chaotic after that," Mrs. Popova said dryly. "The ship crashed against the rocks. Most of the sailors wouldn't say anything or accept any help. But they let my brother bring Misha over to this side of the island, where our doctor lived," Mrs. Popova said. "We tended to him. We didn't realize until the next day that everyone else was gone. They'd vanished."

"But that was not the worst of it," Mikhail said. "The worst was when they came back."

Mrs. Popova looked down at her hands. "The last time I told anyone about all of this was when your Dr. Kapoor came back from—from that other place. It's strange to say it out loud."

"All this time, we have kept silence," Mikhail said, turning to Mrs. Popova. "What has it given us? Long life and little joy."

Mrs. Popova sighed. "Very well. As you've probably gathered, my family was among the first to settle Bitter Rock. My father was Russian, my mother was Unangan. She converted to Russian Orthodox when she married him. She died of a sudden illness the winter before the *Krachka* came—and sometimes I thank God for that. She didn't have to see what happened.

"In any case, the day after the crash, we found Belaya Skala empty. We searched, of course, the sea and the land. Looking for bodies or for some explanation. We found nothing except a hole in the hillside. Wide enough for a man to fall in. Deep. Too deep to climb down. The edges were . . . It's hard to describe. It was like a wound. I was there with my father, helping. I was a young woman at the time. Nineteen."

"It is hard to remember we were ever so young," Mikhail said.

A slight smile played over Mrs. Popova's lips, but she kept up the tale.

"We searched the whole island. And then the mist came. We were there—my father, my sister, and me. My sister's husband had been on Belaya Skala. He was among the vanished. When we heard his voice calling her name, we were overjoyed. She ran out into the mist to meet him. I was right behind her. I saw her run into his arms. I watched him snap her neck with a twist of his hands. Like it was nothing." She shut her eyes and shuddered.

"My father had his gun. My sister's husband died smiling. And then we heard screaming. He was not the only one that had returned. We fled across the water, but not all of us made it."

Mikhail nodded. "After that, no one went to Belaya Skala. But sometimes the mist would come and cover the island, and you could hear them calling in it."

"Most of the others left," Mrs. Popova said. "Many right away. Others within a few years, when they realized it wouldn't stop."

"Wait," I said. "If you were nineteen in the 1880s . . ."

"Time doesn't pass here properly," Mrs. Popova said. "At first the effect didn't reach past the headland. But it spread. Sometimes I wish it had bothered to get this far before I was quite so gray in the hair." Her lips twisted at the feeble joke.

"But why would you stay?" I asked. "If it was so dangerous—"

"My daughter is still there," Mikhail said. "And so I could not leave."

"And someone had to be here to warn people," Mrs. Popova added. "To tell them about the mist."

"Your daughter," I said. "You mean her echo?"

Mrs. Popova looked over at Mikhail. He was silent. She put her hand over his. "At first the children seemed to grow up normally, but then . . ."

"They would walk out into the mist," Mikhail said, staring at the wall. "We tried to stop them. We locked them in their rooms. Tied them up. They fought. Broke their bones to escape the ropes. Clawed the walls until their fingernails tore. And even if we stopped them, they died. And so we stopped trying to keep them. We let them go."

"Whatever the Six-Wing is looking for, I have always thought it requires a child," Mrs. Popova said. "A very particular child." The look she gave me was sharp-edged.

"And now you know the truth," Mikhail said. "You know, and so you can leave."

"No, we can't," I said. "I still don't know what happened to my mother."

"She's gone, Sophia," Mrs. Popova said. "Let her go, and leave. While you still can."

But I couldn't. I had to know what happened. I had to know who I was. What I was.

Even if it killed me.

VIDEO EVIDENCE

Recorded by Joy Novak

AUGUST 14, 2003, TIME UNKNOWN

*The group descends deeper into the bunker. The stairs creak
and groan beneath them, and Novak has a particularly hard
time navigating them. When Carreau offers the girls his
hands to help them down, they shy away from him, sticking
to Novak's side. Hardcastle hangs behind briefly to wran-
gle the camera settings, and then edges past the rest of the
queue to take the lead. The stairs lead down and down and
farther still.*

KAPOOR: I think I can almost make out the words. We must
be getting closer.

NOVAK: It's not really that I can make them out, it's more
like I'm starting to understand them.

*Hardcastle reaches the bottom of the stairs. He looks in on the
round room. It is similar to the chamber in which Sophia*

will find Liam, over a decade from now, but its walls are not adorned in paint.

They cross the room cautiously, and the tunnel leading out comes into sight. In this video it is wider, and arched smoothly, crafted with intention and skill. The tunnel beyond seems manmade, wide enough for two people to walk side by side, if a bit uncomfortably.

HARDCASTLE: Only one way forward.

They proceed into the tunnel. No one speaks. No one questions the decision to press onward—and downward, as the tunnel slopes, curves, spirals slowly in on itself. As it has before, the camera cuts out now and again. It is especially difficult to guess how long these intervals might be as there is no difference between one section of video and the next. A slightly different wrinkle in the rock around them, a crack in the floor, a discolored bit of stone—nothing substantial. The video comprises at least fifteen minutes, but they may have been walking for many more by the time they come to the door.

It is identical to the door into the bunker: metal, rectangular, windowless. Hardcastle looks back at the others, turning the camera. They watch him expectantly. There is no question that he will open the door, and he does, grunting with the effort.

The door opens onto the island. Onto the same patch of ground they came into the bunker from. Here, there is no mist. No grass either; only bare rock. Hardcastle points the camera up toward the sky—but there is no sky. Only a reflection of the island and the ocean, hanging above them.

KAPOOR: I should be terrified, but I'm just . . . empty.

She looks up. Her expression is slack, but tears track down her cheeks.

KAPOOR: We aren't getting out of here.

CARREAU: Stranger things have happened, Vanya dearest. Stranger things.

NOVAK: Down there.

She points. Just offshore, a large wooden vessel is mired against the rocks. Even translated into the medium of film, it is a mind-bending sight—it seems, impossibly, to be eternally breaking apart. An optical illusion, perhaps, for there is no beginning nor end to the way the wooden beams crack against the rocks, splitting open. Black liquid gushes from the crack like a wound—a wound that is forever in the process of being rent open.

HARDCASTLE: Is that where we need to go?

KAPOOR: No. I think that is.

She points along the side of the slope and downward—toward the town. Hardcastle steps to where he can angle the camera to follow her pointing hand.

Where the town should be there is only an empty field. Except for the church. It has doubled in size, gained spires that twist in nauseating geometry. Terns swarm around its roof in eerie silence, and where its door should be, the camera captures only random visual glitches and flashes of light

CARREAU: No sense in wasting time.

In wordless agreement, the group starts off down the hill. Car-

reau takes the lead, his gait buoyant, head high, and hands in his pockets.

The glitching of the camera becomes more frequent as they draw closer. As they step over the threshold, the video remains rolling but turns to jagged, discordant shapes and colors.[7] The image resolves thirteen seconds later.

The interior of the church is not a church at all, but a cavern. The walls are gray stone. Columns of rock and stalagmites rise from the floor, preventing a complete view of the space. The vaulted ceiling is covered in a mural not unlike that of the previous echo, though on a larger scale, and wrapped around the outcroppings of rock. A path leads toward the dark interior of the space, and the group follows it.

KAPOOR: Did you see that?

NOVAK: What?

KAPOOR: I thought I saw something moving.

CARREAU: Come on. It's just through here.

KAPOOR: What is?

They step through a gateway of two craggy columns, and Joy gasps. In the center of the room, suspended in the air, is a massive shard of glass, the size of a human torso. Its edges are jagged, and light refracts brokenly through its clouded surface. It shifts and changes in midair, and sometimes it seems less like a piece of glass, and more like the world itself is the glass and the object in the center of the room is a crack through it.

....

7 Frame-by-frame review reveals signs of multiple images overlapping and/or fragmented. Unfortunately, our inability to retrieve the video files themselves prevents us from further analysis.

From its jagged lower tip weeps black liquid, dripping into a circular pool. Channels flow from the pool outward, threading among the congregation gathered around the shard. For there are people—many people, dozens—arranged in concentric circles. They kneel, heads bowed and backs bent, their hands resting on their laps, holding shallow bowls.

Hardcastle draws close to the nearest man. He wears the uniform of a US Airman circa the second world war. One of his boots is unlaced, his shirt unbuttoned. Black tears run down his cheeks. Every few seconds, one drops into the shallow bowl. It is already half-full.

Most of those nearby are dressed similarly. Some seem to have had more time to dress than others; a few wear only their underclothes. One young man, no more than nineteen or twenty, has only one sock on.

NOVAK: Will, look out!

Hardcastle jerks back from the man he is examining, yelling as a burst of movement comes toward him—but it's only a young boy, and he runs past Hardcastle, ignoring him entirely. The boy, who has a dusty blond mop of hair and a gaunt frame, carries an empty bowl clasped to his side. He stops in front of one of the airmen and exchanges the man's filled bowl for the empty one. He pauses, the bowl balanced carefully on both of his palms, and looks at Hardcastle.

HARDCASTLE: We're not going to hurt you, kid.

The boy approaches with hesitant steps. He holds the bowl up toward Hardcastle. In his eyes is an invitation. An offer.

HARDCASTLE: Uh—no thanks?

The boy nods—and then he sets the bowl to his lips, and drinks.

He drinks thirstily, greedily, gulping down the tarry black liquid. It spills out of the sides of his mouth, down his chin, splashes on his chest and the ground at his feet. Hardcastle makes a guttural sound of revulsion and steps back.

The boy takes the last swallow and lowers the bowl. His skin is red and blistering where the liquid touched it, but he smiles, a contortion of his lips that is almost parody. And then he sprints back toward the rocky outcroppings at the edge of the room, his movements too limber and too controlled to belong to such a young child.

KAPOOR: There's more of them.

Eyes reflect the team's lights. Dozens of eyes, belonging to rail-thin children who cling to the rocks or crouch against the ground. The oldest is perhaps twelve, though it's difficult to tell, given their emaciated state and ragged clothing. The youngest might be four or five.

NOVAK: I know that girl.

She's whispering. She holds the Sophias close against her as she stares at one of the children, a girl with long black hair and light brown skin that had begun to turn a sickly sort of gray.

NOVAK: Mikhail has a painting of her. He showed me once. That's his daughter.

KAPOOR: We have bigger problems.

Her voice is shaking. She points with her flashlight. Around the circle, toward the outer edge, kneels a group of four people, two men and two women, as insensible as all the rest.

They are Joy Novak, William Hardcastle, Vanya Kapoor, and Martin Carreau.

PART FOUR

THIS ROUGH

MAGIC

VIDEO EVIDENCE

Recorded by Joy Novak

AUGUST 14, 2003, TIME UNKNOWN

*Sophia—which one is, at this point, unclear—slips from her
Novak's hold and walks toward the kneeling figures. Joy
grabs for her but doesn't seem willing to move closer to her
double. Sophia reaches out and presses her hands against
the kneeling Joy's cheeks.*

SOPHIA: Mama? Wake up. Mama, talk.

She looks back.

SOPHIA: Why she doesn't talk?

HARDCASTLE: They're doubles. Those are our doubles;
they're not real.

KAPOOR: Don't be obtuse, Will. This explains everything
quite neatly, doesn't it? Vanya and William did go
down toward the beach. We're the ones that came back.
Carolyn—

NOVAK: She must have been replaced before we even got to the church. When we were separated in the mist.

KAPOOR: They tried to bring the real one here, but she got away somehow. And we found her. We killed her.

Her voice is almost clinical—almost. An edge of disgust seeps through.

NOVAK: No, you didn't. I did.

KAPOOR: You didn't know.

HARDCASTLE: I *am* William Hardcastle. I'm me. I'm not some . . . doppelganger.

KAPOOR: That's exactly what you are, Will.

NOVAK: How could we not know? I feel like Joy Novak. I don't remember being anyone else.

Carreau giggles. They look at him sharply. He spreads his hands.

CARREAU: You should see your *faces*.

He laughs—laughs until he wheezes, bending over at the waist.

CARREAU: Caro arrow row oh, such a lovely echo we made of her, and then you put a bullet in its brain. But you were just the same!

HARDCASTLE: Jesus, Martin.

CARREAU: No, neither, I'm afraid.

He stops laughing abruptly and stands up straight. His head gives an avian tilt, and he clicks his teeth together three times rapidly.

CARREAU. We eat their memories, and for a time they seem like truth. But it doesn't last, doesn't last. We can't hold on in the face of the song. And it's so, so nice to surrender.

KAPOOR: Then you know what you are.

CARREAU: Oh, oh. Yes. You'll know soon too. Now that you've done what was needed.

NOVAK: What was needed?

Carreau looks at the Sophias, his grin wide and fixed.

CARREAU: You brought them here. They wouldn't have followed if you didn't believe.

Novak moves now, grabbing both Sophias and pulling them away from Carreau.

NOVAK: What do you want with them?

CARREAU: We need them to open the gate. We've searched so long for the right child. There's something *special* about little Sophie and her shadow, don't you think?

At the edge of the room, the strange children move among the stones, their eyes gleaming with reflected light.

NOVAK: Stay away from them.

CARREAU: Listen, Joy. Listen to the song. Let go of her.

He jerks his head toward Novak's kneeling double. The echo-Novak's throat bobs in a convulsive swallow.

HARDCASTLE: I'm not surrendering to any song. Come on. Let's get out of here.

NOVAK: We can't leave them.

She gestures to the kneeling doubles.

HARDCASTLE: Screw them. I'm not sticking around.

KAPOOR: There must be a way to wake them up.

HARDCASTLE: You're kidding, right? We wake them up and they're going to panic. Attack us. They won't let us exist.

NOVAK: We aren't real.

HARDCASTLE: Speak for yourself.

He looks down at the camera, grunts, and drops it. It hits the ground and rolls, the image going momentarily blank, but the drop doesn't seem to have done too much damage.

KAPOOR: Will, get back here!

NOVAK: Let him go. We need to— Martin, how do we wake them up?

CARREAU: He's right, you know. They'd kill you. And I wouldn't want that, Joy. Oh, how he longs for you, how he loves you. You know, don't you? And you ignore it.

NOVAK: That's not true.

CARREAU: You string him along. You take what you need from him. From everyone. You take and you twist and you watch them dance and it makes you feel so good, so very good, that they love you so, but you love no one but yourself.

NOVAK: Stop it. Martin—whatever you are, you're a copy of him, and there's too much good in that man to be gone completely. Not if you were a good enough copy to fool us. Tell us how to wake them up, Martin.

CARREAU: I—

His hands clench, release, clench, release, a rhythm like the beating of birds' wings.

CARREAU: We're still connected. But it's like a dream. Like a memory. I

He jerks his head to the side.

CARREAU: Here, let me show you.

He steps toward the kneeling Carreau. He reaches for his waist-band. Novak notices the knife a moment too late—a folding utility knife, just a common-sense bit of gear Carreau has probably used a dozen times in front of her, too small and practical to be remembered as anything but a tool.

NOVAK: No!

She's too far away. She knows it; she makes no attempt to stop Carreau, instead turning the girls toward her, pressing their faces against her legs so they can't see as Carreau grabs his double by the hair, pulling his head back, and slashes with the knife.

Blood spatters into the shallow bowl. The real Carreau topples, limbs twitching as he bleeds out without ever regaining true consciousness. The echo steps toward the next person in line—Vanya Kapoor.

CARREAU: This will simplify things.

He reaches for Dr. Kapoor. Her echo shouts.

KAPOOR [*echo*]:[8] Vanya Ellora Kapoor, wake the fuck up.

The real Kapoor's head whips up. She sees the knife and, too fast to be anything but raw instinct, throws herself up and forward, inside Martin's reach. Her elbow connects with his stomach and sends him sprawling onto the ground.

Her echo steps forward into view. She holds one arm out, blood dripping from the cut along the side of her arm. Her other hand grips a shard of one of the shallow bowls, broken to create a sharp edge.

8 For the sake of clarity, echoes are identified throughout the remainder of the transcript where it is possible to confirm their status. In the case of Sophia Novak and her echo, such a determination is impossible.

KAPOOR [*echo*]: Pinch me, I'm dreaming.

KAPOOR: What the hell is—

NOVAK: Joy Serenity Novak, you aren't dreaming. This is real. Sophie is in danger. Wake *up*.

She strides forward and slaps her double across the face. Novak—the real Novak—half topples backward, but catches herself, blinking rapidly and gaping at her echo.

KAPOOR [*echo*]: Look out!

Carreau's echo springs to his feet and charges at the newly awakened woman, brandishing the knife. The echo Novak throws herself in the way. Between the light and the poor angle, the fight is a confusion of shadows. Kapoor's echo darts across the room. She bends down beside a soldier, one of those fully dressed, and straightens up, holding a pistol.

She levels it. Waits. Carreau throws Novak's echo off, looms over her. Kapoor squeezes the trigger.

The bullet passes through Carreau's left eye and exits out the back of his skull. The damage is contained, orderly. A brief puff of blood. He collapses.

Novak's echo lies on the ground, blood soaking her sweater. The real Novak steps toward her.

NOVAK [*echo*]: No, take care of—take care of the girls.

KAPOOR [*echo*]: You're going to be all right.

Joy, looking stunned and a bit sick, turns to the two Sophias. She gathers them up in her arms and whispers to them, pressing her lips against their hair. Vanyu's echo looks up from where she kneels beside Joy's echo.

KAPOOR [*echo*]: What do you know?

KAPOOR: Bits and pieces. I saw—sometimes I thought I was you. Awake. And sometimes I was here.

KAPOOR [echo]: But you know the gist of it.

KAPOOR: I think I can put it together.

NOVAK: We need to get out of here.

KAPOOR [echo]: You do. We aren't going anywhere.

NOVAK: It's not safe here. We all have to—

KAPOOR [echo]: I don't know if you heard what Martin—the fake Martin—said. But what happened to him and to Carolyn is going to happen to us too. I don't know if that means in minutes or years or what, but I'm not taking that chance. My son needs his mother to come home. And I'm not the one he's waiting for.

KAPOOR: What about . . .

She looks over at the Sophias, both in Novak's arms.

NOVAK: They're kids.

NOVAK [echo]: She's different. Even Martin said so. She's not like the rest of us. You have to take her with you. Take care of her. I—I'm starting to understand the singing. You need to get them away from me. But I think—when I listen to the song, I know things. And I think I can open a way back out of the mist for you. Just get to the boat. I'll hold on as long as I can, if you just promise to get them home.

NOVAK: I promise. Of course I promise.

KAPOOR: What about William?

KAPOOR [echo]: Try slapping him. I mean, something positive ought to come out of this.

Kapoor snorts. She crouches down and looks into William Hardcastle's slack face.

And then she leans forward, and whispers in his ear. He shivers. The bowl slips from his fingers, clattering to the floor. Kapoor stands up and holds out her hand.

HARDCASTLE: What . . . ?

KAPOOR: Questions later. How do we do this, echo girl?

She looks at Novak's echo, who still has one hand against the oozing wound in her belly.

NOVAK [*echo*]: Just get me . . . bring me to the pool.

Kapoor and her echo are the ones that help her, Hardcastle still too disoriented to help, Novak holding the crying, confused girls. They bring the echo to the edge of the black pool beneath the glass shard, and she steps in. She staggers free of them. With each step she sinks lower in the liquid. When her fingertips brush the surface, it begins to crawl up her arms. It flows in rivulets along her clavicle, up her throat. It slips between her lips. It trickles over her eyelids, and her eyes fill with that shadowless void.

SOPHIA: Mama . . .

NOVAK [*echo*]: I love you, little bird. Now *go.*

25

MRS. POPOVA AND Mikhail weren't quite looking at each other, as if it was shameful to have spoken all of this aloud. I wondered if they ever really talked about it on the island—or if they pretended their lives were some kind of normal, only sometimes giving a knowing look toward the rocky bluffs across the water.

Outside, a voice howled in rage or pain. Inhuman and unearthly, and horribly familiar. I jumped up, startled, but Mrs. Popova put her hand on my arm. "It's the Warden," she said. Mikhail's double. That was who Dr. Kapoor had been afraid of running into—not Mikhail after all. "The mist is here, but it's all right. He never comes inside."

Footsteps crunched in the gravel along the drive. A new sound came, a kind of guttural *huhhh-uh-huh*, like someone trying to clear a crushed throat.

"Never comes inside because he can't, or he doesn't?" I asked.

A body struck the door with force. The door shuddered with the impact. Liam leapt to his feet, toppling his chair with a crash. Mrs. Popova gripped the crucifix that hung around her neck and muttered a prayer.

The Warden slammed into the door again. Wood cracked. Mikhail stayed in his seat, eyes fixed on the wall opposite. It took me a moment to recognize the look on his face. It was the grim acceptance of a man who has been waiting a very long time for the inevitable to arrive.

"Do you have your rifle?" Mikhail asked Mrs. Popova.

"Sure, I just tucked it down the back of my pants," she said sourly. "It's in the truck."

Bang. Another impact, and then the slow scraping drag of a footstep. A voice, low and garbled, came through the door. "*Soooophiiiaaaa,*" the Warden said, and coughed wetly, a meaty hacking that cut off with a wheeze. "Ty k nam vernulas."

"'You came back to us,'" Mikhail translated. The tortured voice went on, and Mikhail murmured the translation. "'We saw you in the boy's memories. She tried to hide you from us, but we know you have returned. Come outside. Come with us.'"

The voice stopped. There was a long pause, an unbalanced kind of silence, made to break. And then the Warden slammed into the door once again.

Mikhail stood, pressing his palms flat against the table. "You must run," he said.

Bang. The frame of the door splintered. One more good hit and it would give. There was no back door, no other way out. The windows were too small to fit through. The Warden roared.

"My truck's out front," Mrs. Popova said. Her voice was shaking, but she dug for her keys. "We just need a clear path out."

"Where do we go?" I asked. "If they can get in here, is anywhere safe?"

"The LARC is built like a fortress," Liam said.

"The LARC is a fortress. That's why it's built that way," Mrs. Popova said.

"He will be inside in a moment," Mikhail said. "I will fight. You run."

"He'll kill you," I said.

Mikhail rumbled a laugh. "I am long past due to die, Sophia Novak. I thought for a long time the reason I lived so long was to save you, that day on the water, and I wondered why I persisted still. But now I know. I was not done saving you." I could only stare helplessly, words a tangle in my throat. "But after this, you will have to save yourself."

Then the door burst open, and the monster came in.

Sometimes when terrible things happen, time blurs. Sometimes it slows, every moment crystallized and indelible. This time it stuttered, chaotic smears of movement and panic interspersed with shards of clear memory:

The Warden in the doorway, eyes fixed on me. I had time to think that he looked nothing like Mikhail, and wonder how that could be, and then he charged me.

Mikhail, pushing me out of the way.

Liam's hand in mine, both of us sprinting up the gravel path

302 KATE ALICE MARSHALL

toward Mrs. Popova's old truck, my laptop, still hot, in my hand.

The cabin framed in the rearview mirror as Mrs. Popova floored the gas pedal. A man stood in the doorway, backlit and obscured by mist. I could not tell which man it was.

The truck jolting over a pothole halfway up the hill, throwing me against the window, and a woman in a gray dress standing at the edge of the road, her eyes blackened sockets.

Time untangled itself at the top of the hill, as we threw ourselves free of the truck and pelted toward the LARC. We were hardly three steps from the truck when a large woman staggered out of the mist toward us. Her blonde hair stuck to her cheeks under a crust of salt, tears, or sea spray dried to scales. She reached for Mrs. Popova.

The rifle crack came before my alarmed shout could even leave my throat, and the echo toppled to the ground. Mrs. Popova's face was a mask, but her hands shook.

"There's more," Liam said.

Shapes in the mist, moving with clear purpose. Mrs. Popova moved backward as we crossed to the entrance, sweeping the rifle left and right. Spectral shapes drew toward us through the mist. Liam fumbled with his keys, dropped them. He swore and bent down, his nails raking across the concrete as he scrabbled for them.

"Hurry up," I said, grabbing his shoulder. "They're coming." The echoes moved in short bursts, violent grace interspersed with stumbling confusion. "Liam!"

"Got it," Liam said. His eyes were wild and his breath thin between his teeth. My heart galloped in my chest. Liam flung the door open, and we piled inside, Mrs. Popova taking up the rear as the nearest of the echoes cleared the mist. A man this time, his face overgrown with fleshy mushrooms. He took a dragging step and then leapt forward, graceful as a dancer. Mrs. Popova slammed the door behind us, and Liam turned to me. My eyes were wide, my breath quick. "Sophia? Freakish calm would be useful right about now."

Trying to keep control was like trying to keep my grip on an eel, but I didn't want the calm. I didn't want to be that person. "Promise me you'll—"

He pressed a kiss against my lips, a rough, half-wild thing, and he leaned his brow against mine. "You're you," he said. "You're real. And I'll remind you every time you forget."

It was like carving away a piece of myself—the fear was so deep, I had to cut to the core to get it out. And what remained was a cold knife between my ribs. Cold, and still, and calm. "I'm good," I said. I blinked away the last haze of emotion and pulled away from Liam.

Mrs. Popova was staring at the door. She gave a sudden, jerky nod. "Right," she said. "That will hold most of them off, but some of them can still think and reason. Especially the newer ones. They might find a way in." She winced. "I hope Mikhail found his way to safety."

"I'm sorry," I said. I didn't feel it beyond the surface level, but I knew it was true.

"None of this is your fault, dear," Mrs. Popova replied with a sigh.

"I'm still sorry it's happened," I said. "I'm sorry this came to your island at all."

Fists thumped against the door. It didn't give, but we all drew away from it.

"They'll hold. I'll go check the rest," Mrs. Popova said. "You two stay put."

I almost protested, but then I saw Liam. He was pale. Exhausted and running out of adrenaline to keep him moving. He needed to sit down, and in my frigid clarity, I recognized the importance of rest. I didn't have panic and desperation to convince me we needed to keep moving whatever the cost. I sank down onto one of the benches in the foyer as Mrs. Popova headed off, letting my own exhaustion be Liam's excuse to rest. He sat beside me, shoulders slumped.

The thudding against the door stopped. They must have gone to find another entrance.

"We should . . ." Liam started, but I covered his hand with mine. I tried to think of the right thing to say, but that was the trouble with being empty. I knew what was practical to do, but without feeling anything myself, I couldn't tell how to soothe his emotions.

Then my hand tightened over his. We weren't alone.

My echo was standing down the hallway. Her hair was soaked, the golden strands darkened to brown. More water dripped from the hem of her skirt—one of Mikhail's wife's—and the cuffs of the LARC sweatshirt half-zipped over her thin frame. She smiled. It was a fragile smile, half-broken, tangled up in hope and in sadness. "Hello," she said softly.

"Hi," I replied, managing a small smile of my own. I tried to remember her, but every time I got close, my thoughts filled with dark water and my lungs began to burn.

"It knows you're here now," she said.

"Yeah, I'd say my cover's been blown on all fronts," I said.

"Sophia?" Liam asked, hesitant.

"It's okay," I assured him, standing up. And then I saw what she was holding. Abby's camera. "Where did you get that?" I asked.

"She wanted me to bring it," the other girl said. She held it out. "You have to see."

I took it from her, shivering as my fingertips brushed against her skin. I opened it to check the data slot. There was an SD card inserted. Which meant . . .

"That's it," I said. "This is the data card we found at the LARC. Abby must have put it in her camera." I turned on the camera. The screen might be cracked, but the innards were clearly still working, because I was able to pull up a list of video files.

Videos from 2003.

The files went on and on. Someone had started filming and stopped so many times, and the videos weren't short. They'd filmed so much. What had happened? I needed to find the beginning of the thread.

I sat back down on the bench. Emotion boiled at the edge of my awareness, but I clung to the calm. *Breathe steady. Don't think, don't feel.* Because if I started to feel anything, I would feel it all, and I would truly drown.

Yet even with the hungry void, my hands were shaking. Liam reached over, resting his hand over my forearm to steady me. I tried to speak but my mouth was hopelessly dry. I swallowed down a sob, my control fracturing.

"This is it," I said. "Whatever happened, it's on this camera."

"Play it," Liam said.

"I can't," I said softly. As long as I didn't know, anything could be true. She could be alive. Out there, waiting for me. As soon as I played those files, the possibilities would collapse into cruel truth.

"It's okay," Liam said. "I understand." He took the camera from me gently and selected the first file.

We watched in silence as the tale unfolded in fragments, and my hope shattered piece by piece.

VIDEO EVIDENCE

Recorded by Joy Novak

AUGUST 14, 2003, TIME UNKNOWN

In the final file of the 2003 LARC excursion, the group retraces their path: out of the church doors, up the flank of the island. The ground seems to fold itself to shorten the way, and while the camera—held now by Kapoor—catches glimpses of shapes both human and otherwise, they seem frozen in place. Whatever Novak's echo meant to do, it seems she is succeeding.

Hardcastle, apparently recovered, takes the lead. The wariness in his posture says that he is not only thinking of what beasts might lurk out of sight, but also of the other threat out here: his own echo.

They climb the stairs. None of them remark on how there are far fewer now than when they went down. They've moved past the expectation of a consistent reality.

Some things persist. Joy makes the girls turn away when they pass echo-Baker's body.

They have almost reached the shore. The possibility of escape has nearly teetered into probability, fear giving way to the wild blossoming of hope. There is the empty shore, the gray water. There is the boat, their boat, not some twisted mimicry but a solid, certain thing. Novak lets out a sound of relief.

KAPOOR [*echo*]: This is where I leave you.

Kapoor nods, unsurprised. Her echo looks down at the gun.

KAPOOR [*echo*]: I don't know if I can . . .

She swallows.

KAPOOR [*echo*]: Will. I know it's a lot to ask.

HARDCASTLE: What do you—? Oh.

He looks sick.

KAPOOR [*echo*]: I'm still me, or very nearly. That's the note I'd like to go out on, not babbling away with a mad song in my mind.

HARDCASTLE: Not here.

NOVAK: Don't do this.

KAPOOR [*echo*]: My choice. And I don't know how long I'll be able to say that about anything, so let's get it done before I hurt anyone.

She and Hardcastle walk together. Not far—Hardcastle stays at the edge of the mist. Vanya's echo walks a little farther, behind a rocky outcropping and deep enough into the mist that they won't be able to see. Still Joy looks away, whispering to the girls. Kapoor keeps the camera trained on Hard-

castle, *as if it can provide some extra barrier between her-*
self and the act.

When it's done, Hardcastle walks back slowly, his face set and
hard.

KAPOOR: Will . . .

HARDCASTLE: Don't. It's done. Let's not talk about it.

NOVAK: Let's just get out of here.

She stands, holding the girls' hands. Hardcastle steps between
her and the boat. He looks at the ground, the gun in his
hand, his jaw tense.

NOVAK: Will?

HARDCASTLE: We can't bring them both back.

NOVAK: Of course we can.

HARDCASTLE: Those things are time bombs. Eventually,
she's going to go off.

NOVAK: She's a toddler, Will.

HARDCASTLE: We don't know what they're capable of. You
really want that in your house? They've gone after their
doubles first, Joy. You want your little girl's throat slit by
a monster with her face?

NOVAK: Will!

HARDCASTLE: The double stays.

KAPOOR: Will, calm down. We can—

She steps toward him. He points the gun toward her.

HARDCASTLE: I've killed you once today, Vanya, and I really don't want to do it again. But I am not bringing that
monster back. I won't be responsible for what it does.

Kapoor lets out an angry hiss of breath, but she doesn't try to get closer. She grips the camera so tightly the whole view shakes, as if by witnessing she can somehow prevent what is happening.

NOVAK: We don't even know which one of them is which.

HARDCASTLE: You do. You know. You're her mother. You *know.*

He swings the gun around and lowers it. It points at one of the girls. Novak makes a startled noise and pushes both girls behind her.

HARDCASTLE: If you don't tell us which one it is, I won't have a choice.

Still she doesn't move.

HARDCASTLE: Okay.

He steps to the side, getting an angle on the nearest girl, and his finger starts to tighten on the trigger. The girls shriek and quail.

NOVAK: No! Don't. I'll tell you. I'll tell you, just don't hurt them.

She crouches down. She makes soothing noises, holding each girl's arm gently. They calm slowly, though one is still crying softly, tears running down her cheeks.

NOVAK: Listen, loves. We can't stay together. I know it's scary, but it's going to be all right.

She pushes up their sleeves. Her fingers run over the bruises on one girl's arm—the bruises from Baker's attack. This is the girl who came home out of the mist, the one who traveled to the headland on the boat. If she was replaced the day she got lost, this is the echo.

NOVAK: The day you were lost and heard the song, you're the one who came home.

The girl nods. She seems the far calmer of the two; the other girl is still whimpering.

NOVAK: She's the echo.

She turns toward the other girl, cups her cheek.

NOVAK: Hush. Stop crying now, little bird. It's going to be okay. Come here.

She hugs Sophia close, stroking her hair.

NOVAK: Auntie Vanya and Uncle William are going to take you home, okay?

KAPOOR: What?

Novak stands.

NOVAK: I'm not leaving my daughter here alone.

HARDCASTLE: She isn't your daughter.

NOVAK: I can't leave her here, Will. I can't. Just . . . get Sophie home safe, okay? Now give me a minute. I need to say goodbye.

The scene that follows holds nothing supernatural, only a raw and terrible grief. A child taken, screaming, from her weeping mother, her cries pure terror and desolation. There is nothing unreal in it, and yet it is the most unnatural, the most horrifying thing the video log has captured.

Time does not run properly in the mist, and it is both seconds and an eternity later that those who are leaving are on board the boat. The motor is running, Hardcastle tending the rudder; Sophia huddles against the side, her tears spent, only the occasional whimper left. Vanya sits at the prow of the boat, the camera on her lap.

HARDCASTLE: Look.

Vanya's coat rustles as she twists in her seat; a moment later she picks up the camera and trains it on the water ahead. There is an end to the mist. The rocky spit that connects the headland to the rest of the island pierces it, offering a guide, a path back to the world they came from. Not one curl of mist touches the mainland. If they can reach the shore to the other side of the yawning bay, they will be safe.

HARDCASTLE: That's it. That's the way out.

He cuts the motor.

KAPOOR: What are you doing?

HARDCASTLE: It's good that Joy isn't here. It'll be easier.

KAPOOR: What will be easier, Will?

HARDCASTLE: We can't be sure. She might have been switched weeks ago. Or it might have been while we were here. We just can't know for certain.

KAPOOR: Joy was sure.

HARDCASTLE: Joy was guessing. This has to be done. Turn off the camera.

He moves forward. Hardcastle lunges forward, grabbing Sophia by the shoulder and hauling her back.

KAPOOR: Don't you dare.

But Hardcastle still has the gun.

HARDCASTLE: Turn off that camera, Vanya. I don't want to hurt you. But I will if I have to. Turn. It. Off.

Three seconds pass in perfect stillness.

Then the recording ends.

26

THE VIDEO WENT black. "I remember," I said softly. "I remember him drowning me."

"And my mum didn't do anything to stop him," Liam said.

"We don't know that," I replied. "She's not one of them, at least. Not an echo."

Complex emotions warring in his expression. Guilt and hope and love and fear—fear at what might lie beyond that blackness, beyond the end of the recording.

I looked up at my echo, standing uncertainly before us. "You've seen this?" I asked her. She nodded. "Abby gave it to you." *Or did you take it from her?* I didn't ask.

"She said. She said bring it," my echo said. The corner of her mouth trembled. "I brought you something else. It's yours. I held it, but I think you need it back."

"What?" I asked, bewildered. "What do you have?"

She beckoned. I stood, leaving the camera with Liam, and approached her warily. She tilted her head, an invitation to come closer. A drop of salt water tracked from her hair and down her cheek. I stepped toward her, and she leaned in, her lips nearly brushing my ear.

"Memory," she whispered—and the ocean roared.

I couldn't breathe. I had no lungs for it, and the water was everywhere, black and cold. I could feel the whole expanse of it, this ocean—the water, the salt, the decay, the life flashing quicksilver through it. The water was ever-changing, and it was constant.

I was drowning, and then I wasn't. The water let me go and I crouched in the bottom of a boat in the dark, watching two giants struggle. Not giants—just people, but I was small. A child. The stars were shimmering back into existence above me, and the boat rocked violently as William Hardcastle threw Vanya Kapoor down. Her head cracked against the bench. She moaned—conscious, but barely. Her eyes fluttered and her hand grasped feebly for Hardcastle. I shrank against the flat stern of the boat as he turned toward me.

We stared at each other. Was this a dream? The cold air biting my cheeks and the press of metal against my back said no. My left eye throbbed with a hot, dull pain.

"Don't," I said in a child's voice, and with the words, the sense of who I was, who I had been in the years between me and this moment, flowed away. I was only Sophia, three years old and terrified, crouched in front of a monster.

"I'm sorry," he said.

He grabbed me by the front of my jacket, fist twisting the fabric. I screamed and kicked, clawed at his arm, but I was nothing next to his bulk. He started to lift me over the side. I thrashed in blind panic, and he dropped me.

My shoulder hit the edge of the boat with a jolt of pain, and then I was in the water. For a moment it closed over me, and then I kicked and my head broke the surface. I grabbed at the only solid thing before me: the white side of the boat. My cold-numbed fingers closed over it. And then he was there again, hands around my wrists, prying my fragile grip free.

"I'm sorry," he said again. "I have to."

He threw me away from the boat. I went under again, the water closing over me, and this time when I kicked, I didn't break the surface. A roar shuddered through the water—the motor. I knew how to hold my breath, my mama had taught me that, how to kick and how to move my arms to swim, but not with my clothes on, and they were so heavy and it was so, so cold—

There were wings in the water. Wings and a song, and a whisper against my ear. *Hush, little bird.*

I rose through the water, carried by unseen arms. The water turned to ice, then turned to wood, and I watched a boat weave itself from nothing into something. I crouched, shivering and afraid, as the ocean lost its grip on me.

A creature hovered in the air before me. Its wings beat slowly, and its empty eyes blazed down at me. I wasn't afraid. Not of that.

Hush, little bird, it whispered. And then it vanished, and so did the memory.

I was in the hallway again. Staring at my reflection who was not a reflection, my wild echo. It wasn't just the memory that she'd given me. I stared at her, knowledge swirling through my mind. She didn't have the words for it, didn't know how to tell me.

I did have the words. And what I knew was terrifying.

"Sophia," Liam said, uncertain.

"I'm all right," I assured him, stepping back. Though I didn't know if I would ever be all right again.

"There's another video," he said. I turned to him, startled. "It's not from 2003. It's from 2018. It's from *today*."

"Abby," I whispered. I glanced at my echo, but she made no move to stop me, so I returned to the bench. "Play it," I told him.

"What if it's . . ."

He didn't want to watch her die, which I understood. I squeezed his shoulder. "We have to see."

He pressed play.

VIDEO EVIDENCE

Recorded by Abigail Ryder

JUNE 30, 2018, TIME UNKNOWN[9]

Abby pants, watching the space beyond the camera. Her lip is split and bloodied.

ABBY: I got away—no. No, it let me go, but I can't figure out why. It told me to run. So I did. I ran. But there's nowhere to run to. There's no way out of here. Sophia was right. There's never just one echo. It's one after the other, and I think I've gone pretty deep.

She shuts her eyes for a moment. Her lips roll under, pressing together until they turn white. A thin whine starts in the back of her throat, and then she takes a gulping, gasping breath.

ABBY: Okay, that's enough. I'm going to keep looking for a way out of here. And in the meantime—in the meantime,

....
9 As in the Novak recordings, time metadata is corrupted.

I'm going to talk to you, little camera of mine, because otherwise I'm just going to start screaming.

She pushes herself to her feet. She turns the camera around, revealing Belaya Skala—or a version of Belaya Skala. The basic landmarks seem to be the same; she is standing near the entrance to the bunker, and at the very edge of the frame, in the distance, are the rough rocks of the isthmus. But in the place of a sky, a second sea seethes overhead, and massive, ropy creatures writhe within it.

ABBY: I should call Sara[10] when I get out of here. I bet she never saw sea monsters in the sky. Okay. Okay. Keep it together. I— Oh, shit.

She steps around a small boulder, revealing a gruesome scene. Dozens of terns lie on the ground in various states of destruction and distress, mangled or half-dissolved into black liquid. Wings flap weakly; claws grasp at the grass; heads flop and glassy eyes stare at the sky. In the center, splayed on his back, is a young man. One leg is bent the wrong way at the knee. His hands curl against his chest, his fingers misshapen. Half his face caved in, reduced to that viscous tar, and more of it oozes from where his skin splits.

Even so, he is recognizable as Liam Kapoor.

ABBY: That is not Liam. That is not Liam, it's an echo.

She draws a step closer. Some of the birds are not just beneath the young man but growing from him, their feathers giving way to flesh, the places where human and bird meet weeping blue-black liquid.

10 Refers to Sara Donohue. See File #74, "The Massachusetts Ghost Road."

LIAM: Abby.

It's not the boy that speaks, but the birds, a wheezing mockery of Liam's voice.

LIAM: Abby, you left me. You left me alone.

His head jerks toward her. One hand splays and grasps, but he can't extend his arms.

ABBY: What's wrong with you?

Liam coughs. His body shakes.

LIAM: We can't—can't—can't—she got inside us. They won't come out right anymore. Abby, it's me. It's Liam. Don't you know me?

His voice is a scream from three dozen throats.

LIAM: Get away from her!

Abby swings around. Sophia—no, Sophie, the echo-girl— stands a few feet away.

SOPHIE: Don't touch him.

ABBY: Wasn't even tempted.

SOPHIE: They come out wrong. Sometimes. More and more.

ABBY: Why? What's happening to him?

Sophie's hands knot together, and she furrows her brow.

SOPHIE: Hard to . . . to say. Explain. I'm not good—I can't . . .

ABBY: Not much of a talker?

Sophie nods.

ABBY: Can you get me out of here?

SOPHIE: No. But . . . a better place. Safe. Maybe. A little while. Harder to find you.

She beckons. Abby hesitates.

LIAM: Sneak thief liar brat bring her back I know she's here.

I see her in this mind. You hid her.

SOPHIE: Please.

ABBY: Yeah. Okay. Between the two of you . . . I'll take the one with the face.

There is a loud shriek and the sound of massive wings beating.

SOPHIE: Hurry!

The video cuts out.

27

LIAM'S FACE WAS pale, gray tones in his brown skin as all the blood drained from it. "It made an echo out of me," he said. "When I touched that black stuff, when I felt like I was getting walled off in my mind, it must have been . . . I don't know. Learning me."

"But something went wrong," I said. I thought of Rivers, the back of his skull caved in. "I don't think it can make echoes the way it used to," I said slowly. "Something's changed."

"You," Liam said. "It's all been about you. Both of you." He looked at my echo. She shrank back under his gaze, eyes fixed on her hands, which she twisted around each other with a whisper of skin against skin.

"Because I'm—we're—like Abby said. Attuned. *Special*." I spat out the word. "I'm what the Six-Wing has been looking for since it came to this place, but it lost me." I shook my head in frustration. "We still don't know how I survived. I remember drowning. I remember *Hardcastle* drowning me. But Mikhail found me in a boat— What boat? Where did it come from?"

A door banged open down the hall, and we jumped. A moment later Dr. Kapoor came striding into view, Kenny trailing. "What the hell is going on here?" Dr. Kapoor demanded. Kenny halted, gaping at my echo.

"What are *you* doing here?" Liam demanded. He put himself between us and her. *That's sweet of you,* I thought inanely.

"I went to find you, before the mist," Dr. Kapoor said. "You weren't at Mrs. Popova's, and you weren't at home. The echoes are everywhere out there, and when I heard the gunshot . . ." She took a sharp breath. "But you're all in one piece."

"For now," I said. "You locked the door, right?"

"Yes, much to the consternation of those creatures out there." Dr. Kapoor said.

Mrs. Popova returned then, and she and Dr. Kapoor shared only a brief glance as greeting. "Everything's secure," Mrs. Popova said.

I swallowed against the taste of seawater. "What happened on Belaya Skala?" I asked Dr. Kapoor. I held up the video camera, and her eyes widened. "I remember you tried to stop him when he drowned me, but I don't remember how I survived."

She stared at me. And then she shut her eyes. "I knew we wouldn't be able to hide from it forever. And I knew that I hadn't done nearly enough to make up for . . ."

"At least you tried," I said.

"And then I let him bury it," she growled. Her hands balled into fists at her sides. "I helped hide all of this, because I was afraid of what it meant and I was afraid of what I'd done. When we got back, Dr. Breckenridge explained everything to us—that Theresa Landon founded the LARC to watch the island, not just the birds, and to try to find a way to destroy what her husband had worshiped. That is the work."

"That's what you're trying to do with the sound equipment?" I asked.

She nodded. She had the same stiff posture as when she'd lectured me about counting chicks. "It was the military that realized the birds could travel into the echo worlds. And there was the song. They theorized it was sound frequencies that let the birds navigate, slip through. And those same frequencies bind the echo worlds together, bind them to this one. We thought if we could find the right frequency, we could create enough interference that the link would be severed. The bridge between the worlds would collapse."

"Okay, hold on," Kenny said. "Can someone please tell me what you're all talking about? This sounds bonkers."

"It's a really long story," I said.

"There's a fucked-up supernatural world on the islands full of evil doubles of everyone here and a big fuck-off evil angel, and they want Sophia for some reason," Liam rattled off.

"Decent summary," Mrs. Popova noted, a touch amused.

"Oh. Huh," Kenny said. I gave him an incredulous look. He spread his hands. "It explains a lot, you know? Everyone knows that island's haunted."

"I know why it wants me," I said. I glanced at Sophie, but she had shrunk back. She didn't have the words, so I would explain for her. "Abby told me there are people who are attuned to other worlds. The Six-Wing needed someone that was attuned to *its* world. To make an echo of. There's a connection between us, the same kind of bridge that links the echo worlds to ours, and to the Six-Wing's world."

"You're like a tuning fork," Dr. Kapoor said. "The birds have learned to mimic the echo's song, but it's in your *bones*. You do it without thinking. If you strike the right note, you'll make the link between the worlds strong enough that the Seraph—the *true* Six-Wing, the Eidolon beyond the gate—can wrench open its prison and step into our world."

"Then why let me come?" I asked. "You knew who I was."

"We haven't been able to find the exact frequency we needed," Dr. Kapoor said. "I thought if I could get you and Sophie in the same place, I might be able to isolate it. I knew it was a gamble, but . . ."

"But the echo worlds are expanding. At first they only touched Belaya Skala, and then all of Bitter Rock. By now they extend into the ocean. They'll reach the mainland soon. People will die," Mrs. Popova said.

"It was a hell of a risk," I said.

"The Six-Wing can't control Sophie. It can't see inside her mind. I knew we'd have time before it realized you were here," Dr. Kapoor replied.

"But it made an echo out of Liam. It saw inside *his* mind. It saw who I was," I said. "That's why the echoes are attacking. It's coming for me."

This was bigger than filling in the mystery of my past; bigger than finding Abby; bigger, even, than finding my mother, that lonely voice echoing down the corridors of my memory.

"I've done what I can to help. All these years—" Dr. Kapoor said, and anger flared through me. All these years, she'd sat and fiddled with her equipment and kept her secrets. She'd kept the secret that had poisoned this island, had preyed on it. That had destroyed my life.

The rage was like a storm, but there was no point in being angry at Dr. Kapoor for what she had or hadn't done—I had to focus on what came next. And so I pushed that anger away. Into the void.

And my echo's lips peeled back from her teeth. She let out an angry growl and rocked forward, digging her fingers roughly into her upper arms. Her eyes, the whites showing starkly around her irises, met mine, and a fraction of my anger washed back into me.

"Oh," I whispered. "Oh, I'm sorry. I'm so sorry."

The anger ebbed. She made a mewling sound and drew back against the wall, pulling in on herself.

She'd borne it all. All my anger, all my fear. It hadn't been an empty, uncaring void that held my rage and terror for me. It was *her.*

"I'm sorry," I said again. But she shook her head, as if it didn't matter.

"It's all right. Because you've come back," my echo said. "You've come back and now it ends, but how it ends, we don't know."

I could see my reflection in her eyes. My true reflection, mirrored as it should be. And I knew, from the faint vibration in my bones, that I could slip as easily into that other world as I could step through a doorway. "We'll end it," I told her.

"What if we can't?" she asked.

"Then we can't," I replied. I took her hand and helped her up.

One of us was real.

One of us was the echo.

One of us had been saved.

One of us had been abandoned.

But was I the real girl? Or was she? And was the abandoned child the one who had stayed in the echo, her mother's arms around her, or the one cast out on the sea?

Neither of us had chosen our beginning or the shape of our lives. But we could choose an ending.

"What do we do?" Liam asked.

"I—" I said. I was uncertain. And yet I felt the answer, a lump in my chest waiting to force its way out, the way I had answered Lily without knowing how. I had known the answers because my echo did. *Sophie*, I thought. She called herself Sophie, not Sophia. She might have aged, stayed the perfect reflection of me, but time didn't pass in the echo world. She was still Sophie. Still the child left behind.

We were connected. I knew the things that she knew. And then, standing there with our hands linked, reflected in one another's eyes, I remembered.

28

"PLEASE," I SAID. The girl with the camera was afraid but trying not to show it. There was a ghost with her, but she couldn't see it. It shimmered beneath her skin, haunting her, but the sunlight would not let it breathe and be.

"Yeah. Okay. Between the two of you . . . I'll take the one with the face," said the girl.

The screaming came across the hills, chased swiftly by the thunder of the angel's wings. It was a gift and a warning, and it meant we had little time. "Hurry!" I cried.

She was a clumsy thing, scrabbling over rocks and catching herself on her palms when she stumbled. But she followed. Not toward the traps: the throat of the bunker, with only one way in and one way out, or the church, the false haven where the angel watched. I brought her toward the north, where the birds roosted. The cliffs were silent now; the birds tended their young beyond the echo, where the persistent sun would let them grow.

We were nearly there when she fell. I grabbed for her, caught her wrist, but the camera tumbled from her hand and skidded down the side of the hill. She lunged for it. "No!" I told her. "No time." We were almost to the cliffs. We were almost safe.

"I have to get it back," she said.

"You'll die."

She gave me a vicious, wild look. She wasn't afraid of death. More than that. She thought she'd earned it.

"She'll be lost," I told her, desperate.

"Who?" she demanded.

"The girl in your bones," I told her. "It will drink her down."

"What girl?" She shook her head in confusion.

"She's shining in you," I said. "She never let you go."

"My sister. Miranda," she whispered. The kind of love that shone like that, you wouldn't mistake. She ran with me, over the gray rock to the white, and I led her along the foot-wide track that hugged the bluff.

"These rocks," she said. "They're—salt? Why? Is it some kind of—" She stopped as I turned to look at her. "There isn't a reason, is there?"

"There is," I said. "But I don't know . . ." I waved my hands. I didn't know how to tell her that the angel feared the touch of salt, and feared this place, and so this place was salt. That the angel feared this place *because* it was salt. That both of these things were true, because cause and effect were the snake devouring its own tail, the bird laying the egg from which it hatched.

The birds flocked here because the angel feared it. The angel feared it because the birds flocked here. The thing and its reflection. Who could say which was which?

The screeching came again. Closer now, but we were almost safe. "Here," I said, and I stepped into the cliff face, into the crack where white against white concealed a passage just wide enough for a single slender figure. The girl had more trouble with it, scraping her back and her hips as she negotiated her passage. But then she was through.

My home: a cave, carved from the salt with rocks and broken shells and fingernails, a centimeter scratched out at a time over the years. We stood in the first chamber, littered with the detritus of my wounded life. A broken chair brought over from the LARC. The wooden birds Uncle Misha gave me every winter. Bits and pieces I'd stolen from other people, other lives.

I'd never shown it to anyone before. I looked at her expectantly. The light from the passage was enough for me to see her wobbly smile.

"It's . . . nice," she said.

Outside, the angel screeched again. This time it was not the warning sound, but the red sound, the rage sound. The girl flinched.

"Safe," I told her. I took her hands and walked her to the chair, sat her down in it. "Safe."

"What is this place?" she asked.

"Home," I said. "It doesn't come here."

"You brought her." The voice was dry and rasping. The girl's eyes widened. *"I want to see her."* The girl stood, looking toward the back. Toward the second room, toward the shadows from which the voice came.

"It's all right," I told her.

"*Come closer.*"

The girl swallowed and walked toward the voice. I remained, sitting on the salt of the floor, biting my thumb hard enough to hurt. The girl crept closer and closer to the dark. She cast one last look over her shoulder at me, and then vanished within the second chamber, out of the reach of the light. I wrapped my arms around my knees.

I did not go into the dark anymore. My fingertips were still scarred from the effort of clawing out the salt of the walls, digging a space where the light would never touch.

It was impossible to say how long the girl was back there. This was not a place where time found purchase. But when she emerged, she looked pale, and she wetted her lips several times before she spoke.

"She told me what's happening. That this world is going to spread. That that thing—the Six-Wing?—is going to use you and Sophia to do it. And every person in the world will suffer."

"Not just people," I said. I trailed my fingers along the salt, sending loose grains skittering. The words were in my chest, a recitation, mimicry giving me more eloquence than I possessed. "Magpies hold funerals for their dead. An albatross flies ten thousand lonely miles and never forgets its mate. We are not the only ones that would be mourned."

I wished the words were mine. I wished I had words to put to all the thoughts that flew in a great murmuration through me, but I had trouble holding on to spoken things. I had only pieces of them, the trailing edge of echoes.

"She told me what I have to do," the girl said. "And she said that you have to bring Sophia here, and then we can try. I can go with you. Help you."

I shook my head. "You stay. Safe."

"You won't be."

"Stay with her," I insisted. "It's not good alone."

She looked back over her shoulder. Bit her lip. "I'll stay," she promised me. "Until you get back, I'll stay."

I padded away, the salt scraping at the soles of my feet. She didn't follow as I slipped back out into the sunlight.

Two terns had fallen through the echoes to this one, and they glided lazily out over the water. That meant the mist was rising, in the other world, the barriers grown thin. It was time to go.

29

SOPHIE SQUEEZED MY hand. She looked grateful, and I understood why—she didn't have the words to tell us what had happened or what we had to do, but I did. She could use my words, and I could use her memory, and together we were almost whole.

"Abby is still alive, or she was a few hours ago," I said. "She's with—" I swallowed. The voice in the dark. I remembered scraping at the salt to make that room. I remembered her voice. But Sophie had walled off the memory of the sight of her, and I didn't know why. "She's with my mother. They can help us get into the echo, as deep as we can go, and then we can close it. Sophie and I."

"How do you know all of that?" Dr. Kapoor asked. "Some kind of psychic transference?"

"We're the same person, sort of," I said. "We can remember each other's lives." Our memories bled into each other. And now I knew why I had so often woken with the taste of salt on my lips, why every rock on this island felt so familiar.

"The mist will fade soon," Dr. Kapoor said. "Getting over the water should be easy enough. Can you get us into the echo world?"

I met Sophie's eyes, the image of myself reflected in them. "Yes," I said.

"We should move quickly," Mrs. Popova said. "Mist's gone."

"How can you tell?" I asked. We weren't near any windows.

"You get so you can feel it," she told me. "The Visitors don't linger after the mist leaves. Or at least they haven't before, but things that have held constant for a hundred years have gone haywire with you here, so who the fuck knows." Mrs. Popova was Very Done With This Shit.

"You can stay here," I said. "You've done enough."

"It should be safe in the LARC," Dr. Kapoor said. "Liam, you'll stay with Mrs. Popova."

"No way," Liam said. "I'm going."

"You are not," Dr. Kapoor said. "I shouldn't have let your mother leave you here in the first place. I don't know what I was thinking."

"I'm eighteen," Liam said. "I don't need your permission. If you want to stop me, you're going to have to tie me up."

Dr. Kapoor looked like she was very willing to do just that, but Mrs. Popova grunted. "No one's safe. Here or there," she said. "And he's got a part in this whether you like it or not."

Dr. Kapoor nodded reluctantly. I was still holding Sophie's hand. She had a distant look on her face. "We need to hurry," she said. "He's gathering his strength. He'll be able to send them through again soon."

Which meant the mist would come, and the Visitors with it. "We can head straight to the dock," I said.

"The *Katydid*'s down there," Kenny confirmed. "We can be over in no time."

"Who's 'we'?" Dr. Kapoor asked.

"Lily vanished over there. So that's where we should be looking," Kenny said.

Guilt went through me like a fishhook. "Lily's dead," I said. "I'm sorry."

"You—you're sure?" he asked, holding on to hope with every bit of strength he had.

It broke my heart to tear it from him. "Yes," I said. "She's gone. I saw her die."

His face crumpled. He looked away and seemed for a moment unable to breathe. Dr. Kapoor put a hand on his shoulder. It was the most tender gesture I'd seen from her.

"Stay here," she said. "If we don't make it back, you can still get help. Warn people."

I wasn't sure what good that would do. But I was glad when Kenny nodded. He'd be safe—or safer than us, at least. It was something.

"I need to go back for Mikhail," Mrs. Popova said.

But Sophie caught my hand, and I knew. "He's dead," I said, grieving for a man I hardly knew.

"You're certain," Mrs. Popova said sharply.

Sophie stepped forward, addressing Mrs. Popova directly. "I saw," Sophie said. "He's gone. The Warden too." Her voice was utterly calm. I might have thought she felt nothing at all if I weren't feeling it for her. Sorrow so deep I didn't know how I would ever find the bottom or break the surface.

"Sophia?" Liam said, and I realized there were tears running down my cheeks.

"I'm all right," I whispered. "It isn't mine."

Sophie couldn't survive her sorrow, and so for her, I wept.

We went down to the shore together, the three of us, Kenny and Mrs. Popova safely within the fortress of the LARC.

"I want to be clear about something," Dr. Kapoor said, fixing Liam with a steely glare. "You survive, or I will kill you myself. I don't care if the whole world drowns."

He gaped but nodded. And I ached. I ached because of what the island had taken from us both—that love, that ferocious love. He'd lost her to the island—not completely, not the way I'd lost my mother, but he'd lost her just the same.

"Okay. Let's—" Dr. Kapoor continued, but she didn't get to finish.

"What do you think you're doing, Vanya?"

Sophie gasped, shrinking back, and my breath stopped in my throat, the world spinning around me as Dr. Hardcastle strode toward us, fury in his face.

I'm sorry, he'd said. Sorry. Like it mattered. Like it could remove even the slightest bit of evil from the act. Sophie's fear and mine crashed together and turned to rage. This man—this man had stranded our mother. Had left her behind and he had promised, he had *promised her* that he would keep her daughter safe, and he had lied.

He had left us on the shore. He had cast us in the cold water. And all he'd said was *sorry*.

The rage filled us both. There was nowhere for it to go. But I—I had lived my life among people. Among rules and society. I knew how to swallow it down. Sophie didn't.

He saw us, *both* of us, and his eyes widened. Was he afraid in that moment? I hope so.

Sophie screamed and threw herself at him. If she'd had a weapon, she would have killed him. She had her fists, though, and her nails, and she flew at him, all fury and agony. Her nails raked his cheek. He yelled in pain and caught her by the wrist. She thrashed, kicked at him, but however much strength her anger gave her, he was still bigger than her, still stronger. He spun her against him and wrapped his arms in a bear hug around her, hands grasping her wrists so all she could do was scream and struggle against him, her hair a ragged veil over her face.

"Aren't any of you going to do something?" he demanded. "This thing—"

"She is not a *thing*," I screamed at him. I grabbed at his arm. "Let her go!"

"Jesus. You're her," he said. "You don't understand. These creatures are dangerous."

"Let her go, Will," Dr. Kapoor said.

He made a noise in the back of his throat, like a scoff, and threw Sophie free of him. She hit the pebbled ground and rolled, scrambling upright to sit, panting, her teeth bared. I ran to her, wrapped my arms around her for both comfort and restraint. I couldn't push my fear away, or my anger, because it would only flow into her. I had to let it submerge me.

And I had to keep going anyway.

I pressed my brow against her hair. "It's all right," I told her.

"He hurt us," she whispered. She shook, and I felt it through my whole body.

I watched the boat vanishing into the fog as my mother wrapped her arms around me and a shriek tore through the air. I felt the cold shock of the water as he flung me away. I remembered a monster.

I stood. "You deserve so many things," I told him. Contempt turned every word to acid, and I relished the way it burned my lips, my tongue. "You deserve to be hurt. Maybe you deserve to die. God knows you deserve to be afraid. But you don't deserve to have one bit of power over me. You don't deserve one more moment of fear or anger. I will not give it to you. And I will not let you keep us from what we have to do. Stay here and rot. You don't matter. You are *nothing*."

His face contorted: rage first. Then contempt. Then—desolation. He looked as if he wanted me to scream at him and strike at him, because if I hated him for what he'd done, it would save him from having to do it himself.

Sophie pulled herself to her feet, clinging to my hand. "He needs to be punished," she hissed at me.

"Yes," I said. "But we can't wait around to do it. Don't let him take anything else from us."

She took three short, sharp breaths between her teeth, her hand gripping mine tight enough to hurt. Then she nodded.

We left him there on the shore. We made for Belaya Skala.

PART FIVE

ALL WHICH IT INHERIT, SHALL DISSOLVE

VIDEO EVIDENCE

Recorded by Sophia Novak

JUNE 30, 2018, 9:16 PM

The island is calm. Almost inert. A gentle breeze stirs the air, and a few birds tilt in gentle crescents above the island, but otherwise there is only the scrape of the skiff against the rocks to break the stillness. But it is the kind of stillness that promises a storm. Sophia, holding the phone that is recording the video, steps out onto the shore. Liam hops out after her.

LIAM: What are you doing?

SOPHIA: Abby would want us to record this. She's putting herself in danger for us. It seems like the least we can do in return.

LIAM: Plus, if we don't make it out . . .

SOPHIA: Yeah.

SOPHIE: It knows we're coming.

*The girl, fey and wild, her callused feet bare and dirty, looks off
     toward the peak of the headland.*

SOPHIE: It will come for us.

KAPOOR: Then we'd better hurry.

*She unlocks a long storage chest at the back of the boat and
     extracts a pair of shotguns, along with a box of ammunition.*

KAPOOR: Right. Any of you know how to use these?

SOPHIA: No?

KAPOOR: Well, all right, then. More for me.

*She slings one strap over her shoulder and carries the other
     shotgun in the crook of her arm.*

LIAM: You have shotguns?

KAPOOR: This island is overrun with monsters. Of course
     I have shotguns. There's a gun in almost every room of
     the LARC, if you know where to look. I have a goddamn
     machete under my bed. I have been coming to this island
     for fifteen years and I do not fuck around. Now. Where
     are we going?

Sophie points up the hill.

KAPOOR: Bunker, then. Good. I'll lead the way.

*She sets off at a march, and the others fall in behind. The climb
     up the flank of the headland is uneventful, and though So-
     phia diligently keeps the camera focused on the procession,
     there is nothing out of place until they have nearly reached
     the bunker.*

LIAM: What was that? Did you hear it? I think it was a voice.

SOPHIA: The mist is coming.

KAPOOR: Are you sure?

SOPHIA: The air shimmers before it comes.

KAPOOR: I don't see any shimmering.

LIAM: She's right. Look.

He points. Mist creeps from behind the hill, rolling southward.

KAPOOR: Let's get moving!

They sprint for the bunker. Shadows dart and dash in the mist as it races toward them. They reach the door. Liam gets hold of the handle, hauls.

LIAM: It's welded shut again. How is that possible? We came through it—

SOPHIA: You were already in an echo when you went through. Just a very faint one. We need to cross over before we can get in. Here.

She hands Liam the phone and turns to Sophie. The girls take each other's hands.

KAPOOR: Whatever you're going to do, do it quickly.

The mist rolls over them. Within it, a dozen voices whisper eagerly, and footsteps draw close.

30

WE HELD HANDS, my echo and I, and I looked into her eyes. I saw her and saw my reflection. The air hummed around us. I could feel every echo in my bones, a different frequency for every distorted version of the world.

"Sophia!" Dr. Kapoor yelled. "They're here!"

"Now," Sophie whispered, and through her I saw what to do. How to take the sound that sang in our bones and amplify it, weave it around the others. We fell through the echoes as the world grew stranger around us, bones growing from the earth, strange flowers bursting from the rock, the sea glazing over with ice and then shattering again.

And suddenly we came to a shuddering stop, both of us gasping, gathered in a stand of trees the color of bone, weeping red sap, branches drooping with swollen fruit.

"This one's different," Liam said. "How can this be so different than the places we've seen before?"

"There are many," Sophie said. "They aren't all real at once." She looked at me helplessly, her words failing her, and I stared at her, trying to put her knowledge into words.

"There are hundreds and hundreds of layers of the echo world," I said slowly. "But most of the time they're sort of— collapsed into each other. They only become real enough to exist in when you . . . well, when you exist in them already. You don't always notice when you fall out of one and into another, but to get to the last one—or rather, the *first* one—you always have to go through there."

I pointed at the bunker. It was where it always was, in every echo. I wondered what had been there before the bunker was built, in the real world. The Six-Wing, and the echo world by extension, had seized on it and embedded it right into the center of this mad architecture.

The door in this echo was made of the same bone-white wood as the trees, and the red sap had dried over it in rivulets that looked disturbingly like veins. Liam hauled it open, revealing the dark corridor beyond, the familiar doors to the left and right. Inside, the bunker looked perfectly normal. It was the connective tissue between all the different echoes. We fumbled with flashlights for a moment.

"Hello?" a voice called.

We whirled around. Dr. Kapoor half raised her shotgun.

"That was Lily," Liam said.

"Lily's dead," I said.

"I know," Liam said. "I know that." And yet he was peering into the mist, something almost as solid as hope in his gaze. Could there be any way—?

"It's a trick," Dr. Kapoor said. "It makes copies, that's all."

"Not anymore," Sophie said. She twisted her hands together. "They come out wrong. They all come out wrong."

"Liam?" Lily called. "Sophia?" She came closer with staggering, lurching steps. There was something wrong about her silhouette in the mist. Something misshapen. "Help me. I got away, but I—" She coughed, whined.

The indistinct outline of her body was solidifying, the shape of her clearer. There was movement where there shouldn't be, something jerking and tugging at her side while her head lolled to the left. "Please," Lily called.

"You don't want to see," Sophie said. She retreated back toward the bunker.

Liam let out a breath, the not-quite-hope extinguished. He followed Sophie.

The thing in the mist screamed. It threw itself forward, racing along on all fours, its grotesquely lengthening arms pulling it along the ground faster than we could react. It leapt from the mist and straight for Liam, its limbs streaked with purplish veins like a blood infection.

It had Lily's face, but it was wrenched to the side, her neck crooked and a tumorous wing bulging from it. Slashes and open sores covered her body as if she'd tried to slice the traitorous growths from her skin.

I didn't think—I just threw myself in her way. She struck me and we toppled to the ground, her hair stringy, her mouth a razor-slash of a smile, too full of teeth. She had one arm around my neck before I could react, and then she was pulling us both back into the trees, scuttling crab-like on limbs that bent wrong and reached too far.

The others screamed. I caught a glimpse of the shotgun muzzle and Dr. Kapoor's furious eyes, but the Lily-thing held me between her and the gun, and then we were vanishing into the mist.

"Where'd they go?" I heard Dr. Kapoor demand. "Did you see?"

The forest was a maze of mist and identical trees. I twisted, tried to pull free, but she held me tight, cooing softly against my cheek.

"One to bring and one more to fetch. Even broken dolls have uses, and I'm oh-so useful now," she whispered, and her tongue darted out, scraping my face with a quick cat's-tongue rasp.

I tried to scream. Tried to *breathe*. But there wasn't enough air in my lungs—

Water closing over me, darkness rushing in—

She charged out of the mist, half-blind—Dr. Kapoor, wielding the shotgun like a club, slamming it into the Lily-creature's elbow. I heard bone crack. Her grip went slack. I rolled free, gasping, and then came the blast, so loud I heard nothing else but ringing as I clawed my way upright, surging to my feet. I staggered, but Dr. Kapoor grabbed my elbow, steadying me.

I didn't look down. Didn't want to see. The ringing in my ears faded.

"Are you all right? In one piece?" Dr. Kapoor asked. The brisk efficiency of her voice was belied by the worry in her eyes.

"I'm okay," I said, though with the adrenaline coursing through me I couldn't feel my body enough to be sure if it was true.

"Let's get—" Dr. Kapoor began, but she didn't finish.

"Help me." Lily's voice. Lily's shadow, off to the left.

"Please." Lily again—but this one was off to the right, this form tall, like it had been seized and stretched by some great hand.

"Help," she called, her voice garbled with the clamoring of birds, her figure a swarm of shadows approaching from straight ahead—a woman at the center with demented creatures flapping crookedly around her.

And there were more. They were everywhere.

"Get back to the bunker," Dr. Kapoor said calmly. "Run and don't look back."

"You're not coming?"

"Maybe I am. Maybe I'm not. But you're not going to wait for me. Clear?" Dr. Kapoor said in the same even tone she used to instruct me in how to fill a spreadsheet properly.

The Lily to the left lurched forward. The blast of the shotgun made my ears ring. The figure dropped with a wet thud. But there were more shadows, more voices, pleading and whimpering and calling.

"Now," Dr. Kapoor commanded, and I obeyed.

I ran through the mist, through the trees, following the thread that ran between my heart and Sophie's. I didn't need to know the way to the bunker, because I knew the way to her. I'd always known the way back to her, but I hadn't understood.

I burst from the mist to find Sophie and Liam waiting at the bunker door. The shotgun roared behind me; the mist lit up. Then again. "Where's my mum?" Liam demanded.

"She said not to wait," I told him, shaking my head helplessly. He leaned forward, as if to run out after her.

"Sophia," someone called. Not Lily this time. Some other voice, some other throat—the voice was a stranger's, but they knew my name. It came from behind us, from up over the hill.

"Sophie, Sophia," another voice sang.

"We have to go," Sophie whispered.

"My mum's still out there," Liam said.

"We can't wait," I said. I had always been good at making people do what I wanted them to, what I needed them to.

Liam nodded. He stepped inside the bunker.

The echoes were coming. I looked again toward the trees, in the direction of the shotgun blasts. Rocks skittered down from the hill up above.

I tore myself away, plunged back into the mouth of the bunker, and slammed the door shut behind me. On the inside, the door was the more familiar steel, and I threw the lock, fighting with the rusted mechanism. Bodies slammed against the outside, gibbering and cackling.

Distantly, a muffled shotgun blast rang out.

Liam slid down into a crouch, fingers digging into his scalp. I knelt next to him, but I wasn't sure what I should do. Touch him? Tell him it was okay? I'd never really been close enough to someone to offer comfort. I didn't know how it was supposed to go.

"A few hours ago I thought she was the enemy," he said. "Now she's gone before I—"

"She's not gone," I said fiercely. "You'll see."

"I thought you were done lying to me," he said. I flinched away, the hand I had raised, almost touching him, curling against my belly instead. And then, aware of the process in a way I had rarely been before, I felt myself step away from what I felt—not fear or distress this time, but what I felt for Liam. Because it was too strange and too immense. Because I didn't know what to do with caring for someone so intensely and suddenly, and I couldn't help his pain if I was lost in it with him.

Sophie took in a sharp breath, but she caught my eye. She could carry that awhile for me.

"Listen," I said, without the weight of grief to dull the words. "If anyone can survive out there, it's your mom. And she's got the guns. She'll make it, and she'll find a way out. She's done it before. But we can't let worrying slow us down. Do you understand?"

He looked at me with hatred in his eyes. But the part of me that cared was safely guarded, safely tucked away in Sophie's heart. And then the hatred softened back into sorrow as he cast away his misplaced anger. I took his hand and helped him to his feet, and if he didn't quite meet my eyes, he at least wasn't glaring poison at me anymore.

A footstep scraped behind us. I jumped—and then I laughed in sheer relief and joy.

Abby.

"Hey, guys," she said. She stepped forward into the light of our flashlights. "What did I miss?"

VIDEO EVIDENCE

Recorded by Sophia Novak

JUNE 30, 2018, TIME UNKNOWN

Abby drops down to one knee at the top of the stairs. From her pocket, she pulls out a pale crystal and brushes white dust from it. Salt, perhaps. She sets it on the top step, and then opens a small knife. She cuts the side of her hand, letting the blood drip onto the crystal.

ABBY: An anchor. It should hold a little while.

Abby starts down the stairs. Footsteps ring on the metal steps.

LIAM: Where are you taking us?

SOPHIA: To my mother. Right?

Abby stops. She half turns and looks at Sophia, and perhaps it is the light of the flashlights, but she looks weary and worn, as if she's spent a month in this place, not a day.

ABBY: She isn't what she was, Sophia. This place has changed her.

SOPHIA: But she's alive.

Her voice breaks on the word. As if it's a dangerous notion to voice. Abby looks grim.

ABBY: I don't know if that's the right word for it.

She continues down the stairs. At every landing she stops and sets out another crystal, and relinquishes another measure of blood.

Abby begins to pant, as if from exertion, though their pace is not strenuous.

SOPHIA: Are you okay?

ABBY: Something's wrong. We should have reached the bottom by now.

LIAM: Do you hear that? Someone's singing.

SOPHIE: It's coming. It's found us.

Metal creaks above them. Sophia trains the camera on the dark above, and the flashlights shine along the underside of the metal steps. Down the walls comes a rush of dark mold.

ABBY: Come on!

They clatter down the stairs, but only keep going down and down and down.

ABBY: The blood and the salt. It's supposed to keep the way open. Keep it the same. It isn't . . . it isn't working. The Six-Wing isn't supposed to be able to stop us like this, but—

SOPHIE: Living blood. It requires living blood.

ABBY. Sorry, do you know something I don't? Because I don't remember dying.

SOPHIE: No. But you carry the dead. You're haunted.

LIAM: Aren't we all?

ABBY: This is no time for poetry, Harry Potter.

LIAM: Harry Potter? Is that seriously the only British thing you can think of?

ABBY: Fish and chips. Bangers and mash.

SOPHIA: Can you two stop bickering for one minute?

ABBY: I don't know what to do.

Something clatters and bangs against the walls up above. Sophie looks up.

SOPHIE: You go. I stay. I can make it let you go for a little while. Long enough.

SOPHIA: Wait a minute. You aren't giving yourself to that thing!

LIAM: Guys?

SOPHIE: It won't hurt me. Not yet.

LIAM: Guys!

They whip around. Their flashlights converge on the landing above. It should bathe the whole landing in light, but the figure there defies illumination. Its edges are like ink dropped into water, dissolving without ever losing its substance. Its body is human in outline, but it is like an absence in the world. Its wings are half-folded, all six of them, made of the same black void as the rest of the being. The image stutters, flickering back and forth like a digital glitch. Not quite there, not quite here.

Sophie steps toward it.

SOPHIA: Sophie, no—

She snatches for Sophie's hand, but Sophie steps smoothly out of reach, walking calmly up the steps toward the creature. She stretches out her hands, murmuring something the microphone doesn't quite catch. The creature retreats a step, the movement uncertain.

SOPHIE: It's all right. It's what must happen.

She looks over her shoulder. There is fear in her eyes, but determination too.

SOPHIE: Go. Find Mother. I'll be ready.

The creature of shadow and void spreads its wings, and leaps upon her. Sophie screams, her calm torn away, but before Sophia or anyone else can move to help her, they are gone— the Six-Wing, the echo-girl, even the mold that covered the walls moments ago.

All that remains is the distant sound of wings.

31

I SHUT MY eyes, not to block out the image of what had just happened, but to focus. There—Sophie was there. The sense of her. The *sensations* of her, her heartbeat quick, mouth sour with adrenaline. Alive, and not in pain, and not afraid—or not *only* afraid, a storm of other feelings clashing within her, too chaotic to tease apart or interpret.

It's okay, she'd told that thing, like she was *comforting* it. What did that mean?

Meanwhile, the stones were screaming.

It was a tortured sound, more tearing than grinding, and we clapped our hands over our ears as it went on and on and on. The walls buckled. The stairs collapsed into each other like a twisting kaleidoscope, and then everything snapped into brutal focus. The Six-Wing's hold relinquished, the stairs led down, as they should, to a concrete floor, to a steel door.

Abby lurched down the last few steps and to the concrete floor. Her knees buckled. She caught herself in a crouch, and Liam rushed to help her back to her feet. Her skin was the same gray as the walls around us, her lips pale and cracked.

Alive, I told myself, looking upward into the dark. *Alive. Stay that way*, I willed my echo.

"I'm good," Abby said, pulling free of Liam's support. She wavered, but stayed upright, and held up a warning hand when he started to reach out to her again. Oil and water still.

I set my hand against the steel door handle. Something soft and wet gave beneath my fingers, but I suppressed my shudder and shoved the door open, revealing the round room. *The memory room*, I'd called it when Lily asked me what lay beyond, and now I understood why. They were her memories, of course. Sophie's. Even her handprints, here and there, growing from the soft, pudgy hand of a toddler to the long, slender fingers of the gaunt girl I knew.

God, what had her life been? Wandering through this tortured world? Had she seen glimpses of my life in her dreams, the way I'd seen hers? No one aged here, but she did, tugged along in the river of time by my passage through it.

"Like Orpheus into the underworld," Liam quipped. "I hope we can sing sweetly enough for Hades."

"You are such a nerd," Abby wheezed. She jerked her chin toward the tunnel. "That way."

It was the *only* way, but someone still needed to say it, or we would have stood forever in that round room. We walked single file, and while we had to squeeze through a few narrower spots, we made it through—through to the last door, set in stone the color of a corpse.

Outside, everything was the same color. The sea, the sky, the stone. Not one blade of grass grew. This whole island was a grave. And it was the nearest thing to the world the Six-Wing wanted to unleash.

"This way," Abby said, setting out. Liam took my hand. I looked at him, startled.

"I'm sorry," he said. Sorry for the hatred in his eyes before. But he didn't need to apologize. He didn't have an echo to bear the horrible things that thrashed and snarled within him. He had to tame them himself. I was the lucky one.

But now I was alone.

Abby led us to the white rocks, along the track worn smooth by years of Sophie's passage. It was a miracle that she'd survived. A miracle that she'd stayed sane—or mostly sane.

I reached for my flashlight, but Abby put a restraining hand on my wrist. "We'll wait out here," she said. Not understanding, but unwilling to disobey, I handed her my flashlight and faced the shadows of the second chamber. I remembered this place. I remembered her voice. But I couldn't remember the sight of her. Her face. Her touch. Sophie had hidden those from me, and I was afraid to find out why.

"It's . . ." Abby began. *It's okay*, maybe. But it would have been a lie, I could see that in her face. "It's bad," she said instead. "But she's still her. And she's been waiting for you." Liam met my eyes, and it was as warm as if he'd wrapped his arms around me.

This is what I'd come here for. And so I walked into the dark.

The angle of the walls almost completely blocked the light from outside from reaching the small space. Only the light that reflected off the white walls managed to filter in, and as my eyes adjusted, I could make out the contours of the room. The craggy walls. The low ceiling that I had to duck to avoid. And the form at the back of the room, against the wall, sitting with her knees to one side, arms limp at her back, head hanging low.

"*Sophia*," she said. Her voice was the hiss of the tide across a forgotten beach. "You came back." She lifted her face. Her hair hung in stringy, stiff sections around it, and salt tracked down her cheeks, the accumulation of a lifetime's tears.

"I came for you," I whispered. She looked skeletal. She wasn't just leaning against the salt wall—it had grown over her, turning her clothing into firm plates like armor, coating her skin, which was red and raw beneath.

But she was my mother. She was the face I saw when I closed my eyes. I had always wondered if that face was a real memory, or if it was a composite of pictures and stories and imagination, but here she was in front of me and it didn't matter.

"I'm sorry," she whispered. "I'm sorry I couldn't go with you."

"You had to protect Sophie," I said. "I know that now."

She reached for me, but I was too far away. I hesitated—hesitated just for a moment, staring at that salt-rimed skin, those sunken eyes, those brittle limbs. Her face crumpled. "You're afraid," she said despairingly.

"Yes," I said. My voice broke. "I'm afraid. I'm afraid of this place. I'm afraid of what you've turned into. I'm afraid of what's going to happen to me and what that *thing* wants me for. I'm afraid, Mama, and you weren't *there*." A sob tore free of me. She stretched out a hand for me again—but she couldn't reach me. I was the one who had to move.

Step by halting step, I did. She caught my hands and drew me down, drew me against her. Her heart beat erratically. Her skin was cold and sharp with salt. She smelled of sea and stone, and there was nothing soft in her, but she held me, and I wept, and my tears made channels in the salt.

"Little bird," she said. "I thought you would be safe."

"I wasn't," I said. "He threw me in the water. You weren't there, and he tried to kill me. I don't know how I didn't drown." Blame was a thorn in every word. I couldn't help it. I knew why she had stayed, and still I hated her for it. I hated her for choosing Sophie over me.

"Neither do I," she said. "But you didn't drown. You lived, and you'll live now. Both my beautiful girls will live." She said it like she was making a promise to herself.

"The Six-Wing took Sophie," I told her.

She stiffened. "No," she said. "No, no, no, that can't—she can't—"

"She said it wouldn't hurt her," I hurriedly added. "She said it needed both of us."

"Yes," she said with some relief. "It needs you both. But once it has you both, it's done."

"But we can stop it," I said. "Sophie and I. If we're together, we can destroy this place."

I sat up, pulling away from her. She pressed her palms to my cheeks, her smile fragile.

"I have dreamed of you a thousand times," she said. "I wish that you had stayed away. But I know that you can do this."

"I will," I said with all the boldness I could muster. "And then we'll go home. You and me—and Sophie."

"I can't go home," she said. "I wish I could, little bird, but there isn't enough of me left."

My eyes had adjusted in the dark. And so when I looked at her this time, I saw what I hadn't before. Broken, ragged black wings, growing from her back. They were grafted to the salt, vanishing beneath it. Blood stained the wall around them, and fresh wounds wept where the skin had opened.

"This place gets inside of you," she whispered. Her pupils were pinpricks; her irises filled her whole eyes. "It gets inside of you, and you'll never scrape it all out."

32

I STOOD ON the gray rock, the taste of salt on my lips where I had pressed a kiss against my mother's cheek. *Live*, she'd told me. *Please just live*. But I hadn't wanted my last words to her to be a lie. *I love you*, I'd said instead.

Abby held my phone now, recording; Liam held my hand. We faced the ramshackle village, and we steeled ourselves one last time as we started forward.

"It's quiet," Abby murmured. "Not to be cliché, but—"

"They don't need to come for us," I said. "We're coming to them, remember?"

"If it's what they want, doesn't that mean it's a bad idea?" Liam asked.

"There isn't a good idea in this scenario."

There was a shadow in the doorway of the church. I expected wings and empty eyes, but it was a man, his shoulders slightly hunched and his face obscured by the dark. We walked forward.

"We can't let them take me," I said. "I don't know exactly what happens if they do. But I have to make it inside with my will intact."

"We've got you," Abby assured me.

"All the way to the end," Liam added. He squeezed my hand. For a moment I saw, as vividly as if it was truly laid out in front of me, the future that might have been. The future that belonged to Sophia Hayes: a summer of endless sunlight, of hard work, of evenings learning Liam Kapoor by heart. A future flung open to possibility, hers to choose. And she'd choose him. They'd travel, drink coffee in cafes, wander side streets, hike trails. They'd go everywhere until they found the *here* they wanted to stay in, and having seen the world, they'd build their own.

But I was Sophia Novak, and my future was not one of endless possibility. It was as unyielding as the rock beneath our feet. It was the church, and it was what lay inside, and there was nothing else beyond it that I could see. That I could even hope for.

We'd reached the church. It seemed larger than it had before, grander—and the shadows within it were far too deep. The man in the doorway stepped forward. William Hardcastle's echo looked at me and smiled.

"Welcome home," he said, his voice like the scrape of rocks. His clothes were patchy, moldering, and his skin was patchy too—peeling from wind-carved sores. I stood rooted in place.

It wasn't him, but it didn't matter.

He was the echo of the man who'd tried to kill me, and my body didn't care that those weren't the hands that had done it. It feared them just the same.

Help me, I whispered silently, and Sophie replied—replied with all the rage and fury that had sent her at Hardcastle on the shore. Anger was better than fear. Anger was fire, and I needed fire. "Get out of my way," I growled, advancing. If I'd had one of Dr. Kapoor's guns, I wouldn't have hesitated an instant to use it.

But Hardcastle only kept smiling. "Come on. I'll take you to them," he said.

I shook my head. If he took me, I was lost.

"There are other ways," he said. "Less kind. But come with me, and they can live. Your friends."

"You really think I'd believe that face?" I asked. "You should have worn someone else." Hardcastle's echo laughed.

I flung myself at the empty space beside him, thinking to force my way past. He caught me around the waist and tossed me back onto the rocky ground. My back took the impact, knocking my breath out of me. Abby yelled something, and Hardcastle came at me.

I bunched up my legs and drove both of my feet, in their heavy boots, into his stomach. He let out a whuff of breath. His torso gave oddly, and I could feel something soft tearing, something brittle cracking. He staggered back and swiped his hand across his mouth, smearing black liquid across his palm. He grinned, and his teeth were black with it. He came at me again.

This time when I kicked at him, he caught me by the ankle and dragged my body forward. I rolled, scrabbling at the ground to find some purchase, and the angle gave me a glimpse of what was happening behind me—and why Abby and Liam weren't helping.

More echoes had appeared. Some of them were twisted beyond recognition, corrupted echoes like Lily's. Others wore the faces of the Landontown residents, or air force uniforms, or LARC ID badges swinging around their necks on lanyards.

Abby and Liam had spread out, darting in opposite directions to avoid the attackers. There were too many of them. We were going to fail, I realized. We were going to fail here and now, and they were going to die, and I was going to be taken, and my defiance would do nothing.

And then came a croaking cry, and the sky filled with black wings, so vast for a moment I thought the dark would swallow me, thought the Six-Wing had come—but no.

Moriarty.

The raven's talons raked the back of Hardcastle's head and he yelled in pain. Blood and black ichor splattered around us.

Dr. Kapoor had put Moriarty back in his cage before we left. Mrs. Popova could have let him out, maybe. But I didn't think she would. Which meant—which meant maybe Dr. Kapoor had. Which *meant* that she was alive, that she had escaped.

I kicked out. It broke Hardcastle's grip, and I scrambled to my feet. He lurched toward me, but the raven was there, clamoring around him. I grabbed a rock from the ground—bigger than two fists, one edge sharp. I held it in both hands, above my head, and swung it hard against the side of his skull.

It crunched—not like bone but like a branch giving under your foot. He dropped. I didn't stop to see if he would get up again. I ran.

I knew what was coming, the transition from church to cavern, the straight beams of wood turning to rough stone. Still I stumbled. My palms slapped against the ground. I heaved back up and kept running down the twisting path. Past knobby columns of stone, through the hollow, liquid sounds that plopped and pinged around me. The path twisted and looped, its shape more serpentine than I remembered.

And then it stopped. My breath was loud. The air was cool and damp. The path bottomed out into the wide chamber, with its weeping congregants, the pale children flitting between them. The shard—the heart of the echo—hung suspended above the black pool, dripping the blood of that other world. And before it was Sophie, blank-eyed, a wide bowl balanced on her palms—and with her was the Six-Wing.

33

I FROZE, BUT the Six-Wing didn't react to my presence. Its wings bent forward, encircling Sophie. Through the gaps, I watched its long arm extend, its fingers brush against her shoulder. It sang, the words not from any language I'd ever heard—and yet I almost understood them.

Sophie lifted the bowl to her lips and drank, and acidic cold trickled down my throat. With each swallow, I understood more of the song, and things beyond the song. This is how it would reclaim us. Change our hearts so that we obeyed only its whims. And then we would sing for it in turn, and wrench open the gate that bound the Eidolon.

Sophie drank, and I crept forward, my fear dissolving into peace. The black liquid slid down Sophie's throat. I passed between soldiers and sailors and men and women. I took my place across from Sophie, the Six-Wing between us. A child appeared, a girl no more than seven or eight, and she placed a shallow bowl in my hands, filled to the brim with black liquid. I smiled and lifted it to my lips.

The Six-Wing turned to watch.

Suddenly the Six-Wing wasn't the matte black of empty shadow—I could see it. See it truly. Its face was blurred, indistinct. Its eyes—the pupil and iris shivered, splitting in two, merging again. And that was what was wrong with its face, too, shuttling rapidly from one to another.

It had my mother's face. She surfaced from the shadows, submerged, then broke the surface again—and I heard her in the song, too. The Six-Wing sang of the shard and the broken world and the gate.

My mother—my mother's echo—sang of me, and of Sophie. She sang of the black, of sinking into it, of pulling it inside of her and being pulled inside of it. It had tried to unmake her, but her daughters needed her, and she would not let go. If Sophie and I were special, it was because we were Joy Novak's daughter. She was different. Her echo was different too. The Six-Wing had created Joy's echo, but it could not control her. Instead, she had sunk into the black pool, the stuff from which all the echoes were born, the stuff from which the Six-Wing's echo had arisen. And *she* had taken control.

Not completely. But enough. Enough to let Dr. Kapoor and Dr. Hardcastle escape. Enough to corrupt the new echoes into unstable, mad things, obviously inhuman and barely functional.

Enough to save me.

With every beat of those great wings, with every word of the song, she became less *her*, more *it*, but somehow, somehow, she had remained.

The Six-Wing reached for me. No, *she* reached for me, my mother's echo.

Our hands met and I saw, I *remembered* as she poured the memory into me through the song.

She cannot persist against the fury of the Six-Wing, but she must. She must stay herself, she must remember, because her daughters are running and they will not live if she fails. She holds and she holds and she holds and go, *she whispers,* go. *They reach the shore—*go—*they reach the boat.*

And William has the gun. William has the gun and she almost lets it loose, this monster, this winged beast, this servant of a broken prince, because if she lets him loose, together they can tear William apart. But there will be no end to the blood, then, and so she watches as Joy whispers her love to one of their daughters and she hates this woman, this flesh-and-bone version of herself—she hates her for choosing one, until she sees what Joy means to do.

What Joy does: she stays. She stays, because both these children are their daughters and Joy and her echo are both their mothers, and of course she stays, and they will protect her, this child of theirs who must remain.

But the echo of Joy Novak watches the ship on the water. She watches them reach the very edge of this false world, and she opens for them a way out. And then, with all her effort trained on that gap, that tear for them to escape through, she can only watch, helpless, as William throws her daughter from the boat.

She is rage and she is fear, and she is the Six-Wing, and there is so little room left to be Joy. And yet she holds, because she cannot keep the way out open and still strike at him.

She holds, because if she does not, he dies and so does her daughter.

She lets the boat slip away, slip through the mist. And she plunges beneath the waves, into the deep water where her daughter sinks, eyes open, lungs empty, on the edge of the breath that will end her. She holds. She lifts the girl up. She kisses her lips to fill her lungs with breath.

She pulls her from the water, but it is not enough, because the ocean is cold and hungry and the shore is so far away. And so she gathers her will and makes it a solid thing—her arms encircle her daughter and turn to wood, her words whisper their way into a wind to coax the sea into carrying her. She uses all of the Six-Wing's power, all of its control over this place to craft a ship out of nothing.

The Six-Wing screams, for it wants the child. It needs the child.

But it made a mistake. It made too perfect an echo. It stole Joy Novak's face, her voice. Her love. And that love is strong enough to bend this false reality. It is strong enough to keep the Six-Wing caged.

The boat she has made for her daughter floats away, the girl shivering, curled up in its bottom.

Go, she whispers. Go.

Time works differently here. For the echo of the woman who was Joy, it stutters. Sometimes she sees her daughter: singing by the water, skipping rocks, running from the echoes who hunt her, always. Joy's echo distracts them. She blinds them. She walks them into the ocean to be battered by the rocks.

She holds. For years, she holds.

She cannot protect her daughter alone. But she is not alone, and Joy Novak tends the girl well.

It is moments later. It is a lifetime past. Her daughters are both here, and she cannot hold any longer. She is so tired.

"Help them," I whispered. I gave her memories of my own. Abby and Liam and the echoes outside, Moriarty with his furious darkness. "Help them, please."

She could not help them. Not alone. But she was never alone here, because my mother stayed. Together they protected Sophie. And together, they can do this.

I felt her cast herself out over stone, over salt, the Six-Wing stripping free of her as she crosses where it cannot. She finds Joy Novak, half-broken, half-human. My mother's echo isn't made of flesh and blood anymore—she's made of will and anger, love and rage, and she sinks into Joy's skin, lending her strength. Unmaking herself to make Joy whole. I heard her whisper one last word, and then she was gone.

Go.

VIDEO EVIDENCE

Recorded by Abigail Ryder

JUNE 30, 2018, TIME UNKNOWN

Abby and Liam crouch behind a stand of rocks. Abby breathes heavily, but has her forearm pressed against her mouth, her sleeve muffling the sound of her breathing. Her face is white as paper, drained of blood. Liam fumbles with the phone, then extends it out around the side of the rock. The crowd of echoes stands in front of the cave. Moriarty circles high overhead, calling. Hardcastle's echo lies facedown near the church entrance, motionless.

ABBY: One of those guns would be nice about now. We have to get in there.

LIAM: I know. How are you?

ABBY: Think I just broke a few ribs, no biggie.

LIAM: Can you move?

ABBY: Not fast. I'll distract them. You get past. Help Sophia.

LIAM: I'm not going to leave you.

ABBY: You gotta pick one of us, Liam, and we both want it to be Sophia.

LIAM: Goddammit. If you—

But Abby surges to her feet with a yell of pain and charges around the rock, toward the echoes. They charge toward her. She screams at them, a wounded battle cry—and the scream is redoubled.

Joy Novak is there, is coming, mangled wings crusted with salt growing from her back. Shadows flicker behind her, almost like wings themselves. Her irises and pupils are doubled, filling the whole of her eyes so almost no white shows.

She looks at Liam and Abby.

NOVAK: Find her.

She spreads her full wings, black as a raven's, salt falling from them like snow.

Abby and Liam run for the church.

34

THE SIX-WING SCREAMED and staggered. Joy's echo was gone from it now—there was only the one face, its features crude as if chiseled out of gray-black stone.

Abby and Liam were shouting nearby. They'd made it past, but they couldn't help me now—I knew what I had to do. I'd heard it in the song. And I had to do it alone.

I dodged past the Six-Wing and grabbed Sophie. I jerked her arm, sending the bowl of black sludge clattering to the ground. "Sophie!" I yelled. She blinked. I wrapped my arms around her once, fiercely. And, almost without thinking, I slid our mother's wooden tern into her pocket. The talisman that had reunited us. "Get out of here alive," I told her.

I didn't have time to stop and see if she understood. Abby and Liam were coming. They'd help. They'd protect her. I had to go. I listened to the music in my bones, and I let it fall into perfect synchrony with the song of the echoes. Jagged lines of light striped the air, and the world heaved around me. The Six-Wing reached for me, but it was too slow. I was already gone.

The world vanished, and a different one formed around me in its place. The cave was gone. Instead, I stood on a field of stone, flat and seamless, stretching in all directions. It was night, as far as I could tell, but there were so many stars I could still see clearly. The stars seemed too low, too bright. Too watchful. In the distance a storm churned, lashing itself with lightning, but here it was quiet. The world of echoes had pretended at our world, but this was an entirely alien place. I had slipped through the bars of the gate, I realized—into the realm where the Eidolon, the Seraph, was trapped.

I knew where I was headed. The shadow against the stars.

It was a massive structure, like a castle. Like a cathedral. I scaled the steps. They rang under me like crystal. Deep gouges in them resolved into words when I peered closer, carved in a language I didn't understand.

The massive stone doors, thirty feet high at least, were shut, but when I pressed my palm to one it swung inward just enough to step through.

Inside, the light of the stars was replaced by the light of blue-petaled flowers, growing from vines on all the walls, on the pillars that supported the cavernous roof. They lit the broken mosaic scattered over the floor: a pattern that made my head ache when I tried to look at it, shapes snarling and twisting and writhing.

The throne sat at the back of the room, on a dais with seven steps. On the throne sat a man, his skin gray, his six great wings white. A metal loop pierced each wing-joint, and a chaotic mass of cord and chain held the wings out, posed, as the man slumped inert in his seat.

This was it. This was the monster that had made the Six-Wing in his image. The Seraph.

I walked up the steps, my heart hammering. I could still feel Sophie, but for once, I didn't push my fear away. She was still in danger. I had to hold on to all the fear I could bear, in case she couldn't.

I reached the top of the stairs. The Seraph was breathing, but barely, his breath so slow and shallow it hardly stirred his chest. Dust had settled on his shoulders and his arms, even his eyelids.

I lifted a trembling hand. My fingers brushed a gray cheek.

His eyes flew open. His lips parted, and they worked as if to shape a word, but all that came out was a rasp like sandpaper.

He drew in a wheezing breath and spoke again. This time I could almost make out the words. I leaned close.

"We will return." He looked upward. The ceiling above was covered with a mural. Seven thrones, and seven indistinct figures on them, blazing with light. Tiny, humanoid shapes cowered in poses of fear and worship at their feet. "We will return," he said again. "And you will worship us."

"Not today," I told him, my voice thick with everything I had cast away from myself for so many years. The love I had been denied and the love I had denied myself, because to feel that love would be to feel the grief of losing it. But there was no grief now. Everything that I'd lost I had found again, and so much more beside. William Hardcastle couldn't take a thing from me, and neither could this monster.

I had never felt so fierce a rush of feeling. Sophie had seen

Abby's sister haunting her, shining from within her, and I understood that now. Because they were in me—my mother and her echo, and Sophie, and Abby, and Liam, and even Dr. Kapoor and Mrs. Popova and Mikhail and Lily and Kenny—the living and the dead, those I'd known since my first breath and those I'd only just met. I had frightened away so many people, I'd stopped trying, and I'd made myself hollow. Only now did I see the foolishness of it.

I was wild with love, drunk on it. It roared through me, and I didn't need to push away fear, because I was so much stronger than it was now. So much *more*.

The man on the throne swiped at me, grasping with fingers that had too many joints. I danced back to the edge of the dais with a feral laugh. He hit the end of the chain that bound his wrist and halted, chains clanking, muscles straining. Then he slumped against the chair.

He wasn't the only monster. This wasn't the only dying world trying to claw its way back to life. Abby's work proved that much. But someone had done this to him, long ago. Someone had known what he was, and how to stop him. We could learn again. We could stop whatever was coming—and whatever was already in our world, hiding in the crevasses and shadows. We were so much stronger than they thought we were.

I wished Abby could see this place. She would understand what it meant so much better than I could. But she wouldn't see it, and I couldn't tell her.

I shut my eyes. I felt the thread, the hum, that connected me to Sophie. Felt *her*. She was alive. That would have to be enough.

But maybe . . . *Sophie*, I thought, and reached for her.

Sophia. I felt her hand close around mine. We were running for the water together, and it didn't matter which of us was real, which of us the echo. We were on the island, surviving by hiding and fleeing and finding scraps of comfort, moments of affection. We were far from the sea, alone in every crowd, adrift without past or future. She wasn't Sophie and I wasn't Sophia—we simply were *us*.

Memory ebbed and flowed between us, the border eroding, our selves spilling into each other at the edge. The barrier between us was a fragile thing.

I shattered it. I let myself pour into her—my memory, for her to guard. My words, because she'd need them. My love, because she'd need that too, she'd need that most of all, and however much spilled into her, there was more, as endless as the rushing sea.

I let all of myself flood into her. Except one thing. I kept my courage. She had her own, and I needed mine still, because I had heard the song and there was only one way to end this.

"You are no one," the creature on his throne said.

I held my courage tight. "That's all right," I told him.

I let the song in my bones, in Sophie's bones, swell, shifting to match the song of this place, of all the many echoed worlds. I let it fill me, until it felt as if it would spill out from my mouth, from my skin, until my whole body was a cathedral for that glorious, hideous sound.

And then I silenced it.

INTERVIEW

Sophia Novak

SEPTEMBER 2, 2018

Ashford settles back in his chair. He adjusts his glasses.

ASHFORD: You believed that silencing the song would destroy the echo worlds. Destroy the connection between the Seraph's realm and ours.

SOPHIA: Yes.

ASHFORD: But it did not succeed.

SOPHIA: It did. Or it seems to have.

ASHFORD: And yet you are here. How is that possible?

SOPHIA: Is it really the first time you've heard someone narrate their own death, given your line of work?

ASHFORD: No, I suppose not. You do not, however, appear to be a ghost, given that it is broad daylight and I can't see your bones, so I must ask—how did you get out?

SOPHIA: I didn't. Haven't you been listening?

Ashford does not seem shocked by this information—it is as if he knew it but hoped to be contradicted.

ASHFORD: You're Sophie.

SOPHIA: My name is Sophia Novak.

ASHFORD: But you are an echo. Correct?

SOPHIA: Maybe. Or maybe she was. You're not afraid of me now, are you?

Ashford raises an eyebrow.

ASHFORD: No. Did you think I would be?

SOPHIA: She said you wouldn't be.

ASHFORD: Sophia did?

SOPHIA: No. Abby.

ASHFORD: Where is she, Ms. Novak? Please. Just tell me that she's all right.

Sophia looks down at her hands.

VIDEO EVIDENCE

Recorded by Liam Kapoor

JUNE 30, 2018, TIME UNKNOWN

The scene in the cavern is chaotic, caught at first in glimpses as the phone in Liam's hand swings wildly. Sophia leaps toward the shard and vanishes. The Six-Wing claws after her, but it recoils from the heart itself, and screeches futilely at the empty air where she was a moment before.

It has nowhere to turn except on Sophie.

ABBY: Move! Sophie, get away from there!

Sophie turns and stares blankly at Abby. The Six-Wing reaches for her with six-fingered hands, each digit a knuckle too long, clawed at the end. Liam hesitates, but Abby flings herself forward, despite her broken ribs. Her knife is already black with echoes' blood.

LIAM: Come on!

He grabs Sophie's arm as Abby draws the Six-Wing's atten-

tion. *She at last seems to wake, to move. Together, she and Liam race to the inert forms of the kneeling figures. They are no help, but some of them are armed. Sophie has the same idea. Liam fumbles a sidearm from a soldier's belt, and Sophie finds a long knife, a fish-gutting knife, on a sailor with rotted eyes.*

The Six-Wing knocks Abby aside with one wing and stalks toward Sophie.

The camera drops. The struggle plays out in shadows on the wall, in crashing and shouts.

Suddenly: stillness. And then Sophie and the Six-Wing scream.

35

SOPHIA HAD VANISHED, and I couldn't follow. It was wrong—all wrong. It should have been me in there. She was the real one. The one with a life, with a voice, with a soul. The Six-Wing advanced on me.

In the moment before it ended, I heard her. It wasn't words but a feeling. A *knowing*. The connection between us hummed.

Sophie—listen.

She washed over me. I gasped, as desperate for air as if I was drowning. It was too much—she was emptying herself, and I couldn't hold all of that for her and stay myself.

And so I stopped trying.

Sophie.

Sophia.

We are here.

We are.

We—

And then, in one bright instant of pain, she was gone, and I was only myself.

It was like an electric shock—the connection between us broken so suddenly, so violently, that the energy of it rebounded. The shard flared with brilliant light.

And then it shattered. It fractured into a thousand pieces and they burst apart. I ducked instinctively, but the slivers halted, hovering in a cloud of scintillating fragments.

The Six-Wing screamed, wings beating in the frantic arrhythmic tempo of a dying bird. It hunched, clawing at its face.

"We have to go!" Abby yelled. She clasped one hand over her shoulder, wounded in the fight, though I hadn't seen it.

"Sophia," Liam said simply.

I looked at the shattered heart of the world. Somewhere in those many facets, I almost imagined I caught a glimpse of a face staring back at me. My reflection, maybe.

Maybe not.

"Gone," I whispered. "She's gone."

We fled.

VIDEO EVIDENCE

Recorded by Dr. Vanya Kapoor

AUGUST 14, 2018, 12:29 AM

The camera is trained on the ocean, and at the mist that cloaks the island in the distance. At the edge of the frame, Dr. Kapoor sits, her arm in a sling. Kenny Lee appears, walking out with a thermos. He sits beside her, pours a cup, hands it over.

LEE: You should let me take a shift.

KAPOOR: Soon.

LEE: You've got to rest.

KAPOOR: The only thing waiting for me back there is an empty house and a phone with my son's mother on the other end of it.

LEE: And a bed. There's a bed too.

KAPOOR: I don't—

There's a blast of air that rocks the camera.

LEE: What was that?

Kapoor and Lee leap to their feet. A cacophony of bird calls fills the air. White forms flash from the mist, flying straight toward them—toward them, and overhead. Lee picks up the camera, tracking their movement as the huge mass of birds wings south.

LEE: That looks like all of them!

The mist begins to clear, revealing the bay, the water empty and still, untroubled by the slightest wave.

KAPOOR: Come on. Come on, Liam. Don't do this to me. Don't do this to her.

Out of the mist, a final bird flies: a raven, massive and black as pitch. Kapoor sucks in a hopeful breath.

LEE: There!

Lee points excitedly, and zooms the camera in on the small blot in across the water, floating at the edge of the mist. A boat, with three figures sitting in it. The sound of the motor makes its way to the shore, and Lee whoops.

KAPOOR: Is Liam there?

LEE: Yeah! Yeah, you can see his stupid haircut!

Lee continues to yell and wave his arms. Kapoor sinks down, as if the weight of relief is more painful than the fear.

KAPOOR: Three. There are only three.

LEE: Wait. There's someone else in the boat. Lying down.

The figure is in the bottom of the boat, covered in a blanket. The boat draws up to the shore. Liam leaps out, and Kapoor grabs hold of him, crushing him to her.

LIAM: You're alive. You made it.

KAPOOR: Of course I did. That island tried to kill me once already.

LEE: Here, let me help you.

Lee sets the camera down as he moves to help Abby haul the skiff farther up on shore.

LIAM: We found the boat—we thought for sure that meant you hadn't . . .

KAPOOR: I stumbled out of the echo on Belaya Skala, and Maria and Kenny were waiting for me. I thought—I thought that if you managed to get out, you'd need a ride back. Left the boat for you.

NOVAK: Vanya.

Kapoor jerks. She turns toward the boat, toward where Lee and Sophie are helping the fourth passenger from the boat. She stands on the shore, unsteady, her arms still striped with salt tracks.

KENNY: Oh, my God.

NOVAK: It's good to see you, Vanya.

Novak's smile is weary but genuine. The blanket drops from her shoulders. Her ragged wings hang, broken, bloodied, from her back. She shuts her eyes and lets out a soft sigh as the light of this world shines across them.

Black spreads like frost over the feathers, the patches of exposed skin and fractured bone. They flake away, soot scattered in the wind, leaving only skin behind.

Sophie laces her fingers through her mother's.

KAPOOR: And which one are you, then?

The girl looks at her steadily, and does not answer.

The mist fades. The waters are still. The birds are gone.

36

TWILIGHT FELL, AND I stood on the porch of Mrs. Popova's house, watching the moon play over the rippling water at the shore's edge. For the first time, there were words in my mind to wrap around what I saw, what I felt. But there was no one to speak them to.

My mother was asleep inside. We'd found her, bloody and nearly unconscious, as we raced from the cathedral. We'd tried, briefly, to help the people inside. But with the Seraph gone—dead, or shut away, we didn't know which—they were undone. Their flesh gave under our fingers, scattered to ash like my mother's wings.

The strange children raced beside us. They raced into the sunlight outside, where the earth was littered with a thousand, a hundred thousand dead, malformed birds. The children leapt into the air, laughter turning to the cawing of crows.

We'd run, and there she was. My mother, or maybe both of them, the way I was Sophie and Sophia both. Her echo had merged with the Six-Wing to protect us all those years, and when she needed to, she tore herself free. She poured herself into the living woman and gave her strength enough to come, to help.

We gathered her up. Liam and Abby had to carry her, hurt as they were—I couldn't, for I felt at once as substantial as tissue paper and also as if I carried an unbearable weight on my shoulders.

Sophia.

She was there and she wasn't, as we ran.

I shut my eyes against the memory of running. The climb up the steps. We'd made it out. We'd stepped from the bunker into the light of a true sun, filtering down through the mist. Like stepping through an open door. Easy.

Easy, because the echo worlds were dying. Collapsing into each other. Falling into silence.

"Sophie?"

I opened my eyes. Liam stood on the beach, hands in his pockets. He'd cleaned up. Gotten his injuries bandaged. Called his mum. Twelve hours on and we were already getting good at pretending that normal was a possibility, after all of this.

"Hey," I said. "I didn't hear you."

"You've got a lot on your mind," he said.

I smiled a little, a pleasant-painful feeling hooking me just under my heart. "Is everything okay at your place?"

"Yeah. Dr.—Mum fell asleep," he said. "I guess she's been awake for most of six weeks. Which is how long we've been gone, by the way. In case no one thought to tell you before you, say, called home and got an earful from a concerned parent."

I laughed. "I'm sure you charmed your way out of it."

He looked at me, head tilted a little to the side. "You sound different."

"I know."

"How much of her is . . ."

"I'm not sure." I bit my lip. Enough that when I looked at him, I remembered every second she'd stolen with him. There weren't nearly enough of them. Enough that I could not tell which thoughts were mine and which were hers, and whether there was any difference at all. We had never quite been different people, she and I, and now any effort to imagine *two* where there was *one* seemed wrong.

"Do you think she might have survived?" he asked. There was still hope in his voice, though I didn't think even he knew it was there.

"Her body? No. She's dead," I told him. There was hope in my voice too. Because if she wasn't, that was worse. To be alive and to be trapped in that place, trapped with that thing— But I was as sure as I could be. She'd given me as much of herself as she could, and that was all that survived of her. *I* was what survived of her.

He walked up the steps of the porch, standing just below me. We were almost eye to eye. "We'd barely gotten started," he said. "It's not fair. She shouldn't be gone."

"I should be," I said. "I was the one who . . . She was real."

"Are you sure about that?" he asked. "Are you sure you were the echo?"

"I . . ." I shook my head. "It has to have been me."

"And now? You can't be an echo. There's no one to be an echo of," he said. "So what does that make you?"

"I'm Sophie. But I think . . . I think I'm Sophia too. So maybe that makes me both of us. Or maybe it makes me someone new," I said.

"I think," he said carefully, "I'd like to get to know that person."

He didn't hold me in his arms. He didn't touch me at all. We only stood together in silence and in memory. Neither of us knew who I was, not yet, but we would learn. I didn't know what we would find or what that would mean, and there was freedom in that. A future not empty but undefined, full of every possibility.

The door opened. Abby stepped out onto the porch, a blanket around her shoulders like a shawl. She looked between us but didn't ask. Still, my cheeks heated a little.

"How's Mrs. Popova?" I asked.

"Tired," she said. "She says time is catching up to her."

"What does that mean?" Liam asked. "Is she going to die?"

"We're all going to die, sooner or later," Abby said. "She's already put it off awhile. But she hasn't turned to dust yet, so I'm guessing she's got some time before the reaper double-checks his list and comes knocking."

"Soon you won't be able to tell there's anything strange about this place," I said.

"Soon there won't be a place here at all," Abby replied. "The birds are gone. I could be wrong, but I don't think they're coming back. Which means no LARC."

A thrill of panic went through me. Because I hadn't really thought it through until just that moment—I would be leaving too.

I might have Sophia's memories, but I had never left this place. Not once.

"You'll be okay," Abby said, catching my expression. "You survived in the echo world for fifteen years. You can survive civilization. And you won't be on your own."

"I already heard my mum on the phone making 'arrangements,'" Liam added. "Having spent her fifteen minutes of allotted emotion, she's in full problem-solving mode. Her way of making up for leaving you behind, I suppose."

"She's always been kind to me," I told him. "She's always taken care of me."

He gave me an odd look. "I think you may have more of a relationship with my mother than I do," he said. "I hadn't really thought of that."

"You should get to know her better," I said. "I think that you'll like each other once you do. I like both of you, after all."

"And I dislike both of you," Abby added with a grin to show she didn't mean it. *Oil and water*, I thought, and it was *Sophia's* thought, but it was also mine.

In the darkness, stars began to shine overhead. Too dim, and too far away—but no, that was the way they were supposed to look. I was too used to strange worlds and strange skies.

"Nighttime," Liam said. "It's been a while."

I reached into my pocket. My fingers bumped against the slender wings of the wooden tern, and a memory and its reflection surfaced. Sophia, embracing me in the cave. Slipping the bird into my pocket.

"You should take this," I said. I held the little bird out to Abby.

"It already led me here," she said. "I don't think I need it anymore. You can keep it, if you want."

"It isn't the one you had," I told her. "This is Sophia's bird. She still had yours with her when she . . . So I thought you should have it."

Abby took it from me, her brow wrinkled in confusion. "I don't understand."

"What's not to understand?" Liam asked.

"This is the same bird," Abby said. "The wing's broken, see? And there's a stain on the side. Sophia's wasn't damaged."

I reached into my pocket. My fingers bumped against something small and hard, and I pulled it out. It was the tip of the wing, broken off. "It must have happened while we were running," I said.

"Then it is Sophia's bird," Abby replied. "But it's exactly the same as the one my sister gave to Ashford. Which means . . . I have no idea what that means." She snarled in frustration. "What were my father and my grandfather doing here? Why did Miranda send me—to help you? Or was there something else? I don't understand. I thought I would understand."

"Maybe that means you aren't finished yet," I told her. "Whatever brought you here, it isn't done with you quite yet."

She closed her hand around the bird. "It's done for tonight," she said. "Tonight, let's just be done."

"Well, we've already spent most of the night out here talking," Liam said jokingly. "Want to stick around and watch the sun rise?"

"I'd like that," she said. We sat on the steps, the three of us in a line.

Dawn was coming. We'd made it through the dark.

INTERVIEW

Sophia Novak

SEPTEMBER 2, 2018

Silence lingers as Sophie—or Sophia—finishes her story. Ashford frowns, but it takes him some time to compose a question.

ASHFORD: That is an astonishing tale, Ms. Novak. And a well-put-together file. Did you assist in that?

SOPHIA: Liam did the titles.

ASHFORD: I thought he might have. *Tempest*. It seems fitting. You know, Ms. Novak, I don't know that I've ever met someone whose life has been so thoroughly steeped in the extra-normal.

SOPHIA: But there are other people who are in tune with the other worlds. Like me. Like Abby and her sister. We're drawn to those other worlds, and they're drawn to us. Because we're useful. The Six-Wing wanted to use me. The thing that's after Abby, that killed her sister—it wants something from her too, doesn't it?

He doesn't want to have to ask; you can see it in his face. But it is the question he has been trying not to demand answers to this whole time, and it is finally too much.

ASHFORD: Where *is* Abby, Ms. Novak? She made it off the island. So why isn't she here? Why send everything like that? Not a word of explanation. She won't answer her phone or her email. No one seems to have seen her. Do you know? Can you tell me?

SOPHIA: I know.

ASHFORD: Then where is she?

SOPHIA: She went to find out what you've been hiding from her. She went home.

Ashford looks grim.

ASHFORD: That is what I was afraid of.

SOPHIA: Because you don't want her finding the truth?

ASHFORD: No, Ms. Novak. Because I don't want it finding her.

ACKNOWLEDGMENTS

FIRST, I'D LIKE to thank my parents. They have been a constant, un-vanished presence in my life, have not in fact met a grim demise, are emotionally and practically and in all ways extremely supportive, and deserve none of the cruel things I do to their counterparts in fiction. The next parents I write will spend the book baking, happily far from danger, I promise. (This is a lie. I'm sorry.)

Thanks also to my wonderful mother-in-law, Rosemary, and her partner, Mike. Writing during a global pandemic has been challenging to say the least, and without sending the kids off to Grandma Camp there would be far fewer words in this book. And to my husband, Mike, who really should be at the top of the list every time, for splitting the workday with me, taking meetings with a toddler on his lap, and somehow, so far, getting through this with our sanity mostly intact. Special shout-out to Ms. Bean and Mr. O, along with coconspirators Vonnegut and Octavia Pupler, who tried their hardest to keep me from getting a lick of work done (sometimes through actual licking) but without whom my life would be very dull indeed.

As always, thanks to the usual suspects who helped in one way or another to get this book from lumpy little idea to workable draft: Shanna Germain, Erin M. Evans, Rhiannon Held, Monte Cook, Corry L. Lee, and Susan Morris; to Lisa Rodgers and Louise Buckley for their advocacy and expertise; to Maggie Rosenthal, with apologies for not fitting in that extra defiled corpse you asked for; to Marinda Valenti, Abigail Powers, Delia Davis, and Krista Ahlberg for their diligence; and to Dana Li, Kristin Boyle, and Jim Hoover for yet another a fantastic cover and interior design. Special thanks also to SB Divya for her work as an expert reader.

And of course thank you to all of my readers. Without you, none of this is possible.

© Alice Marshall

Kate Alice Marshall started writing before she could hold a pen properly, and never stopped. She lives in the Pacific Northwest with a chaotic menagerie of pets and family members, and ventures out in the summer to kayak and camp along Puget Sound. She is the author of the young adult novels *I Am Still Alive*, *Rules for Vanishing*, and *Our Last Echoes*, as well as the middle grade novel *Thirteens*.

Follow her on Twitter @kmarshallarts or visit her online at katemarshallbooks.com.